MARY RUSSELL'S WAR

AND OTHER STORIES OF SUSPENSE

LAURIE R. KING

INTRODUCTION BY LESLIE S. KLINGER

Allison & Busby Limited
12 Fitzroy Mews
London W1T 6DW
allisonandbusby.com

First published in Great Britain by Allison & Busby in 2016.
This paperback edition published by Allison & Busby in 2017.

Published by arrangement with Bantam Books,
an imprint of The Random House Publishing Group,
a division of Random House, Inc., New York., NY, USA.
All rights reserved.

A CIP catalogue record for this book is available from
the British Library.

10 9 8 7 6 5 4 3 2 1

ISBN 978-0-7490-2152-8

Typeset in 10.5/15.5 pt Adobe Garamond Pro by
Allison & Busby Ltd.

The paper used for this Allison & Busby publication
has been produced from trees that have been legally sourced
from well-managed and credibly certified forests.

Printed and bound by
CPI Group (UK) Ltd, Croydon, CR0 4YY

PRAISE FOR LAURIE R. KING

'The Mary Russell series is the most sustained feat of imagination in mystery fiction today, and this is the best instalment yet'
Lee Child

'These . . . are bestselling books because Laurie R. King captures the voice and character of Holmes as well as any of the thousand and more pastiches that have been written in imitation of Conan Doyle. But this is more than a mere copy. The narrative . . . is completely absorbing and motivates the reader to want to read the rest of the series'
Historical Novels Review

'Excellent . . . King never forgets the true spirit of Conan Doyle'
Chicago Tribune

'Outstanding examples of the Sherlock Holmes pastiche . . . the depiction of Holmes and the addition of his partner, Mary, is superbly done'
Mystery Women

'All [Laurie R. King books] without exception, leave me with a feeling of immense satisfaction at the quality of the story and the writing'
It's a Crime Blog

LAURIE R. KING lives in northern California. Her background includes such diverse interests as Old Testament theology and construction work, and she has been writing crime fiction since 1987. The winner of the Edgar, the Nero, the Macavity and the John Creasey Awards, she is the author of highly praised stand-alone suspense novels and a contemporary mystery series, as well as the Mary Russell/Sherlock Holmes series.

By Laurie R. King

The Beekeeper's Apprentice

A Monstrous Regiment of Women

A Letter of Mary

The Moor

O Jerusalem

Justice Hall

The Game

Locked Rooms

The Language of Bees

The God of the Hive

Pirate King

Beekeeping for Beginners

(a novella)

Garment of Shadows

Dreaming Spies

The Murder of Mary Russell

Mary Russell's War

Touchstone

The Bones of Paris

This volume is dedicated to the
Friends of Russell,
who just won't let me rest
when it comes to
Mary Russell

CONTENTS

An Appreciation   9

Mary's Christmas   15

Mary Russell's War   41

Beekeeping for Beginners   157

The Marriage of Mary Russell   206

Mrs Hudson's Case   254

A Venomous Death   270

Birth of a Green Man   274

My Story   278

A Case in Correspondence   293

Stately Holmes   334

Acknowledgements   373

Publication History   375

An Appreciation

By Leslie S. Klinger

MARY RUSSELL ISN'T MENTIONED in the stories of Sherlock Holmes penned by John H. Watson (and attributed to Arthur Conan Doyle). Yet she was as inevitable – as predictable – as the Ninth Planet discovered in 2015 by Caltech astronomers. 'From a drop of water,' said Holmes, 'a logician could infer the possibility of an Atlantic or a Niagara without having seen or heard of one or the other.' So, too, was it possible to infer from Holmes's work and character that Mary Russell – or one much like her – would enter his life when he was ready.

Judge from these statements of Holmes from *The Sign of Four*, probably in 1888: 'Women are never to be entirely trusted – not the best of them.' 'But love is an emotional thing, and whatever is emotional is opposed to that true cold reason which I place above all things. I should never marry myself, lest I bias my judgement.' Later, probably in 1894, he said, 'I have never loved, Watson' ('The Devil's Foot'). But by 1907, six years into his retirement, Holmes's attitude seems to have softened: 'Women have *seldom* been an attraction to me, for my brain has always governed my heart . . .' [emphasis added] ('The Lion's Mane').

Certainly by this time, as Holmes penned his masterwork, *The Whole Art of Detection,* it is clear that he was yearning for a student, someone who could share his lonely days and learn from him. It is also clear that the student could be a woman, for Holmes had never been one to underestimate women. Like all great artists, he lived for his art's sake. To find one who could appreciate his art – who could *learn* his art – must have been his heart's desire. O lucky man, to have a Russell cross his path at the precise moment when he was ready to share his wisdom!

When the established world of Sherlockians, those worshippers at the feet of Holmes, first heard that one Laurie R. King, a fledgling writer from California, had come into possession of manuscripts purporting to be records of the relationship of a fifteen-year-old girl with Holmes and that – gasp! – Holmes had (after a decent interval) married the girl – a tremor ran through that world. Not only was this heresy, it was patent balderdash. What could a girl, a half American to boot, possess that Holmes would wish to share?

The answer, it turned out, was that Mary Russell possessed a brain and a heart to match those of Holmes himself. While those who judged Ms King's early reports of Russell's life only on a superficial level were horrified at the thought of Holmes sharing a cottage (and eventually a bed) with this . . . *child*, others – those who actually read the reports – were delighted to learn that here was a pupil fit for the Master. Here was a mind as brilliant and encyclopedic as that of Sherlock Holmes, and here was someone with a soul as large, courageous, and generous as his. The fact that Russell was a woman was not only neither drawback nor handicap, it was a positive asset, adding new dimensions to the Great Detective's understanding of humankind. And as to her youth, it allowed Holmes to travel past the era of Victoria and Edward in which Watson attempted to circumscribe him, both literally and intellectually.

That Laurie R. King is now embraced by the Baker Street Irregulars as a member and by Sherlockians as a scholar of note is tribute to her vital role as the chronicler of Mary Russell. Without Ms King's efforts, not only would the myriad admirers of Ms Russell have been deprived of their knowledge of this young woman's life and adventures, the friends of Mr Holmes would be the poorer for having these unexpected dimensions of Sherlock Holmes hidden from view by Dr Watson and his contemporaries. Holmes himself, reflecting on his professional record in 1891 ('The Final Problem'), claimed, 'The air of London is sweeter for my presence.' He was far too modest, for with his partnership with Mary Russell, we can truly say that the air of the world is sweeter for their presence.

Since the appearance of *The Beekeeper's Apprentice* in 1994, Mary Russell and Sherlock Holmes have been a partnership as real as the earlier association of Holmes and Watson. The Friends of Russell are many and far-flung, enthusiasts who play the 'Game' with all their hearts. The rules of this community sporting event are as follows:

Mary Russell is as true as Sherlock Holmes.

Her Memoirs are history, not fiction,
despite being classified as such.

Holmes's obituary has yet to appear
in *The Times of London*.

Therefore, he is still alive today.
And, if Holmes lives on, so does Mary Russell.

The stories that follow, nine of which have been published elsewhere (details at the end) fill in various gaps in the larger Memoirs, but are no less real or essential.

Enjoy playing the Game.

– Laurie R. King
(EDITOR OF THE RUSSELL MEMOIRS)

MARY'S CHRISTMAS

Mary Russell seems to have had a happy childhood before the events that overtook her family in the fall of 1914 (*The Beekeepers Apprentice; Locked Rooms*). It was also anything but conventional, as one might expect of an American Christian father and English Jewish mother who are raising two terrifyingly intelligent children in homes on two continents. A typical eccentricity is the gilt young Mary receives – and carries into her adult years – that becomes her iconic equivalent of Holmes's deerstalker hat: the throwing knife she wears in her boot.

EVERY LITTLE GIRL SHOULD have an Uncle Jake.

The black sheep, the family rogue, whose exploits filled my childhood with admonitions over the dire and delicious consequences of misbehaviour. When Uncle Jake wandered away from a family train-trip at the age of four, he was taken by Indians. When an adolescent Uncle Jake ran away to join the circus, he was nearly eaten by the lion. When Uncle Jake received a collection of Sherlock Holmes stories for his fourteenth birthday and began following suspected criminals around Boston, one of them turned his pistol on the boy at his heels.

Most astounding of all, every one of these cautionary tales turned out to be true.

'Russell, I find that difficult to believe.'

I blinked, pulling my gaze from the fire to the man slumped into the basket chair across the hearth. 'Lower your eyebrow, Holmes. All those stories were quite true. At least, they all had factual elements.'

'Why have I never heard of this mythic uncle before this?'

'And how many years did you know Watson before you told him you had a brother?'

'That is not at all the same thing.'

'No, of course not. Perhaps I wished to be certain you could not flee in horror, and needed to wait until you had made an honest woman of me.'

At that, his other eyebrow went up, either at the idea of Sherlock Holmes fleeing in horror, or at my being made honest. I relented.

'Jake's been gone a long time. And I suppose . . . well, I tend not to dwell on things that remind me of my parents.'

He returned to the pipe he had been filling before my thoughts had broken into the amiable murmur of the evening fire.

'Although I'll admit,' I continued, 'you may be right to some degree: I have little way of knowing if all the stories told about Jake were completely true. But I did confirm some of them, and I did know the man. Little about him would surprise me.'

Holmes dropped his spent match into the pieced-together Roman bowl that Old Will had dug up in the garden. 'He died?'

'I think so.' The outstretched hand paused, the right eyebrow quirking upward again. 'Jake loved me. I can imagine nothing short of death that would keep him from coming to see me.'

'Truly? There could be any number—'

'Yes, I know. And it's true, prison is by no means impossible. Perhaps I should simply tell you about him.'

The basket chair emitted a symphony of creaks as he stretched his long legs towards the fire. He threaded his fingers together across the front of his once-bright dressing gown, preparing to listen.

However, once interrupted, my tongue hesitated to go on. What could I say about my father's brother that did not come back to: '*He* left me, too'? Uncle Jake had tried hard to keep me from pain, but in the end . . .

'So,' prodded Holmes, 'did those stories about the lad's troubles help to keep you in line?'

I had to smile at the thought.

The cautionary tales about Jake's near-disasters had quite the opposite effect on my impressionable mind: namely, the temptation to follow in his footsteps became irresistible. Especially after he was banned from family mention in 1908, following an episode too shocking for consideration – 'family' meaning, in the hearing of my grandparents.

For some reason, my mother had a soft place for her brother-in-law. His few actual appearances were memorable – no doubt explaining why they were few. I could have been no older than seven or eight when he arrived on a summer breeze, borne across the Channel to Sussex in an air balloon. He even managed to come down a) on dry land and b) within a mile of the house.

Because there was the other thing about Uncle Jake: even my

mother, who had theological objections to the concept, was forced to agree that Jake possessed a guardian angel. The Indians returned him, the lion did not like the taste of his shoes, the criminal's hand was stayed by young Jake's blonde, blue-eyed innocence – and, years later, the changeable breeze of the Channel held steady for the requisite hours of the crossing. By the time the dot on the horizon had grown, neared, become recognisable, then begun to descend, half the population of East Dean was scurrying along below, eyes lifted and feet stumbling.

Had this been 1914, he'd have been shot down. But war was half a dozen years away, as far off as any tragedy could be, and so the amateur aeronaut came down towards the earth, skipping over rooftops, narrowly missing a collision with the church tower. The basket snagged among the tops of the trees along the Eastbourne road, shook itself free without quite coming to grief, and cleared a very solid wall by the breadth of a hair before the great bag collapsed, its basket thumping down in the Padgetts' front garden. It would be hard to say who had the widest grin: the small man who climbed out of the wicker gondola, or the children bouncing around him like an overturned bucket of hard-rubber balls. Even my father, attempting an expression of adult disapproval, found it difficult to keep his mouth under control. Uncle Jake pressed through the front row of witnesses, patting excited heads all the way, to come to a halt at the toes of the taller, older man. My father stood firm, enforcing the scowl on his face. Uncle Jake cocked his head, the mischief on his face only growing, until Papa gave up, meeting his brother in a hard embrace.

Jake stayed with us for a week that time, teaching us how to make those miniature hot-air balloons called sky lanterns, foot-wide paper shells lifted by the heat of a tiny flame: it was pure magic, watching a glowing orb lift into the night sky and meander away. For the rest of that summer (which, fortunately for the fields and thatch rooftops, saw regular rain) it was difficult to find a candle in any shop of the South Downs.

Then on the eighth day – again, typical of Jake – he was gone, leaving behind the folded-up balloon, a community of fervent young lantern-makers, and a wistful awareness of having been the recipients of a Visit.

Still, my brother and I were more able to absorb the disappointment than others because it was already nearly September, which meant that Christmas was only a few pages away on the calendar.

Some explanation may be required. Levi and I were Jewish, because Mother was. Papa's American Christianity rode lightly on his shoulders, so that when the two were married – or long before, if I know Mama – he freely agreed that any children from their union would be raised according to her traditions, not his.

Except when it came to Christmas. He did not mind what the holiday was called – generally, Mama termed it 'Winter Solstice' in private and 'the holidays' when talking to others, although she had been known to slip and give December 25th its traditional name – but he did insist on most of the trappings: roast goose, mince tarts, mistletoe sprigs, and morning presents – everything short of church services and the more religious carols.

It was, for children, the best of both worlds. Better still, in order to celebrate far from the eye of Mama's rabbinical father, we quietly took ourselves from London to our holiday home on the South Downs for the entire month, there to decorate a tree, fill the house with delicious smells, and wait for Papa to arrive.

You see, we went long periods during my childhood without

our father. My mother, my brother, and I had left our home in San Francisco for England (the full reasons for this I was not to understand until much later) a few months after the 1906 earthquake and fire. Until 1912, when we returned to the Pacific Coast, England was where the three of us lived, while my father, tied to family business interests in California and Boston, would make the trip across a continent and an ocean twice a year: for the long summer holiday, and for a too-brief winter visit.

Thus, even without Uncle Jake's contribution, December was a period rich with significance. As the year faded, anticipation grew. In early December, our tutors were dismissed, our trunks dispatched, and we boarded a southbound train for Eastbourne.

Sometimes, packages were already waiting for us, collected by the village woman who kept the house both when we were there and in our absence: packages large and small, with numerous stamps or none at all, bearing return addresses from London, from America, or from the world beyond. The tidiest – always rectangular – were from our grandmother in Boston, predictably ill-suited for our age (the toys), our bodies (clothing), or our interests (books). Only slightly less boring would be those from the London shops, purchased by Mother, who never really understood that Christmas was about thrill, and thus could be depended on to produce the next book in a series, a packet of our respectively preferred sweets, and any piece of clothing or equipment we had taken care to mention to her in November. Father's were considerably better, although they were as apt to be puzzling as exciting (such as the year he decided I might enjoy learning to fly-fish) and often did not reach us until we had returned to London in the new year.

But the very essence of Christmas throughout my childhood were the well-travelled parcels that arrived with Jake's bold handwriting on them. Never neat, rarely rectangular, almost always from some unexpected corner of the globe, Jake's presents might have been specifically designed for the purpose of driving parents mad. What adult would send a collection of explosive, corrosive, and poisonous chemicals to a five-year-old boy – even if that five-year-old was Levi Russell? Or the shrunken head with the postmark from Ecuador? Or the tall crate covered with mysterious ink designs that arrived late on Christmas Eve, with my name on it, and kept me from sleep all the long night. It proved, once I had burrowed through the excelsior the next morning, to contain an antiquated Japanese air rifle, magnificently engraved, wickedly accurate.

Uncle Jake's gifts tended to mysteriously disappear soon after our return to London. A few of them turned up, years later, in a storage shed down in Eastbourne I had not known the family possessed. Others I suspected had been anonymously donated to one museum or another: one New Guinean spear in the Pitt Rivers looks remarkably familiar. But other gifts were less tangible, and stayed with the family for ever.

For example: one snowy Christmas morning, probably 1909, a knock on our door heralded not neighbours or carollers, but a heavily-wrapped individual (wrapped in woollen garments, that is, not decorative paper) with snow on his boots and a sheaf of pages clutched between his icy fingers. Mother pulled him inside, thawed him out, gave him food and a couple of powerful drinks, then sat in bemusement as the hairy young fellow rose to his feet, cleared his throat, and read to her a series of poems written on the sheets of paper. He then laid down the poems, resumed his garments, tipped his hat to her, and said, 'I am asked to say that your brother-in-law wishes you many happy returns of the day, and much poetry in the coming year.' Then he trudged off through the snow in the direction of Eastbourne.

Another year, a shipment of penguins bound for the London zoo went inexplicably astray, ending up at our front door. Since it was Christmas Day, with limited trains to London, and since the poor creatures were clearly in need of both exercise and a meal, the entire village was treated to the spectacle of seventeen Antarctic natives gobbling English herring and tobogganing in their feathered evening wear along the snow-covered Downs.

'Your uncle was banned from family mention, yet your grandparents continued to support him financially? Vintage air rifles and waylaying a flock of penguins suggest considerable resources,' Holmes commented.

'Oh, yes: Jake was as banned from the family coffers as he was from their conversations. I suspect that whatever it was he got away with in that 1908 episode might have set another man up for life, but not someone who abandons once-used hot-air balloons or gives away Rolls-Royces to a gipsy king. No, Jake lived by his wits – which, while considerable, were weighted towards the larcenous. The final straw, the event that had my mother reluctantly accepting the opinions of her parents-in-law, brought my brother and me into matters. A young introduction into a life of crime.'

'Hence your remark, long ago, that had you not met me, you might easily have become an expert forger or second-storey man. Woman.'

'Precisely.'

It began in the summer of 1911. At the time, there was nothing to suggest that this would be our last year of familial separation. It was a July like any of those previously spent beneath the Sussex sun, weeks of running wild through Downland lanes and villages. I was eleven,

Levi six, and by this time we were well known to every farmer and housewife in the triangle formed by the Lewes road to the north and the Cuckmere River to the west, with the road from Eastbourne to Newhaven our southern boundary. (Thus, slightly outside the customary haunts of our famous neighbour, Sherlock Holmes.)

To most of them, we were simply two of a gang of free-ranging children – with better shoes and manners than some, perhaps, but every bit as likely to be at the centre of any complex bits of troublemaking. Some would drive us away with shouts, a few went so far as to report a misdemeanour to our parents, but most would merely shake their heads at our antics and shoo us off.

Not all. There were two or three among our neighbours to whom we gave wide berth, although we would have loved to torment them, could we have been certain of anonymity. But after a conversation with our parents, Levi and I agreed that the punishment of these few villains was beyond the responsibility of minors.

One of them was an old woman in East Dean with a bitter tongue and a large and vicious dog. The other was the owner of a run-down public house and inn along the Lewes road, whose threat to turn a shotgun on miscreants was all too widely believed.

This latter individual was a person with a blithe intolerance for foreigners of all stripes and newcomers to Sussex in particular, and an open abhorrence for those of the Hebrew faith. I had never been inside his place, although Uncle Jake was a regular whenever he was in Sussex – less for the company, I had figured out the previous year, than for the card games that kept the publican in business. An overheard conversation in the village shop told me that poker, exotic for rural England, was responsible for the shiny motorcars with London plates that assembled outside of the inn on the occasional Friday night: letting out rooms made it easier to get around licensing hours.

My parents had long since forbidden to us the Lewes road for a mile in either direction of the establishment, whenever we were on our own. This was easily enough done, since most of our social life lay to the south and west of where we lived, but then in the summer of 1911, this person made purchase of a motor car, a sleek and shiny machine on which he showered all the care and attention he did not show his place of business. He drove too fast, and after rumour began to spread that he had deliberately swerved in the direction of a neighbour's affable and arthritic dog, Mother warned us to take great care along the better-kept roads and lanes, where his tendency to speed might give two Jewish children little warning of his approach.

Fortunately, the summer passed without so much as a close call, or I'd have ended up in an uncomfortable conversation with my father about a stone going through the publican's windscreen. We returned to London for the autumn, my father sailed for America, and Mother, Levi and I buckled down to the twelve long weeks that lay between us and our next freedom.

December came at last, and with it, a sensation I had never before felt in the Sussex air: a touch of bitter to the sweet. The next summer, we would *not* board the train to Sussex. We would not spend three blissful months running wild, swimming with Father at Beachy Head, picking wild berries, and transforming into brown-skinned, scabby-kneed, wild-haired urchins. Instead, Mother had agreed, after six long years, to join Father in San Francisco, reuniting our family at last.

We were overjoyed – and yet . . .

This December might well be our last time here, at my mother's beloved Sussex farm.

The three of us went down a few days earlier than usual,

since the prospect of an extended absence would require a lot of planning with the farm manager, Patrick Mason. Or so Mother said. It seemed to me that Patrick ran the farm quite nicely with very little advice from its owner, but I was not about to object to a few extra days in Sussex.

Perhaps Mother, too, was impelled by emotion rather than practicality.

In any event, we went early, which made it one of the years that Father was not there at the start. And because Father was not with us at the start, there were several of his usual tasks that Mother took on instead.

One of those involved a trip to the Evil Publican, to order a small barrel of beer to offer the numerous visitors entertained by both house and kitchen during the holidays. One might have thought that the Russell family would impose economic sanctions against the man, but for some reason, both parents agreed that a campaign of bland kindness might bring him around where open warfare would not. Personally, I'd have dropped rat poison in his tea kettle, but then, I have never been a forgiving person.

Two days after we arrived, under skies leaden with the threat of snow, Mother cautiously steered the motor car down the lane towards the main road. She was not a comfortable driver, but she believed in meeting her fears head-on, which made waiting for Father, or having Patrick drive us, unacceptable. Levi and I huddled under heavy travelling rugs in the back while she peered forward through the misty windscreen, convinced that any instant, a child on a bicycle or a straying pony would dash out before her.

Mother drove at the speed of a brisk walk.

As a part of meeting one's fears, she also preferred to face unpleasant things immediately. So our first stop would be at the home of the Evil Publican – and, lest one think that she might believe children are to be protected, when we came to a halt, she turned and told us to come in with her.

Being a child of Judith Russell was not always an easy thing.

Levi and I stayed well back as Mother walked across the saloon bar to where the publican glowered. She laid down a piece of paper with Father's name on it and counted out the cost of the barrel, making polite conversation to his silence all the while. When the money was on the surface of the bar, she put away her purse, rested her hands on the wood, and looked expectantly at him. Levi and I held our breath, but since his choice was to take Mother's order or lose our family's business, he reluctantly reached down for his order book and wrote down the information.

Mother thanked him, politely added that her friends always enjoyed his winter ale, and turned to go.

One had to know her very well to see how relieved she was.

She was nearly at the door when the man added a parting shot, in a voice that might have been telling a jest. 'Don't know why you people celebrate the Saviour's birth when it was you who killed him.'

In the two seconds before anger came, even a complete stranger would have read the shock on her face. She came to a halt. I expected her to turn and go after the man with all the wits and scorn in her armament – I gleefully waited for it – but instead she merely lifted her chin, gathered us up, and left.

'Why did he say that?' I asked her.

'Ignorant people spout a lot of nonsense, Mary.'

'If he's ignorant, why didn't you stay and argue?' This was, after all, her technique for dealing with the occasional ignorance of her children.

'When there is an emotional element in a belief, argument

26

rarely has much effect. Particularly when it's a man who feels threatened by a woman's words.'

'But, what he was saying! Why does he think we killed Jesus?'

She did not reply, not then and there. Instead, we piled back into the motor and continued the day's tasks – although she did buy us an unexpectedly generous treat in the Alfriston tea-house. However, once we were back home, she sent me to fetch a copy of the New Testament, and we began to work our way through the relevant parts. The next two days were spent addressing my question of why the man blamed us for a political act two thousand years in the past, until the long table in the library was buried in books, maps, and notes in several languages.

Not that the question was answered, exactly, except to convince me that the Gospel authors might have been more careful with their choice of words had they known people would read them as the immortal word of God.

On the third day, life resumed. Father's ship was due the next morning, and none of us wanted to see a look of disappointment at our lack of mince tarts and mistletoe. Every corner of the house smelt of baking – Mother had just pulled Father's favourite ginger cake from the oven, only slightly scorched – when a knock came on the kitchen door. I pulled it open to find a very bedraggled Uncle Jake, wearing a rueful expression, a quarter inch of beard hair, and a beautifully tailored coat, misshapen by damp, which he'd clearly been sleeping in for days.

Also, a black eye going green around the edges.

Mother exclaimed and reached to pull him inside, then let go of his arm when he made a sound of distress. 'Sore shoulder,' he said, taking the step up to the kitchen as if it was a great height. As he went past me, I hesitated about shutting the door: the kitchen no longer smelt so sweet.

Mother put on the kettle, laid a slab of the cake on a plate, and had him fed and refreshed in two minutes flat. It took somewhat longer to get him upstairs to the bath, but she asked no questions, made no protest, merely provided clean clothing, left a napkin-wrapped pair of sandwiches and a bottle of beer on the guest-room table, and resumed her kitchen tasks.

'What happened to Uncle Jake?' Levi asked.

'I'm sure we'll find out when he's had a rest,' Mother said, and directed us back to our construction of many metres of colourful paper chain.

But nothing more was heard from our resident black sheep, all that day and through the evening. The following morning, I came downstairs to find my mother placidly reading, teacup at hand.

'Do you think Uncle Jake has died?' I asked her.

'I heard him moving around during the night,' she replied, to my relief.

'What happened to him?'

'I'm sure that if he wants us to know, he'll tell us. Would you rather stay here when I go to get your father, or come with Levi and me?'

That was a difficult decision, but in the end, my curiosity about Jake (and my conviction that I could get him to tell me first) overcame my eagerness to see Father.

An hour after Mother and Levi had driven away, with the house still silent, I was regretting my decision.

An hour after that, motion came at last.

I managed to get the coffee made before I heard his feet on the stairs. I was sweeping up the last of the spilt grounds when he appeared in the doorway, shaven now and wearing an assortment of clothing – old trousers of his from a previous visit, a heavy sweater with rolled-up sleeves belonging to Father, and a pair of Mother's too-large bedroom slippers.

'Mary, Mary, my favouritest niece,' he said, coming to wrap his arms around me. 'Good heavens, child, you're nearly as tall as I am! Who gave you permission to become such a beautiful young woman?'

It was true that I had to shrink down a little to nestle into his shoulder, but if I had changed, he had not: still tautly muscled, and still warmer than other people seemed to be, his natural odour had returned. I breathed it in, the smell of uncles and exotic places, and I might have stood there for ever had his stomach not given a loud grumble.

'Oh!' I said, standing back. 'You must be starving. Can I get you something to eat?'

'Let's see what there is in the pantry,' he said, and was soon merrily stirring eggs and herbs into a perfect omelette, grating just the right amount of cheese over it, and snatching the toast from beneath the grill a moment before the brown went too dark. He put one serving in front of me, replicated it for himself, and sat down at the kitchen table, emptying his plate in what seemed one rapid swipe of the fork. He washed it down with a swallow of coffee, ignoring the odd bits that floated on top.

We washed and dried the dishes, wiped down the stove and table, talking all the while. Perhaps I did the majority of the talking. In any event, he did not reply to my none-too-subtle queries as to his eye and shoulder (come to think of it, I never did learn what had happened to him), although he did hear all about Mother's decision to return to California. When the kitchen was restored, we went into the sitting room, where I carefully arranged more wood onto the fire (my domestic incompetence, then as now, being largely confined to the kitchen). He lowered himself onto the divan, stifling a groan. I fetched a rug so he could put up his feet.

'So, Mary, what's new in your life?'

Unlike most adults, Jake seemed genuinely interested in what children were doing. He listened with the occasional comment as I told him about my tutorials during the autumn, my decision about the future (I was torn between being a surgeon and a mountain climber, realising that the latter as a hobby might negate the former as a profession, what with the liability of frostbite), and the ridiculous antics of one of my older friends who had recently discovered boys.

He nodded, he shook his head, he sympathised, but he also half-drowsed in the growing warmth – until I started telling him about the Evil Publican. His eyes came open as he watched my face. He said nothing, and although with someone else I might have downplayed the insult, I did not mind Uncle Jake seeing how upset I was.

At the end, I plucked at a frayed spot on my sleeve, and listened to the crackling fire.

'That wasn't a nice thing to say,' he told me after a time.

'It was nasty. Although Mother explained to me the history of what it meant, and how it came about. Uncle Jake, do you have to go there and play cards any more?'

His hand came out to give a sharp tug to the nearest plait. 'I might have to. But if I do, I promise not to give him any of my money. Is that the car I hear in the drive?'

It was.

After my enthusiastic greetings, the handshake between Father and Jake seemed particularly subdued, and during luncheon, some large Presence loomed at the back of the room. When we had finished, Father and Jake left us and walked up to Jake's room, where they spent a very long time behind the closed door, broken at one point by Father's retrieval of the first-aid box and a bowl of water.

Nothing more was said about the black eye, the sore shoulder, or the state of the overcoat.

That afternoon, I heard Jake leave his room to go down the hallway, and after the flush of the toilet, go back. When his door shut again, Levi and I looked at each other, then put down our books and ventured upstairs. I tapped on the door. In a moment, Jake looked out.

'Your father's ordered me to stay in bed today. But he didn't say I had to be alone. You two want to come in?'

We did.

We spent a happy hour playing Faro on the counterpane. When Levi grew tired of losing, Jake had me put the footed breakfast tray over his legs and showed us card tricks – how to snap-change a card, then how to vanish one from the table. His hands were good – in fact, looking back, I can say that his hands were great. Even knowing how the tricks worked, neither of us could catch the card snapping back, or flicking beneath his outstretched arm to his lap. As we practised, he amused himself by shooting cards across the room into the wastebasket, only missing twice out of the entire deck.

I watched in fascination, then demanded, 'Show me how you do that!'

So he showed me. I had a good arm for throwing, but at first the cards flew wildly over. Jake picked up one that had landed on his pillow – well behind my back – and said, 'You're thinking too hard. Don't throw the card; let it throw itself.'

I focused closely on his arm, his fingers: relaxed and sure. On my tenth try, the slick paper seemed to find a pathway cut through the air: instead of fluttering up or sideways, it spun, its corner tapping against the wallpaper twelve feet away.

My whoop attracted attention from downstairs, and Mother came up, sending Levi and me away to let the patient rest. The cards went with me.

By the end of the afternoon, I could hit a wastebasket twelve feet away nineteen times out of twenty. By the time I went to bed, I could get the entire deck in at fifteen feet.

The next morning, Jake was impressed.

That afternoon, he was well enough for a walk over the snow-sprinkled Downs.

And by evening, he felt recovered enough to go up to the Evil Publican's inn for a few hands of poker.

I was, frankly, hurt: why would my beloved uncle turn his back on us to socialise with That Person?

The next day, I asked him.

He and I had graduated to throwing competitions by now: who could get the most cards in the basket, the fastest, and the farthest away. There in the sitting room, in a house redolent with cinnamon and evergreen boughs, I ventured a suggestion that Jake was being a touch disloyal to us.

He did not reply, not directly, merely finished his run of tosses (he missed two, to my one) and then said, 'Let's try something else.'

He took a tall, thin glass vase from the mantelpiece and stood it on the low table. Backing away a few feet, he held a card between his fingers, made a couple of practice runs, then snapped his hand out – and the card magically appeared between vase and table. The effect was like a magician whipping away a laden tablecloth, in reverse. He handed me the deck of cards, watched me knock the vase over a few times, suggested a correction of my elbow, and said, 'When you can feed a sequence of cards under the vase, ask me again about my poker games.'

Perfection took me two days, by which time my fingers were somewhat raw.

It was now December 20th, a Wednesday. I took Uncle Jake into the dining room, balanced a half-inch wooden dowel upright, and let a series of ten cards take up residence between the dowel and the tablecloth, each one shooting the previous card to the floor beyond.

I felt Jake's strong, supple fingers come down on my shoulder, gripping it in approval. I had never felt prouder of anything in my life.

Then the work began.

I listened with something near awe as my uncle casually suggested to his older brother (his experienced, and hence suspicious, older brother) that Charles really ought to take advantage of having another adult in the house and take Judith for a night out. In London, even. Wasn't there something at the theatre that she'd mentioned wanting to see? Yes, he supposed it would make for a late night – unless they stayed in Town. In a hotel even, so as not to face the currently cold and empty London house?

Oh, certainly, whatever Charles thought – it was merely an idea . . .

His apparent indifference set the hook. But when Jake went on to point out that it would of course mean that he couldn't drink or go out – couldn't so much as take his eyes off either of us until we were tucked into our beds – well, then the hook was truly buried.

Maternal suspicions flared when Father surprised her with the proposal of twenty-four hours of adult freedom, but when Jake swore to her that he would be responsible, that he would not have more than one drink, or two at the most, that he would watch over his charges as if they were his own, she let herself be convinced. My parents set off for the Eastbourne station on Friday morning, trailing an air of giddy anticipation.

Jake rubbed his hands together, and put his team to work.

Walking towards the inn that night, well bundled against the cold, we saw the gleam of expensive motor cars from down the road. As we drew near, we heard men's voices, then saw a hand-lettered sign pinned to the door: CLOSED TONIGHT FOR PRIVATE PARTY.

Jake pushed open the saloon-bar door and walked into the warmth and brightness. Half a dozen men in expensive suits looked around at our entrance, their faces first lighting up as they saw who it was, then going confused when they saw Levi and me.

'You can't bring those two in here,' the Evil Publican declared.

'I didn't think you'd be keen on it,' Jake said easily, 'but I'm afraid I'm stuck with them for the night. Playing nursemaid, you know. So unless you want to give them a bottle of lemonade and let them sit in the corner for a while, I won't be joining you tonight.'

Protest arose, most vehemently from the Evil Publican, who had planned this evening for some weeks (and, no doubt, intended to reap financial benefits from it). But Jake stood firm: he'd promised his brother that he wouldn't take his eyes off the kids, so . . .

Having seen Uncle Jake's wiles at work on my parents, I was not surprised when his ploy of innocence worked on men with drinks in their hands and gambling on their minds. Levi and I were settled into a corner with lemonade and a packet of stale biscuits. Since we had come armed with books, we were content.

The evening wore on. Empty bottles collected on the bar, neckties were loosened. For the most part, the men recalled our presence only when one or the other of them shushed some thoughtless language. After Levi curled up on the cushions with a travelling rug pulled up over him, we became even less visible.

That would not have been the case had I been even a year older, but being some days short of my twelfth birthday, I was a child, not a young woman. And when I put down my book and wandered up to look over my uncle's shoulder, one of the men called me Jake's good-luck charm – which that night, Jake Russell surely needed. He won occasionally, but when he lost, it was big. Gradually, he slid deeper into the hole. All the while, the Publican's winnings grew. The room grew warmer. Jake irritably ripped off his tie and loosened his collar. His hand movements grew more clumsy, his voice louder.

I walked back to Levi's corner and picked up my book again, but the voices were growing too loud, the vocabulary a touch uncontrolled. I went back to Jake, leaning against his left shoulder.

'Uncle Jake, can we go soon?'

'Not until I win back my stake, honey.'

'You're a long way from that, Yank,' the Publican sneered. 'You're just about cleaned out!'

But the Yank was not quite without resources.

Jake reached down to his pocket, then laid his fist on the table. He withdrew his hand, revealing a mound of brilliant green and pale gold. I gasped: 'Mama's emeralds! Oh, Uncle Jake, you can't—'

'Just borrowing them, Mary,' he said. 'They'll be back before your mother is.'

The necklace was old, heavy, and valuable – extremely valuable. I watched these strangers pass my mother's treasure along the table, debating its value as if they were talking about horseflesh or a grain shipment. Two of the men had a lot of experience in buying ladies' jewels, and both agreed that the piece was worth more than everything on the table. More than everything *around* the table, for that matter.

'I don't care,' Jake declared, looking flushed and sounding desperate. 'My luck's about to turn, I can feel it.'

The others looked at each other, then sat up with renewed interest. Playing commenced, wagers climbed. One player folded, and another. And then with a convulsive motion, Jake shoved forward his entire bankroll – including my mother's emerald necklace. 'All,' he said.

A third player put his cards down immediately. The fourth mulled it over for a minute before he, too, decided that discretion was the better part of poker.

That left Jake and the innkeeper. As was his habit, well known to anyone who played against him, the man picked up his cards, checked them, and laid them down again on the table to his right side. 'I'm in.'

'Like everyone says, there's not enough on the table to match my sparklies,' Jake pointed out. 'So what'll you add? That pretty new motor of yours? I'd really like a new motor car.' However, I thought that his voice and face did not quite match the confidence of his words. Also, his left leg was jittering beneath the table, a thing I'd noticed he did when his hand was questionable.

The innkeeper saw it, too. 'You're bluffing,' he scoffed.

'Then match the bet. What can you put up but the car? This joint, maybe? Yeah, okay, how about the keys to this place? Or should I . . . ?' Jake wrapped a hand across the heap of gems and gold, pulling it a fraction towards himself. When his arm rose again, the necklace had hit upon a stray beam from the overhead lamp, and sparkled all the brighter.

The innkeeper stood up to go around behind his bar, coming

back with a heavy ring of keys. He unthreaded one and dropped it into his pocket, tossing the remainder atop his banknotes and coins.

He sat down. But just as he reached for his cards, there came a crash and a cry from where Levi had been sleeping. Everyone turned to look, and I detached myself from Uncle Jake's shoulder to scurry around the table to Levi's rescue. The card players, seeing that the damage was more to the boy's dignity than his person, laughed and resumed their glasses, or their cards . . .

The Evil Publican's shock sent an almost palpable wave through the room. He pawed his cards in confusion, then disbelief, before slapping them face-up onto the table and rising in fury. His chair crashed to the floor. Drinks were spilt, curses emitted, and Jake's own cards went flying as he scrambled away from the table, where the enraged innkeeper looked about to launch himself across it. 'What the hell did you do, you little bastard?' the man snarled. 'I had a straight flush with a jack on top! How the *hell* did you—?'

'Language!' Jake protested.

'Look!' The man jabbed a finger at his five cards, which could only have been mistaken for a straight flush if one read the eight of hearts as a jack of spades. As it was, all he had was a pair of eights.

Jake looked with the others, then lifted his gaze. 'You need your eyes checked, man,' he taunted.

The publican did come for him then, starting around the table with a roar while Jake circled nimbly ahead of his meaty outstretched hands. Levi and I joined the tumult with voices raised (me pausing briefly at the two fallen chairs to set them aright) until the other men had extricated themselves from their own seats to seize the Evil Publican, pressing him back into his chair with a glass full enough to sedate a rhinoceros.

Jake returned cautiously to his place, stooping to retrieve his cards.

He laid them out deliberately, one at a time, beside the emeralds.

I thought the innkeeper would explode when the jack of spades appeared. He demanded the whole deck be collected for counting, but there were fifty-two, with no duplicates. And although in the confusion, any number of cards could have traded places, there was no doubt that his claim to a seven, eight, nine, ten, and jack of spades was absurd. How could Jake have touched his cards? He'd been sitting right there until the innkeeper picked them up.

Perhaps if the others actually liked the Evil Publican, his claims might have held a bit more weight. However, his hosting of this card game had always been more avaricious than sociable, and no one put his claimed straight flush against Jake's mere pair of queens. (Two of the four others ruefully admired the skilful bluff, having themselves held hands that could have won.) If they had to lose to someone, make it Jake. At least it made for a good story.

Banknotes, coins, and the set of keys dutifully crossed the table. Jake Russell was now the owner of a derelict public house in rural Sussex.

He gave the inn's former proprietor thirty pounds and an hour to load the shiny motor car with personal belongings. Before first light the following morning, while five mostly contented London poker players snored in their beds above, three Russells stood in the inn's ancient doorway and watched the car's lights fade in the direction of Lewes.

'Quite a gamble,' Holmes remarked. 'There were any number of hands that would have beaten your uncle even after losing a card. And others that your thrown eight of hearts would actually have improved.'

'Credit Jake's guardian angel. And I suppose if he'd lost, the emeralds would simply have vanished from the inn's strongbox, and Jake from Sussex.'

'Which, I suspect, would not have been the first time the police were notified as to his activities?'

'Nor the last. But you're right, it was a gamble. It wouldn't have worked at all, had I not been a child.'

'A highly intelligent, cool-headed, left-handed child.'

I laughed. 'With a brother who could fall off a bench on command.'

'The Russell gang: Scotland Yard's despair. So what cards did your uncle have?'

'It wasn't bad – a full house, three eights and a pair of queens, so he ended up with two pairs and that jack of spades. It was all a bluff, including his nervous leg.'

'He indicated to you the eight of hearts in his own hand, then stretched out play while you stepped aside to fetch that card from a matching deck you'd brought. When you returned and were propped on his shoulder, your little brother conveniently fell off his makeshift bed. Your card toss kicked the jack of spades out of the publican's hand, leaving it on the floor.'

'I retrieved it when I bent down for his chair, then left it with those Uncle Jake had dropped, when I set his chair upright. The fellow knew the change had been made somehow, but since no one saw anything, the only faintly suspicious act was Jake dropping his cards – and even then, everyone else had jumped, too, when the innkeeper came out of his chair. In the end, they decided it was the empty claim of a losing blowhard.'

'I always wondered about that inn's abrupt change of ownership. I was away at the time.'

'Jake sold it for next to nothing to a lady in Eastbourne whose cooking he was fond of.'

'Tillie Whiteneck.'

'She wanted to call the place "Jake's Hand" but he said no, so she dusted off the oldest name she could find for it. Thus, the Monk's Tun.'

'What did your parents say?'

'They didn't find out until after Christmas. Levi nearly let it slip twice, but fortunately I was there to kick his shins under the table. And then Jake was gone – he didn't even stay for Christmas, to our vast disappointment. He never came back to Sussex, although the presents continued for a couple of years, and the occasional letter.'

Before he disappeared, however, my uncle had left behind a gift for each of us. Levi received a set of magician's props, with joining rings, a magic bouquet, and a genuine child-sized folding silk hat.

And for me? An object that I carry to this day, despite my father's disapproval and my mother's dismay: a slim piece of wickedly sharp steel with a rosewood handle that was just a fraction large for my eleven-year-old hand. It rested in a curious sort of sheath with straps at both ends which, after some thought, I fitted to my ankle. There it lay, invisible beneath trouser legs, a long skirt, or a pair of high boots.

Still lies. Now, all these years later, my eyes came to rest on the pile of logs beside the fire. My hand went down to the sheath, and with the flick of a hand, I let the wicked, brilliant little knife throw itself at the target.

Every young woman should have had an Uncle Jake.

MARY RUSSELL'S WAR

On August 4th, 2014, one hundred years to the day after World War I erupted onto the headlines of newspapers the world around, 'Mary Russell's War' began to appear as weekly instalments in a blog kept by Laurie R. King. The journal, like everything else Miss Russell writes, is both autobiography and cool reporting, laced throughout with a vein of her distinctive dry humour. Here, young Mary's commitment to recording the progress of world events weaves in and out of her own personal narrative, the two bleeding into each other until the stories of the girl and the century begin eerily to mesh. The vivid words of the journal, combined with the photographs, newspaper clippings, postcards, and such that Miss Russell slipped among its pages, give us a taste not only of the times, but of this young woman's extraordinary mind – and of the rich and eventful life that is before her.

Since the 1994 publication of the first Russell Memoir, The Beekeeper's Apprentice, a stream of stories (all of them under the 'authorship' of Laurie R. King, for reasons explained by Miss Russell elsewhere)[1] have continued to uncover the remarkable adventures of this young woman and her partner-turned-husband Sherlock Holmes. In addition to the 'novels' that make up Miss Russell's Memoirs, an assortment of supplemental material in the form of 'short stories' and the like offer insight into previously unexplored corners of their lives.

And yet, it is equally striking how often Miss Russell chooses not to reveal matters. Her relationship with parents and brother, for example, is given in small (though illuminating) vignettes; details are sparse of her work with the psychiatric doctor Leah Ginsberg; one searches in vain for the precise locations of houses, or even their physical characteristics.

Yes, one is forced to read between the lines, here as elsewhere in the Russell Memoirs. A reader even begins to wonder if this is not a large part of their appeal: one gets the very clear sensation, even when Russell is little more than a child, that privacy is paramount, and that any conclusions regarding her person will require a great deal of research, a thorough analysis, and a lot of just plain investigation.

As is, on reflection, only appropriate.

[1] 'My Story' and 'A Case in Correspondence'

WAR
EXTRA

San Francisco Chronicle

THIRD
EDITION

LEADING NEWSPAPER of the PACIFIC COAST

SAN FRANCISCO, CAL. WEDNESDAY, AUGUST 5, 1914

Great Britain Declares War

French Warships Sink Teuton Craft in Sea Battle

EMPEROR OF GERMANY'S APPEAL TO NATION

In Speech to Reichstag, Ruler Exhorts His People to Give Support to Government and Bravely Defend Their Country.

EXPLAINS NECESSITY OF COMING TO AID OF ALLY

WAR BULLETINS

GERMAN THREAT FAILS TO COW BELGIUM

The Kaiser Demands That the Little Nation Allow Troops to Go Through to France.

LEAVE DECISION TO ARMS

King Albert of Belgium Asks His Subjects to Be Ready for Instant Mobilization.

LEADERS of British and German Armies: Sir J. French, who will have charge of English troops, and Vice-Admiral Sir John Jellicoe, in command of the Fleet. General von Moltke will be to administer command of the Kaiser's army.

LEGIONS OF POWERS IN BATTLE ARRAY AND ALL EUROPE IN ARMS

Great Britain Issues Declaration of War When Germany Ignores Ultimatum Concerning the Neutrality of Belgium

French Fleet Off Algiers Is Reported to Have Defeated and Sunk German Ships and Captured One in Naval Battle

LONDON, August 4.—Great Britain declared war on Germany at 7 o'clock tonight. The first announcement that Germany had declared war on Great Britain was due to an error in the Admiralty's statement.

MARY RUSSELL: MY WAR JOURNAL

4th August 1914

I WAS FOURTEEN WHEN I first heard about the War. Fourteen years and 214 days, with my nose (as usual) in a book as I walked down the stairs.

At least, that's how Mother says I shall remember this day. And Father agrees: the War will be both long and hard, for all the European countries and the Empire beyond. Flo's parents – Flo carries the role of my best friend, so of course I telephoned her about Britain's declaration of War immediately I had finished my meal, although it was a brief conversation since Mother and Father both wished to use the instrument, yet they would not allow me to go to Flo's house, oh, when will I be permitted to take a simple walk without a chaperone? – at any rate, Flo's parents are of the opinion that England will sweep up the German army in no time. However, since Mother has a dreary way of being right about <u>everything</u>, I thought I might mark the occasion by taking out the journal she gave me for my birthday 214 days ago, and begin writing in it. If she's wrong, I shall show her this, as a demonstration of her fallibility.

Everyone has been talking about war for what seems like my entire life – certainly long before the Archduke and his wife were shot in Sarajevo at the end of June. I have to admit that I have yet to understand precisely what the heir to a Bohemian throne (will I ever be able to hear that name without envisioning Sherlock Holmes and Irene Adler?) has to do with an invasion of Belgium. Judging by the conversation of many adults and the cross-purposes of the newspaper editorials, I am not the only one to whom the sequence is unclear.

Still, one thing is clear: the fuse of the powder keg that is Europe has been set alight.

Looking at what I have written here, I realise that I must decide how much explication a diary requires. Do I explain to a stranger the basic facts of my life? Or do I make notes that might remind a future, absent-minded self that, it being 1914, I live in San Francisco though I was born in England? That my mother is Jewish and my father Christian? I suppose that the possibilities of unfamiliar eyes seeing this means I ought to introduce myself. Very well: my name is Mary Judith Emily Russell (though I never use the name Emily), daughter of Charles Russell (of Boston, Massachusetts) and Judith Rebecca Russell (née Klein, of London, England). I am a day younger than the twentieth century, and in addition to being fourteen years and 214 days old, I am tall for a girl, short-sighted, with blonde hair the same shade as my father's (although considerably longer) and the blue eyes that often go with that colour. I have a brother, Levi, who is nine years old and resembles our mother, being dark of hair and eye, sharp of tongue and wit, and irritatingly right about things. Especially mathematics. He's something of a genius. I'm merely very smart.

I probably shouldn't have written that, since if he finds this he'll take it as an admission that he has the superior mind. If you are reading this, Levi, remember that even Sherlock Holmes wasn't as bright as a woman.

I HAVE DECIDED TO WRITE in this journal, not daily (as the name suggests) but once a week. There is so much turmoil, so rapid a shift of events, that thoughtful reflection requires a week's span.

It is appalling to think what is happening in Europe. Every morning's paper shouts the headlines: BRITISH AND GERMAN FLEETS IN BATTLE. GERMANS OVERCOME BELGIANS' DEFENCES AT CITY OF LIEGE. Even AEROPLANES PLAY BIG PART IN LIEGE ATTACK. The fighting in mid-air was desultory, but deadly. A huge Zeppelin sailed over Liege during the early fighting, but was pursued by a Belgian aeroplanist who risked and lost his life in destroying it. GERMANS BAD SHOTS, SAY PILOTS.

Long Trains of Supplies Accompanying the German Armies in Belgium

Noble little Belgium. Father put up a map of Europe in the library, and places pins at each new report. He tells me the Germans are following a war plan that depends on rapidly overrunning the countryside between them and Paris, and in the past week, Belgium's grim defence has slowed the Kaiser. May God grant that this has given France time to prepare for invasion.

America, of course, has declared herself neutral, offering to negotiate between the parties: <u>TENDER OF GOOD OFFICES BRINGS NO RESPONSE.</u>

This despite atrocity: in one conquered town, the Germans took fourteen residents, shooting eight, hanging two – but letting the mayor go, since the Germans had been his dinner guests the previous evening. I do not understand military thinking. I suppose that when many of those fighting one's soldiers are, in fact, civilians with weapons, there is no division between uniforms and not.

Gigantic British Gun Used to Check German Advance

There are some portions of the world not in flames: <u>PEACE IS NEAR IN WAR-TORN MEXICO</u>. And the newspaper corner advertisements that in the early days were for maps of Europe and a rather tasteless advert for spectacles (<u>Will War Advance Price of Glasses?</u>) have returned to weather reports and apartments for lease on Nob Hill.

But the world appears to be in flames. And not only in Europe.

My parents are arguing. At night, and behind closed doors, but they are arguing, long and hard. Even Levi has heard them, although he has been as unable to hear what they are saying as I.

My parents never argue.

Never.

I WAS AT THE GREENFIELD house last night (the daughter, Florence, was more or less assigned me as a friend when we came back to San Francisco two years ago, since our mothers share many interests and organisations – although truth to tell, I find more to talk about with Flo's brother, Frank) and found the family almost completely detached from the War. Mrs Greenfield seems more concerned at the potential disruption of their travel plans for next summer than any political turmoil or loss of life: she is convinced that fighting will be over by Christmas, but worries over damage to monuments and shortages of wine and foie gras. When I told her that in Father's opinion the War would be a long one, she merely gave one of her ear-splitting laughs and told me not to worry my pretty head. I left before I could say anything rude (which would invariably subject me to one of Mother's lectures) and collected Frankie for a rather violent game of kick-the-can.

The Parents' ongoing argument, I have determined, concerns the War. Mother wants to go home, to England. Father absolutely refuses to permit it. Or rather (I've located an attic corner with a section of plaster thin enough that sound travels up from Mother's dressing room), Father refuses to permit her to take Levi and me with her. And although the two of them are habituated to spending long periods separated by the Atlantic, with Mother and us in England while Father comes and goes from his business concerns in America, she has never been separated from Levi and me for more than a few days. And as their overheard conversations have made clear, she does not intend to be now.

So, it looks as if we are to be stuck in neutral territory – America – until the War is over. (On one point they agree: this will not be a matter of weeks, despite Mrs Greenfield's opinion.) When I told all this to Levi (who although only nine, is nonetheless more intelligent than most of the adults I know), he very rightly pointed out that, as half-English citizens, we had a responsibility to serve the King in any way we could. And (as an article in the Chronicle described last week) if a woman on the train from Antwerp could discover a German spy on the point of releasing carrier pigeons hidden in a bag, surely we could do no less.

Thus, two nights ago, when we heard four brief blasts of a ship's horn, we both suspected it was the German cruiser that has been lurking out at sea, waiting to fill its coal stores. A newspaper article five days ago reported that the <u>Leipsic</u> had wirelessed for permission to enter the harbour, and had also sent ashore two of its sailors for medical attention, so we knew it would slip in sooner or later. When the horn sounded, we were ready. I met Levi at the front door, and we made it almost all the way down Gough Street before a patrol spotted the pale coat Levi had insisted on wearing, and took us home again. Mother was not happy. Father pretended to be angry, but I could see that he was also amused. It will be difficult to slip away for the next couple of days, to keep an eye on the Leipsic, although it is reported to be lying between Fort Mason and Alcatraz Island, so I may be able to see it from the rooftop with Father's field glasses, once Mother goes to her meeting this afternoon.

I am cross with Levi. I fear that my brother, bright though he may be, lacks the instincts of a criminal – or of a good detective.

(Which reminds me – there is to be a new Sherlock Holmes story in The Strand, beginning next month! A serial novel that begins, 'The Manor House of Birlstone, Chapter I, The Warning', with Sherlock Holmes making snappish remarks as he stares at a slip of paper he has drawn from an envelope! Oh, how is it possible to simultaneously adore and loathe a thing – a good long story, but one that demands months of waiting? Petty of me, I know, but I do hope the magazine continues to cross the Atlantic without delay during the hostilities. At least during the period that The Valley of Fear is being published.)

As if to confirm the need for citizen spies, this morning's Chronicle brought the War's proximity into focus. I shall copy the article:

SEA FIGHT IS HEARD ON SOUTH COAST

MONTEREY, August 17th – Firing at sea was heard this evening by J. Lewis, superintendent of instruction at the

YWCA camp at Asilmar. It was in the direction of the heads, near Santa Cruz, north-west of here. A heavy fog has obscured the view.

Lewis says that the firing started at 7.20 and lasted until after eight o'clock. It is believed the French cruiser *Montelam*, which left San Diego on Saturday, has engaged with the German cruiser *Nurnberg*.

Several others at Asilmar, Pacific Grove, and New Monterey have reported hearing heavy firing at sea.

I believe that the War will require service from us all before the end, even fourteen-year-old girls.

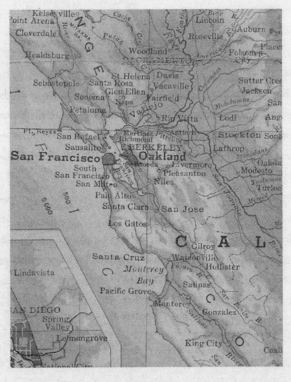

R EADING THE HEADLINES, A rational person must wonder precisely what it means to be a 'neutral' country. We in California are not at war, but at the same time, even a casual observer (is there such a thing, in this age?) can see that the United States are merely undeclared allies of England. It is the unspoken truth behind the wording of such newspaper articles as this:

CRUISER LEIPZIG STANDS OFF SHORE

Fear of Seizure by the Germans May Halt
Departure of the Royal Mail Liner *Moana*

The German cruiser *Leipzig*, which left port early yesterday morning after taking on coal and stores, ostensibly bound for the German port of Apia, via Honolulu, was still off port at 9 o'clock when spoken by the incoming liner *Wilhemina* . . .

Laden with a million-dollar cargo, the *Moana* would make a rich prize for the *German* and, it is said in shipping circles, would be just the seizure that would aid the *Leipzig*, both as a shield and a coal supply ship if the foreigner intends to proceed to Apia. The *Leipzig* has only coal enough to steam 3,500 miles, and it is more than 4,000 miles to the German port.

In the event that it is the intention of the *Leipzig* to continue her cruise on the Pacific coast she would need plenty of fuel, and to this end might lie in wait for coal-laden windjammers and steamers, which at frequent intervals come here from Australia.

That was Wednesday. Thursday's paper all but accused the German-registered steamer <u>Mazatlan</u> of plotting to transfer much of the coal and provisions it had taken on board into the <u>Nurnberg</u>. Now, I am no friend of the Kaiser, but regarding America's so-called neutrality: were the <u>Mazatlan</u>'s country of registry to be Great Britain, would this question even arise?

Levi went to ask Papa to take us down to Pier 17 for a look at the Mazatlan, but Papa refused. Had he suggested a jolly ride in the new Maxwell, it would have been an easy matter to urge our path towards the waterfront, but overt reconnaissance of a suspected warship was unacceptable. Levi will never learn that with Mama it is possible to be direct, but when it comes to Papa, particularly when he is in a temper as he has been this week, the oblique approach is better.

Matters appeared to have reached a head on Saturday, all of which Papa spent behind the closed door of his library, typing furiously[2] without so much as a break for luncheon. When he came out, late in the afternoon, he had a stamped envelope in his hand (too flat for an entire day's worth of typing). I did contrive to glance at it while he was putting on his hat, and saw that it was addressed to the War Office in Washington, DC. Papa was gone just long enough to walk to the nearest posting box, during which time I naturally made a thorough search of the library, but found no sign of his long labours. This can only mean that he had locked his manuscript away in the safe.

(Note to self: locate a safe-cracker willing to teach the trade to a young girl.)

---

[2] This may be the document given in *Locked Rooms*.

After Papa had gone upstairs to bathe and shave (both of which he normally does in the morning), he came down, poured himself a drink half again as generous as his usual serving, and gave Mama a kiss on the back of her neck. I note this because the past two weeks have seen the two of them decidedly cool, and although I have no wish to encounter the sloppy emotions parents occasionally reveal, I admit that it is more desirable to have parents in accord than parents at odds. My own are, in general, of an amiable and co-operative disposition, although there have been times, particularly before we moved back here from England in 1912, when walking around them was like sailing into port through a field of mines.

Sunday, Levi and I took breakfast on our own, with Mah (our cook) in the kitchen. Sunday afternoon, Papa took us down to Golden Gate Park, where he produced a quite marvellous Chinese kite, which rode the stiff breeze like some magical creature.

Monday seemed almost ordinary, by comparison with the last two weeks.

The War news seems to be either triumphant or disastrous, depending on which headline one reads. Last night, I made the mistake of asking Papa how long it might be before we had a chance to travel through the new canal in Panama, since the Germans seemed determined to lock us behind a fence of warships. My innocent question led to an hour spent with the new War Map (19¢ from the San Francisco Chronicle: is this not war profiteering?) spread out over the table in his library. This key point, it seems, is why Japan's entry into the War yesterday was such a blessing, particularly for those of us on the Pacific Coast: the Japanese navy are keeping the German Pacific fleet bottled up in their port on the southern peninsula of China, leaving only two ships – the <u>Nurnberg</u> and the <u>Leipzig</u> – free to threaten coastal cities and make raids on Allied shipping.

That is something of a relief, although even the presence of those two ships will prevent the Russell family from sailing for the Panama Canal anytime soon.

However, the week's news has also provided me with a weapon against the parents. The next time a lecture looms on the horizon, I shall be ready with a very different article with which to distract an uncomfortable mother or father:

YOUNG LOCHINVAR KIDNAPS GIRL IN AUTOMOBILE

Youth Steals the Object of His Affections,
but Is Captured in San Jose

There follows the tale of a seventeen-year-old nurse-girl kidnapped at the point of a revolver (from Baker Street, which is not far from here – shades of the 'Solitary Cyclist'!) and driven to

San Jose, where the man planned to force a county clerk to issue a marriage licence, and a minister to perform a marriage. 'Throughout the seizure of Miss Broadhurst was of the most exciting nature. Screams and shots aroused the entire neighbourhood . . .'

This young man does not sound like Walter Scott's hero to me – 'faithful in love and dauntless in war'. However, he does seem potentially useful, since questions about the incident could serve to loose me rapidly from the parental presence, if needs be – certainly when it comes to Papa, who turns quite endearingly pink when certain topics come before us.

THE GERMANS CONTINUE THEIR advance on Paris, despite the valiant efforts of Belgium. <u>LOSSES ARE HEAVY ON BOTH SIDES</u>. The French and English are lined up against the Kaiser along a vast line, digging in their toes against the push. <u>Casualties on Both Sides are Appalling</u>. Aeroplanes, meanwhile, pass over their heads to drop bombs on Paris, hitting near the Gare de l'Est.

On this side of the globe, British ships have captured the German port of Apia, which will give the <u>Nurnberg</u> and <u>Leipzig</u> one fewer source of provisioning. Closer to home, however, the papers talk of the arrest of two burglars: one was caught when his snores woke the woman who had gone to sleep in the bed over his hiding place, and the other was arrested when he got stuck attempting to climb in through a transom.

I do not think the residents of San Francisco are sufficiently concerned with the War in Europe. Could it be merely the readers of the <u>Chronicle</u>? Father came home early from work today, closeting himself in his library again. This time, there was no pounding of the typewriter, merely silence and the odour of his pipe. After an hour of this, Mother let herself in. I contrived to be in line of sight when she did so, and saw him sitting in his leather chair with a typed letter in his hand. I have yet to locate a duct or thin place in the walls that gives me access to library conversations.

<u>Why</u> do parents persist in keeping things from their children? This is a very foolish way to run a family, and is based on the assumption that minors lack either intelligence or common sense. Until recently, I would have thought this a mistake my own parents would not make. It is disappointing to discover otherwise.

Until I can uncover the source of all these familial mysteries, I amuse myself by collecting examples of Wartime absurdities. Such as the following article:

RUDYARD KIPLING IS ARRESTED ON SUSPICION

LONDON – Rudyard Kipling, who lives near Brighton, on the south coast, was arrested as a suspicious person while taking one of his regular constitutionals along the seafront.

He entered into the fun of the thing: in fact, he was delighted at being mistaken for a possible German spy, inasmuch as it proved to him in a most convincing manner that a vigilant watch is being kept.

Kipling was detained for some time, during which he was searched, but eventually his identity was established, and he was set free with apologies.

S CHOOL IS NOW FULLY under way. Not that Levi and I are directly concerned with classrooms, but our tutors follow the schedule of public school, thus rendering us now as occupied with books and chalkboards as any child of the city. I have two tutors this year. In the afternoons, a nervous ex-schoolmaster with dandruff over his shoulders coaches me through the scientific side of the curriculum, while in the mornings, Miss Warren, the same teacher I have had since we returned here two years ago, is responsible for the less meaty part of my education, from American and English history to Greek philosophers. She herself is English, which is a help when it comes to my spelling, which tends to meander between the two systems unless firmly brought to heel. This year she has also taken on the duty of driving some modicum of general knowledge into Levi's single-track mind, an uphill battle. Perhaps I should suggest that if she can find a way to present her material in some form of puzzle, a prime way to capture Levi's attention, she would have better luck with the actual content.

Speaking of uphill battles: several hundred thousand Frenchmen are furiously digging a complicated system of entrenchments outside of Paris. Is the idea that the Kaiser's men will fall into it as they press forward? Trenches seem hardly more adequate than a row of sharpened stakes when it comes to foiling the advance of a modern army, or even slowing it much: every fortress in the north of France is now in German hands. I see on Mother's face, and in the long hours at her War Work, that she dreads one morning to hear the newsboys shout, 'Kaiser crossing the Channel!' Her ladies' maid, Phillips, has left for home, and Mother has said she will not replace her, but instead devote Phillips' salary to buying aeroplanes – that being her War Work (a phrase she pronounces with Capital Letters).

I should perhaps pause to note that Mother has decided to raise funds to buy aeroplanes for British pilots to fly over the Front. She has entered into this with as much methodical devotion as she does any other matter, with the result that her study is now the headquarters of this diminutive organisation, with thrice-weekly meetings and such a quantity of mail that the Post Office has added a delivery to this neighbourhood.

While Parisians dig trenches, on this side of the world, one of the two German cruisers that have haunted the Pacific was finally spotted:

CRUISER NURNBERG WILL SAIL STRIPPED TO FIGHT

Commander of German Craft Says
Vessel May Be His Coffin

HONOLULU – The German cruiser *Nurnberg*, whose whereabouts have been a mystery since she left here early last month, appeared off this port early today.

Inasmuch as the *Nurnberg* left this port thirty-five days ago, just before war was declared between Germany and Great Britain, she is entitled now to take on as much coal and no more as will carry her to the nearest home port and may remain in Honolulu twenty-four hours.

Where that port now is becomes a point for the international lawyers to decide. The British have seized German Samoa, and the Japanese are blockading Germany's naval base in Kiso-Chow bay.

And elsewhere:

Nothing has been seen of the German cruiser *Leipzig*, the only other German warship in the Pacific not bottled up in Kido-Chow bay.

It is difficult to locate 'Kido-Chow' on the atlas of China, that being one of the many foreign cities given half a dozen completely unrelated spellings. Micah, who took a day off work from his bookstore in Chinatown to help Mother in the garden, found it for me. He tells me that the word is something closer to 'Chiaow-show.' Between the typographical errors and its wilful mistakes, the <u>Chronicle</u> is proving less than dependable as a source of geographical knowledge.

I scoured the papers in vain for any further arrests of English literary figures out for a stroll on the coast. Were I a famous writer, I should do my best to be captured staring out to sea, a flag-like scarf clasped in my hand. It would no doubt do wonders for one's sales figures.

Today's paper, which I read after having written the above (one's parents, inevitably, are granted the day's news first) contained an exciting update:

BATTLESHIP PURSUING GERMAN CRUISER

British Dreadnought Australia Reported to Be in Chase of Kaiser's Nurnberg, Which Left Honolulu September 1st, After Taking Coal.

It is believed here that the Australia cable to British Columbia was cut by the *Nurnberg*.

My fellow Californians seem completely oblivious of any threat. Mother has her War Work, Father clearly is up to something (he has yet to explain that letter to the War Office!), but what are those who are technically underage to do? Are Levi and I – objectively speaking, two of the more gifted minds in the city – to concern ourselves with nothing but mathematical problems and English poetry? After much discussion, he and I went to Father in the library this evening to put the proposition before him, and in the end, Papa did at least agree to tutor us in German, one of the languages in which he is fluent.

That will not be sufficient, but at least we have succeeded in planting the thought in his distracted mind.

L AST WEEK, LEVI CIRCLED an article in the news concerning a boy of fourteen years and eleven months who was serving in the German army, leaving it prominently on the library table. Father said nothing. Then this morning, the news included mention of Mrs Vanderbilt washing dishes in the scullery of a Paris Red Cross Hospital. A full range of volunteers, except for us.

As for deaths, the casualties roll includes Honourables, a viscount, a lord, and the brother of a Duke, while Mother has received a third letter concerning the loss of English childhood friends. Closer to home, a dispatch from New Zealand now reports no fewer than <u>five</u> German cruisers in the Pacific! Yet a local company, playing on all these headlines of death and terror, saw fit to compose an advert saying:

WAR-DROBE TRUNKS

Some salesman no doubt thinks himself most clever.

A letter came from my grandmother in Boston, bemoaning the interruption of fashion out of France (!) and the departure of a good friend for Germany, and included a note to me (on flowered paper) asking if I was wearing my hair up yet, and if so did I wish

Granny to buy me some combs for my Christmas present? It pains me to consider that I am related to this person, who has as little sense of the world as Flo's mother. In the meantime, a woman explorer has discovered a new mountain in Canada, Father enjoyed a baseball game at Ewing Field, and the Kaiser has been approached with an exchange of peace terms.

When I complained at dinner last night (admittedly, in a voice of considerable distress) that I felt as if my brain were being torn across like a sheet of paper, Father ordered me to stop reading the news, and Mother suggested I speak with her friend Dr Ginsberg about my distress. (Dr Ginsberg, a woman, is a doctor of the mind, not the body – and although I like her well enough, and consider her the most sensible of my mother's lady friends, I have no wish to strip myself emotionally bare before her.) I excused myself early from the table, and took to my room.

I have not even been able to indulge in my long-anticipated escape into the world of Mr Conan Doyle's fiction, since the two chapters that make up this month's first episode of the serialisation of <u>The Valley of Fear</u> finds even his two protagonists at odds. In the course of these stories, Mr Holmes often expresses affectionate criticisms of his flatmate's abilities, but never have I seen him as openly rude as he is in these pages. 'Your native shrewdness', he sneers, going on to mock Watson's 'innate cunning' and 'Machiavellian intellect'. It is almost as if he desires to drive Watson into moving out of Baker Street. Or hauling off and delivering a good punch to that supercilious nose. 'He was undoubtedly callous from long overstimulation', Watson writes – hardly an excuse for a string of outright insults!

And yet, reading the chapters a second time, I find two clues that might have been put there for me alone, valuable clues of 'that highest value which anticipates and prevents rather than avenges crime', along with a reminder that 'the temptation to form premature theories upon insufficient data is the bane of our profession'.

Or perhaps three clues, because the episode turns around a complex cipher.

Ciphers are a thing Levi adores.

First, however – 'Data! I can't make bricks without clay!' Or rather, Levi can't figure a cipher without material.

<u>One:</u> there are without a doubt German spies in San Francisco – and from certain things Father has let slip, I believe he agrees.

<u>Two:</u> the city's blithe preoccupation with baseball games and ladies' fashion can only be making those spies confident to the point of carelessness.

<u>Three:</u> the very last person a spy would suspect of watching him would be what Mr Holmes would term an 'Irregular' – in this case, a girl of fourteen and her nine-year-old brother.

<u>Four:</u> the newspapers are full of suggestions, for attentive minds.

This morning at breakfast, Father told Mother that he will be going into Chinatown to see Micah Long (which surprised me, and her, since Father has not been as friendly to Micah as he was when I was a child) and will not be at home until perhaps seven. In one of those instances of the mind outpacing one's thoughts, I spoke up and said that Flo wanted me to help plan her birthday party, but that I, too, would be home by seven. Inevitably, Mother said it would have to be six, but after pretending to sulk, I agreed.

This means that I am free to wander the city for nearly three hours this afternoon. Moreover, when the offices of the German consulate close, the streets will be busy enough that few would take notice of a young girl on the pavements behind them.

And with Levi's assistance, I shall also be able to come and go freely after dark. A burglar might get caught in a transom (or sleeping beneath a bed!) but not I.

I could only wish that the author of Raffles the Cracksman had thought to provide hints on the opening of safes in his own stories. As it is, I must hope that any spy I locate will be lacking in care, and leave his papers lying out.

DISASTER! CALAMITY! OH, HOW I <u>loathe</u> dogs!

Who'd have expected a German spy to have a poodle? Father shouted at me – shouted! – and said that I was fortunate it hadn't been an Alsatian, which might have taken off my leg. Mother – well, Mother went silent, and sits in her morning room, white with fury.

It took me four afternoons of following men leaving the consulate on Sansome Street before I located a likely suspect for being a spy, based on the relative affluence of his home, the lack of any signs of a family, and the way he left his street-side curtains shut even during the day. Only because it has been warm was the transom window over Herr Schmidt's (another reason for suspicion: are people actually named Smith or Jones?) front door left unlatched, although as access to the house, that window would have been inadequate for even a medium-sized burglar. For someone of my girth, however, I did not anticipate any problem. With Levi's assistance, I dressed in black trousers and dark shirt, and left the house as soon as the parents were abed.

The poodle caught me standing at the desk of Herr 'Schmidt'. The man himself seized my ankle as I pulled myself up to the transom, and had it not been for his brutish application of force and the arrival of a butler, I might have succeeded in kicking myself free. The police were called, my parents roused from their beds, and . . . I doubt I shall ever rid myself of those memories, so I shall not dwell on them here in this written account. Suffice to say, I am condemned to my house. My War Work, for the time, is over. A recent issue of the Chronicle informed its readers that the Prince of Wales will not be permitted to fight either, I suppose for fear of the consequences should he be taken prisoner. Never did I suspect that I should have anything in common with the next King of England.

I may give up reading the news entirely, for it seems to alternate between joyous declarations that the Allies are pushing the Kaiser back, fearful warnings that the German army is on the point of overrunning key English and French positions, and blithe promises that the Kaiser is on the point of agreeing to talk over peace terms. And as to the regular reports of extreme behaviour on the part of the Kaiser's soldiers, an American writer who visited the Front says otherwise:

ATROCITIES ARE LIES SAYS AMERICAN WRITER

Worst Behaviour of German Soldiers in
Belgium Was Kissing of Pretty Girls

. . . in less than twenty-four hours the Belgian citizens were chatting comfortably with the German invaders, and the allegation of German brutality and demonical torture dissolved into one of the myths which have accompanied all wars. And yet . . .

WILL YOU STAND FOR THIS?

INTO CAPTIVITY—A SCENE IN A BELGIAN TOWN.

Clearly, one cannot trust the newspapers. When, that is, one can find them. Papa has taken to burning the news once he has read it (forcing me to borrow those of old Mrs Adderley down the street, whose house is one of the few places I am permitted, following my plea for the welfare of the poor old woman – who, in fact, is neither poor nor lonely, having a house full of servants and more friends than I).

Mama, when she can bear to address me directly, again urges me to discuss my behaviour with her psychological friend, Dr Ginsberg.

But really, what is there to say to a mind-doctor? It is not I who has gone mad, but the world.

CATASTROPHE HAS STRUCK. IT is the end of everything. And I have no one to blame but myself.

On Saturday afternoon, at long last, the Parents took Levi and me into their confidence. Too late.

The letter Papa sent to the War Office concerned his intention to enlist in the American army. We are neutral, yes, but that does not mean the government wishes to be unprepared. His ability with languages, his family connexions, and some ill-defined (to us, his family) ties with the world of Intelligence (my father, a spy? Surely not!) conspire to mean that he could be of considerable value, to this country and to England, hard at war. Not that they would send him to the Front – even if his limp would allow him to be sent overseas – but rather to an office in Washington, DC.

Both he and Mother have known for some time that this was coming: this, it seems, was the cause of their protracted disagreement last month. Her immediate impulse, on War's declaration, was to go home to England, but Father's utter conviction has finally swayed her into an agreement that England is no place to take a family. Once agreement was reached, they were merely waiting for certain arrangements to be made before revealing their plans to us.

Bitterly, I now learn that she was on the edge of convincing <u>him</u> that San Francisco would be the safest place for us: that she, Levi, and I would remain here, continuing with our schooling and her fundraising for the Royal Flying Corps, rather than (as he wished) have us three retreat to my grandparents' house in Boston. He was, as I say, on the edge of agreeing to this, when . . .

My fault. Had I not tried to do my part for the War effort, had I not gone after a German spy, the three of us would be waving Papa off at the train station next week. Instead, we shall all board the train with him. It seems that he cannot trust his fourteen-year-old daughter to stay out of trouble. Cannot trust his wife to keep control over said daughter. We shall go to Boston, to that fatuous woman, my grandmother, with her small dogs and her flowery hats and her too-warm house that smells of lavender.

Papa had Micah help carry our trunks from the attic. Mama has begun to pack them, without knowing for how long she is packing. Papa wants to go down the Peninsula to the Lodge on Saturday, to retrieve some things we left there on our July holiday, and to close it up for the coming months. Even years. I would like to accompany him – would like the whole family to go, since it is a place where we have been happy, and which we may never see again. But Mama says we may not be sufficiently packed up by the weekend, and that we probably won't have time.

My fault, all of it.

And in Europe, War continues to sink its teeth into civilisation.

UNIFORMS OF FRENCH OFFICERS GOOD TARGETS

Expert Declares Disproportionate Loss Due to Too Much Gold Braid and Lace on Clothes

GERMAN AEROPLANE DROPS BOMBS ON PARIS

Man's Head Blown Off, Child Is Crippled and Damage Is Done to Buildings

A twelve-year-old boy has been fighting hard in the rifle pits in the public gardens at Belgrade. He is the pet of the full-grown soldiers and lives the same life as they do, and takes his full share of the sniping, as he is a first-class shot.

In further news, a Christmas ship full of gifts is being put together for Europe. No one talks any more of the War being over before then.

[A newspaper clipping and two pieces of paper are in Dr Leah Ginsberg's handwriting here pinned to the pages of the journal.]

LIVES CLAIMED ON COAST ROAD
Family Lost in Fiery Crash

Three members of a prominent family were killed on Saturday morning when their car went off the road, just south of the beach-side town of Pacifica. the road, although paved, is widely regarded as one of the most treacherous pieces of roadway any car could sttempt. It is not known whether the cause of the crash was mechanical failure or some distraction, although family friends assert that the car was nearly new, and Mr Russell was a highly experienced driver. Mr Charles Russell, of Boston, was a prominent businessman here in San Francisco.His wife, Judith, an English citizen before their marriage, has been active in recent weeks with patriotic drives raising funds for the war efforts of her native country. Their son Levi was also killed. The family is survived by the daughter, Mary, who is hospitalized with injuries too serious to permit a conversation with reporters.

LATE SATURDAY NIGHT I received a telephone call from Mrs Long, housekeeper to my dear friend Judith Russell, to say that there had been a motor car accident on the road south of San Francisco. At first, I could make little sense of her, other than something terrible had happened – the poor woman was weeping so, her English had all but left her. After a time, her husband, Micah (the Russells' gardener), came onto the line instead, and gave me the details.

The shock of grief is a physical thing, a blow to every cell of the body at once. Three-fourths of a beloved family, gone – and the life of the surviving member uncertain. I have cancelled my appointments and am currently at the side of young Mary's hospital bed, that when – <u>when!</u> – she wakes she will see a known face instead of strangers.

She appears terribly injured. Her doctors cannot say how much internal bleeding there is, but what skin I can see between the gauze wrappings is either scraped or bruised. I watch her breaths go in, and out, and find my own breathing urging her on.

Dearest Mary,

I am so very, <u>very</u> sorry. I have known your mother for thirteen years, since she returned to California the summer after you were born. She was my oldest friend, and my closest, and I cannot even begin to picture what life is going to be without her.

Your father, too, I liked immensely, and admired unreservedly. A strong man, good to his bones, and utterly devoted to his wife and children.

And your brother – but no, I cannot bear to think of that brilliant life cut short.

My dear child, you have family, you have friends. It may

not feel like it at first, when you wake, or indeed for a long time. But there are many of us who love you, both for the family taken from us, and for you in yourself. I will be there for as much and as long as you need me. Anything I can do to lighten your burden even the faintest scrap, you need only ask.

But for now, please, dear child, do something for me: just keep breathing.

Your friend,
Leah Ginsberg

13th October

[In the handwriting of Dr Leah Ginsberg.]

I WRITE THIS ENTRY IN the journal of Miss Mary Russell, who is currently in no condition to do so herself. A journal records a life, and it should be kept.

It is not ten days since the terrible accident that robbed Mary of her family and the world of three good people. Mary is in the hospital with a series of injuries resulting from her being thrown from the family motor car just before it went off a cliff south of San Francisco. The family's housekeeper-cook, a Chinese woman named Mah Long, has asked me to help with various arrangements until Miss Russell is able to make decisions for herself.

One thing I help Mrs Long do is take various items to the hospital for Mary's comfort and reassurance. Inevitably, a cook thinks of food, and although Mary has to be coaxed to eat anything at all, she is slightly more amenable to tastes that are familiar to her. I, being a therapist of the mind, address the less concrete means of healing this young woman. Her own bedding, her bathrobe over the hospital gowns, familiar books and childhood toys (we all become children, under trauma). When I found this journal in her bedroom, it seemed to me she might be interested in recording her thoughts, and I brought it along with the porcelain-headed doll and the worn stuffed rabbit she kept near her bed at home.

As yet, in the four days the journal has sat beside her hospital bed, she has yet to touch it. So rather than allow it to sit abandoned, I have taken the responsibility to sit down with her pen and enter this Tuesday's events, from another's point of view.

The journal up to now appears to have been largely taken up

with the events of the European War (Mary: I have merely glanced over it, but not read it: privacy is a necessary part of any diary). Today's entry has no such headlines, although that war continues, inexorably. There is sufficient conflict here in this hospital room, for the present.

– Leah Ginsberg

20th October

D R GINSBERG HAS BEEN tormenting me to write in this journal, as she has been urging me to weep, and to talk about the accident. My eyes remain dry, I have nothing to say, and I have considered having one of the nurses carry the journal to the hospital incinerator. I suspect that if I do so, a fresh volume will appear. The woman is relentless.

I have now proven to the doctors of all stripes that I am still capable of setting pen to paper. That is all.

October 27th, 1914

[On a sheet of stationery pinned to the pages of the journal:]

Mary, because you seem worried about possible damage to your brain, as evidenced by your occasional lapses in memory, I am adding a page here as an aide-memoire, that you may read it and reinforce your natural recollection of the facts. Yes, your brain sustained an injury, but the doctors and I all agree: you are healing, and there is no sign of permanent damage.

Rest assured, dear Mary, that each morning I personally bring the wall calendar beside your bed up to date, drawing a line through the previous date, checking to be sure the day's appointments and scheduled visitors are accurate. I promise you I will continue to do this until you no longer need my help. I further promise you that your brain will return to its customary sharp state as its physical trauma subsides. Your fretting about it only delays healing.

Your family servants, Micah and Mah Long, visit on alternate afternoons, and bring you the food that you seem to find more appealing than the Western dishes offered by the hospital. Your friend Flo comes two or three days a week, and your father's lawyer needs no more signatures at present. I mention those two people because you seem particularly concerned with them. Similarly, your concern over the post: I have sent brief replies to all the letters in the lidded box on the small table, and between the Longs and me, new letters reach you within a day of their arrival at your home. Similarly, I read you the day's news and anything else of interest each morning, and again – yes, the headaches will lessen, as indeed they are beginning to do already, although it may not seem so to you.

The other things that your mind has fixed upon are submarines, and your mother's canary.

About those two I can only reassure you that there is no indication that the Germans have sent their underwater craft to

our shores, and that I have taken your mother's little pet home with me, where it sings to my large collection of artificial birds from around the world. I shall try to take a photograph of the little yellow thing perched atop the large black hawk carving you have admired in the past.

Please, child: worry not, and get well. Next week you will be moving to a convalescent hospital, where I believe you will find things more comfortable and less troubling. Certainly it will be quieter.

I will place this atop your journal when I come to your room this morning. Also, you will be pleased to hear, the October issue of <u>The Strand</u> arrived at your house, so I will bring it and see if you would like me to read you some of the new instalment of the Sherlock Holmes serial that you said you were anticipating.

(Later that morning: I am not at all certain that <u>The Valley of Fear</u> is an appropriate piece of fiction to read to a convalescent girl, concerned as it is with a brutal murder. However, when I made to stop, you grew agitated, and so I continued. Perhaps the story will be less appealing by the time its November episode appears. At least it has no German spies!)

– Leah Ginsberg

November 3rd, 1914

[In Dr Ginsberg's handwriting.]

THIS PAST WEEK SAW a relapse in Mary's state of mind. At first, I and her doctor both feared a return of the infections caused by the dirt in her injuries, and she did admit to headaches. However, when she showed no indication of fever, and she responded coherently to direct questions, I decided that these were not hallucinations, but agitation. As her body regains its strength, her mind is forced to deal with loss, and it is doing so in a manner typical of both Mary and her mother: ideas.

It began when I was rereading aloud last month's episode of <u>The Valley of Fear</u>, and she began to mutter under her breath. (As noted before, I do not consider this a proper piece of fiction for a young woman in her condition.) At first I thought she was troubled by the story and I stopped reading, but she insisted I continue. At the second interruption, I had the good sense to ask her what was wrong.

'This takes place before the final problem,' she said.

'Which final problem?' I asked.

'The story called "The Final Problem". Surely that happens after this one? How could Watson have forgotten Moriarty in a few years?'

This was a conundrum for which I could summon no reply, so I read on. Moments later, she said, 'They're in conversation. That's slander, not libel.'

Then after a bit, she protested at the series of numbers broken by the words 'DOUGLAS' and 'BIRLSTONE': 'Why bother with a cipher, if those names are freely given?'

At that point I suggested we go on to the next tale in the magazine, but she would not have it, and subsided, with only the occasional protest at some sequence or point of disagreement with an earlier tale.

This was irritation, not distress, and I took the return of intellect as a good sign. Less encouraging, however, was her sudden resumption of interest in a possible German spy ring in San Francisco, evident when I came in to find her hospital room half buried in a month's worth of back issues of the <u>Chronicle</u>, with articles circled and annotated.

'<u>German Shops in London Destroyed</u>' said one. '<u>Germans claim the right to land troops to create a foothold in Canada</u>' another. However, she seemed less than concerned with the enormous loss of life in the lengthy battle going on near Ypres in Flanders. Instead, a theme of her interests emerged:

Oct 26th:

That a European government has commissioned an American girl to purchase firearms for its use along the battle front in Europe developed today, when it was learnt that Miss Gladys A. Lewis of Chicago is the mysterious 'G. A. Lewis' who has been negotiating with the Standard Arms Manufacturing Company of Wilmington, Del., for all military rapid-fire guns that concern can make in the next two years, regardless of cost.

Oct 28th:

DEATH OF GERMAN SPIES CAUGHT IN FRANCE

How They Were Found Out Though Disguised
in Red Cross Uniforms

and:

British Seize Germans on an American Tug

Oct 29th:

1,500,000 MEN IN ENGLAND TO GO TO WAR

and:

Russians Execute German Girl Spy

Death Follows Discovery That Young Woman's
Clothes Were Lined With Plans of Forts

Oct 31st:

TWO EMPIRES PLAN TO SEIZE OUR PORTS

Roosevelt Sounds Note of Warning

'I have seen deliberate plans prepared to take both San
Francisco and New York and hold them for ransoms that
would cripple our country and give funds to the enemy for
carrying on war.'

Nov 3rd:

SAN FRANCISCO ANSWERS CRY OF BELGIUM

Mass Meeting Called for Next Friday
to Launch Plan to Send Food

Spies, the building threat to her mother's homeland, and a reference to her mother's War Work of raising funds for her embattled country.

At that point, I agreed with her attendants that a mild dose of bromide would be a relief for everyone.

– Dr Leah Ginsberg

10th November

I HAVE BEEN NEGLECTING THIS journal in recent weeks. It seemed beyond pointless. However, it begins to appear that my life will continue, and Dr Ginsberg feels that some weekly notation might be of use in the restoration of normal thought. What is there to say? My family is dead. I, however, am alive. And following the increasing number of visitors and letters who insist that I have a future, I admit that plans for it must be made.

I am no longer in hospital, but lodged now in a building that from the outside looks like a private residence. With me here are four other unfortunates who have 1) survived their injuries and 2) lack the resources for returning to a family's care. The staff gently prod us until we move our bodies about the grounds, gently pester us until we have eaten food from our plates, and gently persist in finding things that might restore an interest in our surroundings. All this meek compassion and soft-hearted torment makes me want to curse aloud and throw furniture at the window (as if I could lift it).

However, they are right, my life will be in limbo until I begin to cope with the mounting demands. Hence, I have agreed to see one or two visitors a day, and to work my way through the intimidating pile of condolence letters.

The visitors have proven trying, although fortunately my attending nurses here remain in hearing, and intervene to send the more emotional guests on their way, with many sympathetic pats. But the letters are if anything more difficult, since most were written immediately the news reached the writer, when the shock was raw and no thought of lessening the impact of their words on the survivor had yet occurred to them.

There is an old woman assigned to help patients with their correspondence, and it would appear that she has seen it all before. After a few days, despite making little impact on the depth of the pile, I began to feel as if the entire world were mourning the loss of my family. Following that breakdown, my elderly helper took to reading the letters first, putting some aside for later consideration.

I felt ashamed at this cowardice, but my strength is limited.

Then today, after she left me for my period of afternoon rest (normally I fall asleep like a small child), I found my eyes resting on the small pile she had set aside. They rebuked me, this collection of letters from those who had loved my mother and father. So after a time, I got up and brought them back to bed to read.

And there it was, the one I had been wondering about, the one I had been hoping for since the day I woke in my hospital bed, the only one that really mattered. The words were few, but the bold strokes of his pen might have been dipped in blood, for the agony they imparted:

Mary, Mary, my favouritest Mary. Oh, child, my heart has been ripped from its chest. If I'd thought it would not merely compound your grief, you would have woken to find me at your bedside.

But it is your choice: if you want me there, however briefly, I will come. You know how to reach me.

The note was not signed, but there was no need. However, as if I might have lost my mind – or, as if he knew that sometimes another person read my letters to me – the paper was folded around two playing cards: an eight of hearts, and a jack of spades.

No: I did not need him to come and stand beside my bed, especially knowing – or, suspecting – that the 'grief' to which he referred would be his immediate arrest for some crime or another.

It was enough to know that Uncle Jake[3] was thinking of me.

---

[3] Russell's Uncle Jake, her father's younger brother, appears in the story 'Mary's Christmas'.

HOW DO I WRITE about this? My tumbling thoughts were just beginning to settle down, my mind was starting to feel as if it were moving in a forward direction again for the first time since the accident, when . . .

How can I go on, knowing the deceit of my own parents? Why would Mother have led me astray? Why would Father not have raised an objection?

It began when the November <u>Strand</u> arrived at the end of last week. When Dr Ginsberg brought the post, the magazine was included, and as my headaches have lessened considerably, I did not need her to read to me this third instalment of <u>The Valley of Fear</u>.

So I thanked her, and picked it up – at which point she reached into her shopping bag and pulled out half a dozen of the Sunday Magazines from my father's New York newspaper. 'Would you like to read the rest of it?' she asked me.

'The rest of what?' I naturally enquired.

That was when she revealed my parents' inexplicable behaviour: this story, so teasingly stretched out by the English <u>Strand</u> monthly magazine, has <u>all the time</u> been delivered in generous weekly (rather than monthly) dollops to Mr Conan Doyle's <u>American</u> audience! Worse, my father <u>knew</u> about this, having seen not one but two issues: both the papers from September 20th and from September 27th would have contained Sunday Magazines with portions of <u>The Valley of Fear</u>. And he knew I was looking forward to this tale, since we had just been talking about the (considerably smaller) portion in the September issue of Mother's <u>Strand</u>.

So what happened? Why keep the American version from me? Father usually at least glanced through the Magazine section: had he been too busy? Had Mother missed them as well? Did Mother wish me to participate in the same hardship as her English compatriots – and Father choose not to go against her?

I was just beginning to stand on my feet, and now they have been swept out from under me. My mother deceived me, and my father sided with her. Perhaps even Levi knew. And now my Uncle Jake has decided to keep his distance from me.

I am alone in the world. Time to grow up, I think.

THE VALLEY OF FEAR is a murder mystery set in a moated house. At night, the owner puts up the drawbridge, yet someone gets in and kills him.

England is an island. The moats around her, the seas and channels, only appear to protect her: 'Forty Zeppelins Are Ready for Service', say the papers, and 'British Birdmen Raid Zeppelin Works'.

Why is Mr Holmes so interested in a candle? Why does Mrs Douglas show so little reaction at her husband's murder? Why have British warships seized a load of German toys? Why are the Mexicans shooting across the border at Americans? Why does Dr Ginsberg think I am hallucinating an uncle, just because my parents never told her about Jake?

In the story, the dead man says, 'I have been in the Valley of Fear. I am not out of it yet.'

He speaks for me.

LAST WEEK, O IRONY, was Thanksgiving. Yesterday, I returned home for the first time. Dr Ginsberg went with me, and I admit that I was grateful for her company in the car that drove me through the city streets and up the hill. I was braced for the emptiness of the house, for cold air and darkness – and so I was shocked when the kitchen door came open before my hand and warmth washed down across my face.

Our cook, Mah, had been to see me every few days, but invariably wearing Western-style clothing and shoes that threatened to trip her at every incautious step. Here, she was in her usual trousers and tunic, and when she put her arms around me . . .

It was difficult.

A while later, I went upstairs with Dr Ginsberg. The bedrooms look very strange, with no flowers, no clutter, the beds stripped. Lifeless.

I was there not to stay, but to see the place. Next week I will come back and we will pack my possessions to leave here, perhaps for ever.

Before then, perhaps I ought to have a conversation with Dr Ginsberg about how adults go about negotiating. It is a skill I imagine I am going to need, to keep from being trapped in various impossible situations.

<u>BRITISH MERCHANT SHIPS IN FEAR OF RAIDERS</u>, say today's headlines. And what of her <u>passenger</u> ships? Are they not in danger of attack? I believe there are laws against that kind of atrocity, but do they apply in time of War? And in any event, can a ship that rides beneath the water always tell the nature of the hull ahead of them?

It doesn't matter. I am decided. I shall go to Boston, to my grandparents, but I will not remain there. I belong in England.

A T LAST, THE WHEELS of my life give a sensation of moving, for the first time since I set out to hunt German spies back in October. What a very long time ago that seems. Such a young child she was.

(I still feel that the authorities were very wrong to dismiss my accusations. Before I leave here, I shall post a stern but anonymous letter concerning the dangers. If I type it, on Father's machine, that may add a degree of authority.)

Letters arrive with regularity from Boston, my grandmother's increasingly distraught pleas for me to board a train, with a hired nurse, before another day passes. She has taken to writing to Dr Ginsberg as well, although I imagine that the tone there is less pleading than peremptory. I have just sent a telegram to Grandmamma, saying that I plan to arrive sometime between the 18th and the 21st, and that I shall cable again with further details. No doubt my unwillingness to consult with her as to the exact train I take, in which precise compartment, and wearing which hat will set off a positive blizzard of envelopes, both postal and telegraphic. However, unless I am willing to turn my life over to the woman, here is the time to stand firm and convey the message that I intend to take command of my own life.

No: I shall pack my trunks, have another conversation with my parents' lawyer – <u>my</u> lawyer now – and make the final arrangements for closing up the house.

<u>My</u> house.

Also, have two or three more conversations with Dr Ginsberg. I find that, as my strength returns, my recollection of events is becoming oddly vague, as if my brain will only permit me one or the other: health or memories. It is worrying. I have dreams in which my mother's face is obscured by a grey, mist-like veil. Last night, I shot bolt upright in my bed (which hurt) because I could not recall which of his two mechanical pencils Levi had with him when the car went off the cliff. I did not fall asleep again for the longest time – but, why should it matter in the least which pencil he took? I can only think that some part of my brain is protesting at the obscuring effects of scar tissue (actual or psychological). Since I cannot permit my own mind to rebel against me, I shall ask Dr Ginsberg to help me retrieve the clarity of those events.

Other than this peculiar mental quirk, my injuries are beginning to fade. I can even raise my arm enough to brush my own hair, at last. Dr Ginsberg will take me into the shops this afternoon, since all my shoes pinch and my winter coat is now childishly short. She says that we need not go into the City of Paris, that the Emporium has perfectly adequate clothing. Which is good, since I believe merely walking in the door of Mother's favourite shop, particularly at this season of the year (Mother, perversely, adored Christmas) would reduce me to tears.

So, my trunk lies packed in the house, ready for the final tucking-in of objects – apart from one troubling absence. Someone has stolen the mezuzah from the front door! Who would want that? In any event, I have retrieved the one that graced Mother's door into the garden, and packed that. After a last survey of the house tomorrow (during which I shall type the letter concerning the German embassy's spies) the trunk will be locked up and taken to the train station in Oakland, and I can say my goodbyes to San Francisco.

I need only wait for the arrival of the December Strand before setting off across the country. I am alone now, and alone is how I shall go forward.

In the meantime, my eyes seem to linger over these final issues of the <u>San Francisco Chronicle</u>, although the reading makes for distressing news indeed.

WOMEN VICTIMS OF COSSACK OUTRAGE

Most Fiendish Atrocity in Galicia

French Youths May Fight
300,000 Under 18 to Prepare

FIERCE BATTLES FOUGHT IN FLANDERS TRENCHES

The reporter's 'utter surprise at the absence of movement and lack of noise. Within one's range of vision with a strong glass are probably concealed 100,000 men . . .'

Commercialising Santa Claus Is Something New

It's Positively the Very Latest Idea in
Christmas Celebrations

14th December

M<small>Y COMMITMENT TO WRITING</small> a journal entry on the weekly anniversary of the start of War (it began on a Tuesday) is being put aside this week, for it looks as if my usual writing time tomorrow will be taken up with other things. That is because today – a Monday – my issue of the December <u>Strand</u> arrived. I can now leave on the next train east.

I do not, in fact, know why I so badly wanted to wait for this magazine. It is reading matter for the train, yes, but more than that, the story feels like a last, and rapidly dwindling, series of gifts arriving from my mother. Silly, but true. In any event, I have written to <u>The Strand</u>'s subscriptions department asking them to send future issues to the London house. And if the letter goes down on its Atlantic passage, or is lost in the chaos of Wartime London, so be it: I can always buy a copy, once in England.

My grandmother is not yet aware that my time in Boston will be so brief. It is a battle I shall fight when I am faced with it. In the meantime, I find I am looking forward to this cross-country voyage, where no one knows who I am, what I represent, where I am going. My fellow passengers will know nothing but what I choose to tell them. With my hair up (I have been practising, with Dr Ginsberg's help – although she does not know why) I will even look like a woman rather than a girl. I could invent an identity – any identity at all – and none of the other travellers would be the wiser.

I shall spend this afternoon with Dr Ginsberg – but not for one of her hypnosis sessions. (Which, incidentally, have not been terribly successful. Rather than restore my memories of the accident, as I had hoped, or bring a catharsis of tears, as was her ill-hidden wish, hypnosis seems to have made the events even more distant. Nonetheless, merely attempting clarity seems to have restored a degree of peace to my mind. So much so, I wondered briefly whether the good doctor had manipulated my emotions, implanting a suggestion of happiness . . . ? But I decided that, even if that is so, I may not need to know of it, quite yet. I can always write and ask her, later on.) Rather, today will be our social farewell. She has become my family here (gently, unobtrusively – in comparison with the rather pushy attempts by Flo's mother), and I shall, frankly, miss her. I have a gift for her, wrapped in green paper though she does not celebrate Christmas: a small bird sculpture for her collection, to keep company with Mother's canary.

In the meantime, my trunk awaits me in Oakland. Tickets are purchased, my new travelling outfit is hanging in the corner, my rooms in this temporary home cleared of possessions. I anticipate another argument over the need of a nurse to accompany me – one of many coming arguments over which I shall prevail, through logic and an icy, calm stubbornness.

Another thing I shall miss is the <u>San Francisco Chronicle</u>, with its blend of news and nonsense, petty local concerns beside earth-shaking events. I doubt I will find the London papers so blithely willing to forget War.

ZEPPELIN CRUISER FLEET NEARLY READY FOR RAID

Giant Armed Aircraft to Make Attack on England Soon, Is Reported

NEW PHASE OF THE HORRORS OF WAR

Many Soldiers Go Mad During Terrific Battles
and Suffer Torture

GIRLS THWART BOLD EFFORT AT ROBBERY
DAUGHTERS AS HEROINES

Eighteen- and fifteen-year-old daughters
coolly faced the revolvers and practically
'shooed' them from the house

In the Falklands, the cruiser that visited my War Journal back
in the summer has finally met her match:

SHORE BATTERIES FIRE 200 SHOTS AT BOATS

German Cruiser Nuernberg Caught and
Destroyed by British Warships, and Dresden
Is Cornered in Magellan

And in a move of pseudo-sympathy I cannot but feel is typical
of those with no stake in the matter:

CARNEGIE OPPOSES WAR TRUCE FOR CHRISTMAS

Declares It Would Be Immoral to Stop Fighting
and Then Begin It Again

BOSTON IS COLD. I have not seen snow for years, but here it covers the rooftops, muffles the sounds, clots the shoes of the walker. The cold penetrates the houses, so that despite the festivities of the season, regardless of the cooking smells and shiny ornaments and tentative but growing collection of wrapped gifts, my grandparents remain formal, distant.

But that is not entirely fair. They, too, have lost family. When I stand before them, a troublesome girl who is their son's only survivor, it must be painful. It is certainly uncomfortable. And so where another would extend arms and embrace me, these two are polite and uncertain.

Not that I wish to be embraced. I am no longer a child, and giving myself over to a warm hug might melt my resolve: to be away from here by New Year. To be heading across an ocean for home.

The small section of <u>The Valley of Fear</u> contained in <u>The Strand Magazine</u> that I waited for in San Francisco was hardly adequate to keep me entertained as I crossed this vast nation. In it, Dr Watson comes across a laughing new widow, then finds Mr Holmes most cheerful and 'debonair' over breakfast, and submits to a lengthy diatribe concerning the murder case (much of which is, to my mind, rather dubious – although it was good to see them in agreement at last). There is an intriguing passage, when Holmes reflects that were he ever to marry, he hoped to inspire feelings in his wife that would prevent her from being so easily escorted away from his dead body. I had noticed that oddity when I read the beginning – but his musings opened an unexpected door: imagine Sherlock Holmes with a grieving wife!

However, none of these is what truly caught at my imagination. Instead, my eye kept being pulled to the brief line describing where this conversation took place: 'sitting in the inglenook of an old village inn'.

Such an evocative phrase! Not that I, a minor – and a female – would be allowed to settle into such a portion of an inn. (Unless I were dressed as a man, that is. The thought occurred to me this morning, as I struggled to pin up my hair before the glass of the swaying train car, to give myself the greater appearance of maturity and thus avoid those questions of where my parents were: if I were to hide the length of it under an oversized cap – or even a bowler, like the picture of Irene Adler wishing Mr Holmes a good night – few would know it was there at all. At present, of course, I would merely look like a boy instead of a man, causing the innkeeper to throw me out due to age rather than sex. Still, in a few years when I have wrinkles, I shall have to try it.)

That inglenook calls to me, as I sit in my frigid Boston bedroom with snow whispering down the window. It gives me a point to lock on to, pulling me back to my mother's home. No doubt my father sat in similar inglenooks, in one or another Sussex village. Not London: Sussex is my home. Yes.

There was another portion of that <u>Strand</u> episode that made me even more grateful than the inglenook's evocation of home: humour.

I laughed – yes, laughed out loud, in my snug quarters on the rattling train, for the first time since October – when I read the part where Holmes returns late at night to the inn's room he and Watson are sharing, and – I shall copy the passage directly, allowing me to chuckle again whenever I come across this:

I was already asleep when I was partly awakened by his entrance.

'Well, Holmes,' I murmured, 'have you found out anything?'

He stood beside me in silence, his candle in his hand. Then the tall, lean figure inclined towards me.

'I say, Watson,' he whispered, 'would you be afraid to sleep in the same room as a lunatic, a man with softening of the brain, an idiot whose mind has lost its grip?'

'Not in the least,' I answered in astonishment.

'Ah, that's lucky,' he said, and not another word would he utter that night.

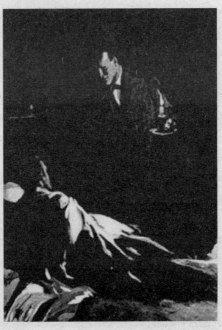

29th December

Two days left in this ghastly year. Four days left for me to be fourteen.

On the third day, I shall slip away.

In the past week, the idea of dressing up as a man in an English inglenook has kept coming back to me, to the point of fixation. On Christmas afternoon, I found myself standing before the looking glass, a child in plaits. A child. With a twist of my arm, I gathered those plaits together at the top of my head, and there before me stood a young lady. Hair down: a child; hair up: the assured young adult seen by my fellow passengers on the train. A child, then with a change of hair and attitude, a person who might well travel all on her own.

I must be quit of Boston. This is no place for me, and my well-meaning, barely educated, humourless, and conventional grandparents in their overheated house will either smother me, or drive me mad. And since they will never approve my leaving, never give their permission for me to sail the dangerous Atlantic, leaving is a thing for me alone, to take into my own hands.

In disguise.

Today I shall dress in clothing more suitable to a woman ten years older than I. I shall go to my father's bank to obtain some funds. Because I cannot be certain they will give me enough, I will take my mother's emeralds in my pocket, to sell at a pawnbroker's.

Once I have money, I will have a ticket. And once I have a ticket, I shall be on the ship to Southampton.

New Year's Day. I tell myself it is a good omen. I tell myself that next year will be less awful. I tell myself a German submarine boat will not see our hull, and we shall put in to Southampton without harm.

I OUGHT TO BE ASHAMED at the exhilaration I feel, walking the decks of this ship. The Atlantic heaves and shoves, concealing German Unterseeboots – U-boats, they call them now – and icebergs and deep darkness. The wind howls, while my fellow passengers speak in low voices, as if the sound might be heard beyond the hull. Despite the hazards lying out here in the deep, one of our engines lies idle so as to save fuel, though it prolongs our crossing by half a day.

I may be the only person on board to whom this was good news. The longer the crossing, the greater the delay in facing London and all she holds.

Were I, in fact, the twenty years (twenty-two? -five?) I appear to my fellow passengers, I would entertain the idea of staying in Southampton. Finding employment, perhaps – I understand many women now work in England, from constabulary duties to munitions factories. I could even enlist for driving an ambulance on the Front! I would be good at that, I am sure.

However, I cannot be certain of my ability to maintain an appearance of age. Plus that, simply disappearing from the world would not only inflict pain on what is left of my family, it would also be the act of a coward.

Also, I admit: I lack the mental and physical stamina for a sustained adventure.

No: I shall face London. I shall prevail against my aunt, who I am certain will be clutching a dozen telegrams from Boston by the time I arrive on her front door. My grandparents will have received my letter by now (I paid an acquaintance to post it the day after I left, for fear that they would find some way of discovering which ship I boarded, and force it back to New York!) and my aunt – my mother's sister – would have been the first to hear from them, with (I have no doubt) a series of escalating demands that she instantly place me back on the first ship heading west again. Which no doubt she would delight in doing, were she capable.

Even considering my condition, there will be small chance of digging me out of England, once I'm there.

Last night at dinner the purser (the thought occurs – perhaps I have not mentioned in this journal that I am travelling under a false name?) walked slowly through the dining room, gazing intently at every passenger under the age (the <u>apparent</u> age) of twenty. I had been practising the skill of manoeuvring around the ship without my spectacles, so as to avoid that giveaway, and my hair gathered beneath its very grown-up hat is a far cry from the description of blonde plaits that he no doubt was given. (There is not much I can do about my eye colour, but blue is not exactly rare here. And clearly, no one has yet discovered my theft of my cousin's passport, thus there has been no enquiry about an 'Emily DuPont' on the passenger list. I did not even need to tell the man examining my papers that, no, I was not one of The DuPonts, because clearly my Emporium coat and pinching shoes had told him that already. Although, why oh why are my shoes shrinking?)

So, with the perfect freedom of anonymity and adulthood, I walk the corridors, I sit in the first-class salon making shallow conversation with other ladies, I dutifully blush at the jovial remarks of the men. Admittedly, I am not good at the techniques of flirtation that one might expect of a woman of twenty-two, but in a flash of inspiration, on my second evening I dropped my eyes to my soup plate and murmured a vague sentence about the tragic loss of a junior officer with whom I had an unofficial understanding. As a result, my fellows now sympathise with my lack of interest in the opposite sex, while at the same time looking with approval on any pleasure or attempt at social intercourse that I may venture.

I suppose I should also be troubled by this previously unsuspected knack for confidence trickery – but I believe I have been sufficiently troubled in recent weeks, and I will no doubt be facing an entire barrage of other troubles once we make landfall, from a Wartime countryside to an irascible aunt.

Just for these days of crossing, I shall gaze out across the white-capped expanse of salt, and feel at rest.

12th January 1915

MY DETERMINATION TO DEMONSTRATE maturity is tried hourly. My aunt has an incredible talent for getting under my guard, or perhaps it's more a matter of finding a sensitive spot with her prodding finger.

If only she did not resemble Mother . . .

I gather my patience to me and keep repeating my intentions – firmly, with a commitment to reason, and without screaming at her. (Which is what I want to do, and what I am doing internally. My eyeballs feel as if they are bulging in their sockets, sometimes, with the effort of concealing my fury.)

The best approach seems to be one of icy resolve. No, I repeat to her: no, we shall not open the London house, since I do not intend to stay in London. No, I will not hire servants, for I will be moving to the house in Sussex, and in any event, servants are thin on the ground. Yes, I understand it is inconvenient to all. No, I am not asking you to move to Sussex with me, I am fifteen years old and can manage with the assistance of local help – the same local help that has cared for my family over the years.

In truth, were it not for my aunt, I might consider staying in London. The War is so immediate here, the streets awash in uniformed men, and a sense of . . . purpose, I suppose, everywhere. It feels wrong for a fit (relatively fit) young person to turn her back on need. Surely there is some task that needs doing, even if less exciting than driving an ambulance on the Front?

Realistically, I know that will not happen. I am too young for anything more demanding than the preparation of bandages. Instead, I will find some kind of training that I might do. Of course, from the talk around me it sounds unlikely that the War will continue past the spring, but I keep calling to mind the grim look on Father's face when he told me that the War would drag on. It is impossible to believe that the terrible carnage across the Channel will not burn itself out before a second summer begins, and yet . . .

DON'T

1. **Don't use a motor car or motor cycle for pleasure purposes.**

2. **Don't buy new clothes needlessly. Don't be ashamed of wearing old clothes in War time.**

3. **Don't keep more servants than you really need.**

In this way you will save money for the War, set the right example, and free labour for more useful purposes.

Your Country will Appreciate Your Help.

In case he was right, I will prepare for service, whatever and whenever that may be. And if he was wrong — well, so much the better: who would wish to prolong War? In any event, no skill is wasted, ultimately.

So: to Sussex I shall go, eventually, with or (preferably!) without my aunt. I shall continue my education, I shall devote myself to skills ordinary and arcane, I shall be patient and mature. And I shall prevail.

To Sussex!

MY AUNT IS A perfect virtuoso of the arts of delay. Under our roof the immoveable object has been meeting the irresistible force . . . and it has moved.

The delays of bank signatures and explanations, and the troubles of Wartime shortages, and the foul weather, and the increased risk of German invasion on the South Coast: and more and more.

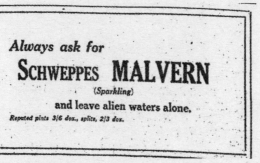

Always ask for
SCHWEPPES MALVERN
(Sparkling)
and leave alien waters alone.
Reputed pints 3/6 dos., splits, 2/3 dox.

However, I believe my aunt has finally accepted defeat. The legal gentlemen have agreed that, young as I may be, I am nonetheless the legal owner of the house she lives in, the coal that fills her fireplace, and the wine in the cellar that she pours into her glass each evening. When my aunt had left us – I would say that she flounced off, but that would be lowering myself to her level – Mama's legal gentleman permitted me a brief look at the record books. He does seem a superior sort of individual, one of the few men I have met who did not seem about to pat me on the head. (Most irritating, to be patted upon the head.)

As I said, I was only given a brief look at the books before he folded them away and had his assistant bring me cocoa and a slice of terribly sweet cake. At some point I shall have to return.

In the meantime, I direct the packing of my possessions, and arrange the purchase of books and a few things I will need (including another pair of shoes, I'm afraid). I go to Sussex tomorrow, and my aunt, or the weather, or even the Kaiser himself cannot stop me.

I T IS DIFFICULT NOT to believe that the current state of the world was designed specifically to thwart the intentions of one Mary J. Russell. I fully realise how utterly absurd, and insensitive, and <u>childish</u> that statement is, but since late October, as my mind flailed around for an alternative to endless suffocating misery, the only thing I wished – the <u>only</u> thing that gave me any glimmer of light in a very dark tunnel – was the thought of listening to a kettle come to boil in my mother's kitchen in Sussex. And now . . .

I know that innocent people have died. A small child was killed in her bed. I have no right to raise a voice in complaint at how the Kaiser has inconvenienced me.

But why could he not have waited, just a day?

Hours before I was to board the southbound train with my reluctant aunt in tow, bombs fell on English soil. At first, the belief was that these had been aeroplanes, although now the reports are of Zeppelins. Whether or not they were intending to hit London (as the Germans have been threatening) and were blown by strong winds up into Norfolk, or whether they chose a lesser target for a trial run – even if, as many say, they were attempting to destroy Sandringham, from which the King returned only yesterday – is of course the topic of huge debate. But however it happened, England has now joined with her European sisters in feeling the blow of explosives, and English civilians have now died along with those of France, Belgium, and the rest. In the wee hours of the morning, bombs and incendiary devices rained down on Yarmouth and King's Lynn.

My aunt is convinced – ridiculously – that the Kaiser's next goal will be the South Coast: Zeppelins working their way across empty farmland from Dover to Portsmouth, with no greater target for their incendiaries than farmhouses and grazing sheep? I have told her that, in fact, London is sure to receive its share sooner or later, and we shall be much safer buried down in the country. She, no country person, is not convinced. She dithers.

So, I have sent a wire to Mr Mason, my mother's farm manager, telling him in no uncertain terms that he may expect me to arrive in Eastbourne as close to midday tomorrow as the erratic schedule of the trains permits. (Whenever there is a particularly harsh battle in northern France, trains are diverted to the coast, to receive the surviving wounded and transport them to hospitals. I am not alone in being inconvenienced by War.) My telegram to Mr Mason did not say specifically that my aunt would be with me. In truth, she will not. Still, I fear that she will follow on my heels before long. Certainly once the Zeppelins come into view over London Town.

And if tomorrow morning Victoria Station is the recipient of a dropped bomb while one Mary Russell waits for her train – well, that at least shall settle the matter of her future.

Thursday will mark the six-month point of this War that was to be over by Christmas. In California, the fighting in Europe is but a distant rumour, while here in Sussex—

But I get ahead of myself.

On Wednesday morning, I left the house in London without being noticed (which required that I make a small diversion in the garden at the back, but I am sure nothing serious was burnt) and travelled to Victoria Station.

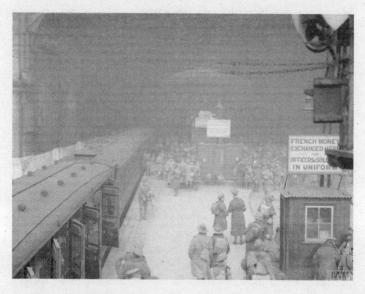

There I bought a ticket for Eastbourne (since there were times even before the disruption caused by War when trains would neglect to stop at the station closer to my home) and was told that the delay would probably not be more than a couple of hours. I settled into the waiting area with my book, and, indeed, it was not

<u>much</u> more than two hours. As it did not take us much more than twice the normal time to reach the town.

Mr Mason was patiently waiting, as I knew he would be. Had the Kaiser's troops crossed the Channel and invaded the coast – had Zeppelins flattened everything from the pier to Town Hall – Patrick Mason would have contrived to find and claim me.

Not that he was pleased to see me, exactly. He took my valise with as ill grace as he could manage, indicating just what he thought of my decision to come to the coast, and unaccompanied at that. It took me most of the trip home before I could distract him from disapproval, by earnest enquiries into the farm, and the horses, and the life of the village as a whole.

I will admit, I nearly broke down when I walked into the kitchen. Mrs Mark, the neighbouring lady whom Mother depended on both while we were in residence and when we were away, had lit the fires and filled the pantry (as well as she could, considering the shortages). I stood there in the warmth and the fragrance of her new-baked bread, and when she came over to give me a hug, it was all I could do to keep from bursting into tears.

Mrs Mark tutted and fussed and made haste to supply me with tea and food, which returned the world to some stability, since I had neither eaten nor drunk since morning. She showed me three times where everything was, exclaimed four times at how grown up I was, and scolded me for my thinness five times. On the sixth recitation of how good it was to see me, I gently ushered her towards the door and told her (for the fourth time) that I would see her tomorrow, and that no, there was no need to send someone over to stay in the house until my aunt arrived.

Then I went through much the same ritual with Mr Mason – who says I am to call him Patrick: I think I remind him of Mother – before finally, the door shut behind my visitors, and I was alone in the house.

In <u>my</u> house.

I walked through all of the well-loved spaces of my past. Dining room, with its echoes of conversation. Sitting room, where we had read aloud and played cards. The hallway with its umbrella stand and empty hatstand. I turned to the stairs, and climbed them to the bedrooms. Everything smelt clean, not at all like a house that had been closed for three years.[4] My childhood bed, looking very small, had been made up, a doll that I had not played with since I was five on the pillow. However, there was also a small crystal vase on the table containing three hellebores: Mother had treasured her garden's winter flowers, exclaiming with glee at any hellebores or forsythia that opened in time for our Christmas table. The bath down the hall had been laid with fresh towels and a bar of my mother's favourite scented soap. My brother's room was next, its shelves holding toys and books that he had outgrown long before he died. Then the next room . . .

It took me some minutes to turn the doorknob. When I stepped inside, although the air smelt the same as all of the other rooms, there was some angle of light through the curtains, some atomic trace of the two that had shared the bed, some imperceptible touch . . .

Dr Ginsberg would have been pleased to see the long-delayed tears loosed at last. It took a quite absurd length of time to bring them under control again. And I did so, in the end, by discovering a more tangible form of comfort.

We had all been in the habit of leaving behind certain items of clothing here in Sussex, whether we were returning to London

---

[4] Events of three years previous are given in 'Mary's Christmas'.

or to America: old, worn clothes suitable only to the most rural of lives. Even after three years, and three deaths, Mrs Mark had been no more willing to clear those garments away than she had my brother's books or my childhood doll.

The wooden chest at the foot of my parents' bed breathed out the remembered cedar smell when I raised its heavy lid. Inside lay two neatly folded stacks of country wear: Mother's on the right, Father's beside it. I could not imagine pulling on her clothing, not yet, but my hand reached out for a tweed jacket that was older than I. My thumb found the small mend in the hem from when he had neglected to put out his pipe before dropping it into his pocket. A very young Levi had noticed the smoke, and had been reduced to helpless laughter by Father's antics.

I put the jacket on. To my astonishment, other than the breadth of its torso, it very nearly fit, being only slightly long at the wrist. I closed the cedar chest and went back downstairs, to let myself out into the garden.

The early winter evening was closing in. Everything was very still. My ears did not know what to do with silence, after so many weeks – months – without it. The convalescent hospital had never been truly quiet, and had been followed with the days of train, then Boston, and another train and then the rhythm of the ship's engines throbbing in the bones, and of course London never slept, but here . . .

The only thing I could hear was a distant, rhythmic murmur that I thought was my pulse. However, listening more carefully, I realised it was external: the constant beat of waves against the chalk cliffs, five or six miles off. I could not remember noticing the noise before, but then, the recent days of gales and heavy storm was only now dying away. And in any event, how often had I, as a child, sat in the garden at night, listening to the stillness? Mother did. Now I knew why.

I lay that night in my childhood bed, feet pressed past its end, hearing the old familiar creaks of the house. I slept eventually. In the morning, before Mrs Mark or Mr Mason – Patrick – could come to check on me, I bundled into my father's tweed jacket and then his greatcoat, which I found in the niche near the front door (even the moths couldn't make much inroads into its harsh wool). My plaits fit under a cap that had been given to my brother by an uncle (who had misjudged the size of Levi's head), a rough lunch occupied various pockets of the greatcoat, and I set off across the Downs in the direction of the Channel. Even if I lacked the strength to make it that far, one must always have a goal.

The air was cold but marvellously clear after the recent storms, an invigorating contrast to the stinking yellow London fogs. A few farmers were out, but at a distance, and I saw only two motor cars when I crossed the main road. For the most part, it was me, the sheep, and the wind teasing the gorse bushes.

The white chalk headlands rise and fall in a series of precipitous cliffs. The tallest of them is Beachy Head, a popular final site for spurned lovers and the otherwise despairing. It took me a ridiculously long time to make it that far, stopping at increasing intervals to rest, the cold and my determination forcing me to my feet. It was after midday when at last I approached the cliffs, to peer cautiously over the precipitous edge at a narrow strip of dry shingle below. No sign of suicides today, fortunately – and if there had been, the incoming tide had already cleared them away.

I retreated from the edge – this is a cliff, after all, which means that bits are falling off all the time, particularly following a heavy beating from the waves – and pulled an apple and a wedge of cheese from my pocket, settling with them on a tussock. My father's coat wrapped me like flexible armour. The Channel was calm, its waters blue, with a few boats off in the distance. So utterly deceptive.

I bit into the apple and wondered how many German U-boats were prowling beneath that innocent blue surface. From this distance, I would not see a periscope coming free of the water, swivelling about, locking onto that approaching steamer. Without a freak glance of sunlight, I could not know if a sailor beneath the surface was examining the great blazing white cliff, noticing a figure seated at its top . . .

I shuddered and got quickly to my feet, turning to walk the nearly invisible path worn by summer ramblers. If the Kaiser decided to launch an attack on England, where would his generals choose? His Zeppelin had flown over Norfolk, but a sea crossing of actual troops? If Germany took France, or at least its northern coast, then any attempt at England would begin here. Hastings, where the last invasion came to shore in the year 1066, was less than twenty miles away.

Would this summer find a return of peacetime rambling, along the chalk cliffs? Or would the War be dragging through its second August? What if the Germans were <u>here</u> by August, the invasion well under way? Would a new generation of cliff-side ramblers speak a language other than English?

No, that was not possible. If invasion threatened, the citizens of England would pour out across the countryside like ants, armed with old shotguns and pitchforks, rallying to throw the invaders off the white cliffs and fill the shingle below with their bodies. Not that shotguns and pitchforks could do much good against the sorts of guns the—

With that thought, my steps slowed, then halted. I heeled

around to face the view, and listened hard, mouth slightly open. That same pulse, sounding in my ears.

Only it was not a pulse. What I had heard the night before, what I heard again now, came not from within my own body. Nor did it rise from the Beachy Head cliffs, where – oh, dullard that you are, Mary! – last night at dusk, the shingle beach would have been dry as could be.

That sound was coming from a hundred miles away. The sound pattering against my eardrums, now as the night before, was the voice of War: the ceaseless, massive throb of artillery barrage.

In a patch of hell on the other side of that calm blue water, boys not much older than I lay dying into the French earth.

M Y BLESSED SOLITUDE, BROKEN only by the occasional presence of Mrs Mark inside and Patrick Mason out, could not last. Indeed, I was fortunate to be granted as many days as I was. But in the end, my aunt descended upon Sussex, bringing with her many trunks and much complaint. Unfortunately, her arrival happened to coincide with the end of a string of fair, dry days. Gales and occasional hard showers ended my freedom to wander the countryside, or as much of the countryside as I can manage before my various ill-healed injuries demand rest (I was near collapse last week when I finally made it home, and spent the next day in bed). The rain and her presence conspire to keep me inside, well supplied with reading material from the shelves of the sitting room. The books here are old, but entertaining – my mind still balks at anything resembling work.

While on the topic of light reading, I must say that I found this month's instalment of <u>The Valley of Fear</u> oddly disturbing. Not due to the accumulations of plot, although the tale does seem to be going in many directions at once. No, what troubles me is the passivity of the heroine. This vivacious young woman has been assigned one suitor, whom she dislikes and fears, then falls beneath the spell of a hot-tempered and troublingly pushy young newcomer. Stories such as this seem designed to drive a reader into contemplation of herself and her future, but the thought of coming under the influence of a handsome young man with a good singing voice and 'pretty, coaxing ways' causes me to feel even more uneasy than the idea of being kidnapped by a 'Young Lochinvar' with a pistol. I may be more intelligent than many girls my age, but evidence suggests that intelligence alone does not render one immune to love's stupidity.

A day or two after reading <u>The Strand</u>, I made my way down to the stables for a conversation with Patrick. Mother's farm manager – my farm manager – is a man with little formal schooling and a great deal of what Father called 'hard sense'. I sat on a bench with my back to the stables door, his old mare dozing at my shoulder, and told him about my concerns. He may have been embarrassed at the unwonted intimacy of my questions, but since he was working on some piece of machinery, he could bury his face in its gears and pretend not to hear me. Until I asked him directly if he thought I should worry about the danger of marrying a man with pretty ways.

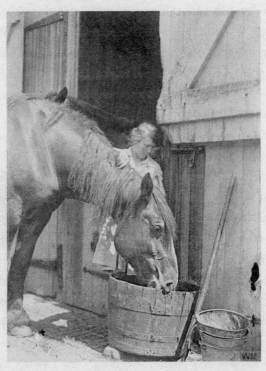

He made a sound very like one of his horses when it gets straw dust in its nose, and told me that I was too sensible for that. But I persisted, asking him what a person could do to ensure they were not in a position of idiotic vulnerability.

He shoved his face even further into the innards of the machine, and mumbled something. 'Pardon?' I asked.

'I said,' he replied, 'seems to me that it's the girls without interests in life what gets into trouble.'

Interests in life. It is true: a lack of goal leaves a person as directionless as a sailing ship without wind. What I need is a goal: to enable me to overlook the caustic presence of my aunt, and to take me beyond my present state of emptiness.

Mother and Father both expected me to go to University. I am fifteen years old. With every week of idleness, I fall further behind my peers. This must stop. Time to bypass the sections of bookshelf that hold the pretty novels and essays, and turn to the meat of the matter.

It seems to me I saw a Latin grammar there, somewhere.

FEBRUARY IS NOT A time of the year where one may easily wander the Downlands with a Latin text in hand. If the pages are not blown asunder, they are rendered into sodden masses of pulp, and in either event, are difficult to manipulate by half-frozen fingers.

So – needs must – I have made my scholar's residence in the warmth and dry of the stables, where my aunt never ventures. Patrick is a pleasantly unobtrusive companion, who does little more than murmur a greeting on his way to and fro. The main drawback is the dimness of the further reaches, making for an oscillation between the bright front of the stables and the warm depths of it.

Three days ago I was surprised to hear voices approach. I hastily gathered my things, preparing to flee into the dark, but neither voice seemed to belong to my aunt. Unless she was a silent partner to the conversation – unlikely – it was Patrick and someone else.

The someone else was a boy. He halted just inside the door, startled by my sudden emergence from the straw-lined manger. Patrick stopped, too, having clearly forgotten that I would be there.

'Ah,' he said. 'Miss Mary. Pardon the interruption, we'll be gone, I'd just—'

'Oh heavens no, you're not disturbing me. In fact, you're saving me from the imperfect subjunctive.' I looked at the boy, and Patrick made introductions.

'Miss Mary, this is one of your neighbours, Second Lieutenant Thomas Saunders,' he said. 'Thomas, Miss Mary Russell, what lives in the house.'

I was surprised, as the young man seemed little older than I. Also shorter. I slumped a bit, having found that males in general and young ones in particular regard height in a female somewhat intimidating, and thrust out my hand.

'How d'you do?' I said, a greeting he echoed.

'Thomas is off to France in a few days,' Patrick said. 'A short leave before he goes to join his regiment.'

'I wanted to come and see how the horses were doing,' the young man explained. 'I used to spend most of the summers here as a boy, helping Mr Mason with the horses. He sometimes let me drive them, when I'd helped him hitch them on the cart.'

'Oh!' I exclaimed. 'I remember you – Tommy, with a sister named . . . Mattie, was it?'

'That's right, though she wants to be called Matilda now. And I remember you – you had the funny brother who knew everything, didn't you? And the uncle who made those whizzer what-you-call-ems. Sky lanterns.'

'But . . .' I stopped. Mattie had been a little younger than I, but I'd have sworn that Tommy was only two years older. A seventeen-year-old officer, on his way to the Front? I thought of the distant rumble of guns, and shuddered.

I must have been staring at him, because Patrick cleared his throat. 'I'll just let—'

'Would you like a cup of tea, Tom – er, Lieutenant Saunders?'

'Please, call me Tommy.'

I fled to the kitchen, finding it blessedly empty of my aunt's presence. I managed to assemble three mugs of tea and a plate of rather hacked-up seed cake, plus a large wedge of cheese and some uneven bread-and-butter sandwiches, and carried the laden tray out to the stables.

Men and boys alike tend to overlook the looks of one's kitchen efforts in favour of quantity, and it was no less so with Patrick and Tommy. They drank and ate, and we talked. About what, I cannot remember, really, although it is now scarcely forty-eight hours later.

We talked about normality, I suppose. Horses and shortages, childhood and California, his sister and my brother. Other than an awkward expression of condolence on his part, death was ignored, both those in the past and the deaths taking part across the Channel. Under the effects of food, drink, and conversation, Tommy's stilted manner faded, and his face resumed something of the animation I remembered.

He went home soon thereafter, but he came back yesterday, and again today. We sat in the stables while Patrick worked, talking about his school and my problems with Latin and where the world was going, and what we wanted to do when it was over. Over those three conversations, his face seemed to undergo an oddly divided change: he began to look both younger, more like the boy I had known, yet at the same time older, more assured.

My mother had been fond of him, I remembered. I could picture her laughing at one of his antics. I was hit by the sudden image of this young officer, half a dozen years ago, handing her a rough bouquet of flowers from his mother's garden.

'Do you need anything?' I interrupted, causing him to look a question at me. 'I mean, a book to take with you, or a packet of tea? Some warm socks, perhaps?'

In the end, he took a small book of poetry and the rest of the cheese. And when he left, he gave me a kiss on the cheek, and pressed my hand in his.

We both promised to write.

Each morning, the young son of the village postmistress comes cycling up the lane to bring us, in addition to the various requests from housekeeper and aunt, the previous day's edition of The Times. My aunt seems to think this inappropriate reading material, given my sex and age, but it is the newspaper my parents used to read, and the font is familiar to me (though the quality of the paper itself seems to have slipped somewhat, as well as the quantity, under Wartime shortages).

It is, I admit, a more challenging way to follow the world's events than the San Francisco Chronicle used to be. That paper's preference for sensational headlines made for a more entertaining experience, more concerned with daring criminal exploits, rum-smuggling, and the abduction of young girls than about the War dead and the dry decisions of Crown Courts.

Still, even The Times acknowledges the need for the softer interests among the hard edges of international affairs. For example, the Queen has been visiting her 'Work for Women' Fund workrooms, a training college where unemployed girls are taught the skills of dressmaking, ironing, and cooking. Only a few, it seems, are deemed capable of learning a clerk's skills.

Elsewhere, a schoolboy of thirteen years has taken ten shillings of his choir money and set off for the Front, sleeping rough and carrying luggage for tips. When retrieved, he was disappointed to hear that he cannot enlist as a drummer boy for another year.

In the meantime, the King has been inspecting a collection of motor ambulances at the Palace. They, too, are on their way to the Front, under the auspices of the Red Cross. Posters urge enlistment, shops arrange goods on sparse shelves, there is talk of gathering scrap metal and iron fences to be melted down into armament – while half the population of Britain sits at home and feeds the children.

Why are women permitted the needle, even the typewriting machine, but not the rifle? Surely chivalry is a dangerous luxury when the enemy is on the other side of a narrow strait of water? Perhaps, if the pressure of having more and more of the men away in the trenches builds, some leeway may open up, that the 'gentler sex' may be granted the right, if not to fire a rifle across no man's land, then at least to drive to the aid of wounded riflemen in those Red Cross ambulances?

My farm's motor car – <u>my</u> motor car, much good will it do me – currently sits upon blocks of wood at the back of the stables. However, even if I were to take it down, fill the tyres, and get it running, I should then come up against petrol shortages. (Oh, why did I not insist that Father teach me to drive, once my feet could touch the controls?) Still, there are motors occasionally to be seen in the village. One of them belongs to the local doctor, who can be seen pressed up against the windscreen with a worried look on his face. This has given me a plan: I shall invent an ailment to get in to see him, and tell him he needs a chauffeur. (Chauffeuse?)

The actual skills of driving will no doubt be quickly learnt – Patrick will teach me, when confronted with the fait accompli of my new position – and once I am expert enough, I can put my name forward for the Front.

All sorts of men drive. How hard could it be?

2nd March

Today is the second day of March, with no sign of the month's <u>Strand</u>. February's issue did not come until the third of the month, and the post seems only to be getting slower. Perhaps the magazine should forswear the serialisation of its pieces for the duration of War, in consideration of its frustrated readers.

Similarly, I received two letters from Lieutenant Saunders on the same day, though they were written a week apart. I found it difficult to decide whether I should read both at once, or whether I should wait a week for the second, so as to duplicate his chronology across the Channel. In the end, I compromised and waited a day to read the second one – by which time two more had arrived.

I shall probably now receive nothing more from him for a month.

Which causes me to wonder if the Post Office could be to blame for my lack of correspondence from Dr Ginsberg? She wrote to me every week when I first left California, although again they arrived in fits and starts. However, I have had nothing since a letter dated on my birthday, 2nd January. That one I did answer, briefly. Perhaps she has interpreted my lack of replies as a wish to be left alone? Or, it has also occurred to me that one of the ships sunk by the Germans could have held my piece of Royal mail, so I wrote again.

Perhaps I ought to send a third, just to be certain that one of them reaches San Francisco? After that, if there is no reply, I shall have to accept that ours were not the close ties I had thought; that her friendship with Mother, followed by her professional care of me after the accident, is not sufficient call on her affections. She is, after all, a busy woman.

If a ship bearing my letter did go down, it would not be the only one. Submarines prowling the waters off Beachy Head have sunk a number of ships in recent weeks. It must be terrifying to look over the rails and see a periscope sticking up from the waters, followed by the track of a torpedo coming at the hull. One of the ships – the <u>Thordis</u> – claims to have made a run directly at the U-boat and damaged it, but either it sank or it limped off because it did not wash up on our shores.

Not that I would know. Although my walks have gotten longer, as my stamina has improved, I have avoided the coast since my one time there, not wishing to see doomed ships or hear the sound of the guns. Instead, when the weather permits, I go northerly out of the Downs and into the Weald, where the trees shelter one from distant rumbles. Last week the weather took a turn for the better, Thursday dawning surprisingly warm beneath a cloudless sky. I slid my book in one pocket and some bread and cheese in another, and before midday I reached the Michelham Priory.

I had come across mention of this ancient moated house, formerly monastic and now private, in one of Mother's histories of Sussex. It reminded me of the moat that surrounds the house in The Valley of Fear, and I took a fancy to see it. As I drew near, I saw that the resemblance was thin, since the Priory moat is quite a distance from the house walls, not directly below its windows as events in the story require. Nonetheless, the place looks intriguing. Perhaps another day I shall knock at the door.

Is it a sign of maturity that I noticed restoration on portions of the structure? I doubt that last summer I should have noticed such a thing. My parents attended a Christmas party at Michelham one year, and I remember Father's concern over the heavy hands of the restorers. Today, this seems a frivolous sort of worry, when a million men are at each other's throats just over the horizon, but a person grasps what small piece of normality she can, these days.

So, I agree with my father: I hope the Priory's restoring hands are gentle.

THIS MONTH'S INSTALMENT OF <u>The Valley of Fear</u> finally came (two days ago!), although I have to admit it has not done much to clarify the mystery around the story's murder. I could see from the very first that any victim whose head was all but obliterated by a shotgun is a victim whose identity the reader should question, and with this current episode, one is led to suspect that the man McMurdo, far from being the criminal and bounder he appears, has another purpose behind his presence in the Valley. In the hands of a more cunning writer, one might begin to suspect a sort of double-bluff, but I fear Mr Conan Doyle is too straightforward for that.

As for 'Birlstone Manor', even with the Michelham Priory off my list of candidates, Sussex has proven rich in alternatives. Brief research through my mother's collection of Sussexiana has given me a plethora of moated houses, the investigation of which will have to wait until the roads have dried enough to permit the use of a bicycle. I was surprised at first, until I reflected on this part of England: as enemies from Norman French to the Kaiser's Boche well know, the South Coast is Britain's open underbelly, and it would well behove any king to have a string of fortified allies between the South Coast and London. War is not a new thing to this land.

As to the current horrors, <u>The Times</u> informs me that 12,369 redyed old sweaters have been sent to the Front, along with countless socks and other bits of knitwear, for the benefit of 12,369 apparently desperate soldiers. In the meantime, the Bishop of London has dedicated a motor coffee stall on its way to France, that he might promote temperance among the serving men: heaven forbid that men clothed in mud-soaked and ill-dyed jumble-sale rejects should be handed a mug of alcohol to warm their bones.

Regular articles on 'Daily Life in the Army' describe a continuous assault of artillery on the nerves, the deadly skill of German snipers, and an omnipresent rattle of machine guns, while wounded officers retreat to the luxury of Woburn Abbey and Blenheim Palace for their recuperation.

This may or may not have to do with the article concerning a 'young woman of independent means' from Bayswater who was charged with assaulting with her umbrella a captain home on sick leave, saying that she had been insulted by men like this.

In Paris, meanwhile, debate continues over the coming width of ladies' skirts and the most flattering way to arrange one's veil.

16th March

THE JUXTAPOSITION OF WAR with an attempt at maintaining the bastions of normal life is at times painful. For example, last Tuesday's <u>Times</u> (which reached me late on Wednesday) contained the following:

NEW PROFESSIONS FOR WOMEN

That section of the field of labour hitherto regarded as the exclusive property of men is being rapidly invaded by women. These include: medicine, railway clerical work, carriage cleaning, grocery, engineering, toy-making, architectural drawing, debt collecting, motor driving, banking, and accountancy.

While nearby was printed excerpts of a diary from the Front:

AT NIGHT

It was quiet when we were in the line. To the right there was the 'devil driving in nails' with a machine gun, and along the line the isolated reports of rifle fire – for firing at night keeps your own sentries awake and worries the enemy. The Germans are blazing away with pistol flare lights, the brilliant pallid flame of which hangs in the sky and then slowly nears the earth, throwing everything within its radius into sharp relief. Their searchlight flashes across every now and again, lighting up the low rain-laden clouds and playing like phenomenal summer lightning along our trench line. When we leave the trenches the night has grown black. We plod heavily up the communication trench, which seems to thirst after our boots, bending low so as to avoid the prying finger of the searchlight.

Thomas – Lieutenant Saunders – is there in the midst of it, his letters giving a picture of truly appalling conditions: freezing mud, swarming lice, and, even in the cold, a pervasive miasma of unburied bodies. I encourage him to write to me of these distasteful details of life, since I am quite certain he cannot send them to his mother and I feel (Dr Ginsberg's influence!) that it must only do a sufferer good to unload some small part of his burden onto a sympathetic friend. At the same time, I try not to read the lists from the Front, lest it remind me how many junior officers lose their lives in their first weeks of duty in the trenches. Thomas tells me that he has a sergeant of the classically grizzled type who has taken him under his gruff and no doubt malodorous wing, going so far as to deliver a slap to his head (assaulting an officer being a court martial charge) to knock it below the sandbags, lest the sniper's crosshairs find a focus.

Would that Lieutenant Thomas Saunders learns his lessons well, and keeps his head down in the future.

I have finally worn down the patience of the village doctor, who has come to accept my offer and agreed to teach me the basic skills of starter motor and gear lever. In fact, these lessons amounted to a demonstration of a) pushing the starter button, and b) a change of the gears, after which he got out of the motor and left me to explore the machine's workings on my own while he (having been up for thirty-six hours attending first a difficult birth and then an emergency surgery) stumbled off to his bed.

I will admit that I was a bit concerned with the effects of my initial trials on the workings of the motor car, but it would appear that the machine is designed to permit much choking, grinding of gears, and bucking to a halt. By midday, I could drive to the outskirts of Eastbourne and back without killing the engine more than a handful of times.

I then presented myself to the good doctor, and told him that I would be available at any time, day or night, and that he had only to telephone to my house or drive past and sound the horn. I assured him that it would be quite convenient for me to be given some hours of enforced reading in the car's shelter while he attended to patients. I am not sure he was convinced (he did, to the contrary, look a bit stunned – perhaps he'd forgotten about handing me his keys?). However, once I have taken up a position outside of his surgery for a few days, springing to his service whenever he makes in the direction of his motor, he will understand that Mary Russell is not to be put aside.

The next thing will be to find someone to teach me the basic workings of the engine itself, since I imagine that the ability to render elementary repairs would be a necessity when driving ambulances on the Front.

THIS WEEK HAS TAUGHT some interesting lessons, both in practical knowledge and – perhaps more valuable in the long run – in the subtle relationships between the sexes.

Dr X and I (I decided I should probably not use his name, since my presence as his driver is probably against a string of regulations and I would not want the man struck off simply because he is too exhausted to argue with me) have forged a reasonable working relationship, in which he agrees to permit me to drive him about the countryside on his daily rounds, while I agree not to lay wait for him outside of his door at night. As a temporary solution, it is most workable, although eventually I shall have to take on the skills of night-time driving.

One of our trips this past week took us to Seaford, where he anticipated a longer than usual visit. As I prepared to settle in with my Latin, I noticed just down the road a small garage, so I set aside the text and moved the motor over to the establishment's forecourt.

I have not reached the age of fifteen years without realising that few men take women seriously – particularly young women. There are two ways around this: one can force matters, asserting one's needs and abilities until the man reluctantly (and resentfully) gives way, or one can manipulate him. The first way is easier on a woman's self-respect, but I have to admit, the second seems both faster and more productive.

In this case, my request – that the man in the greasy coveralls be hired to introduce me to the mysteries of the internal combustion engine – had the result I had anticipated: he laughed.

Had his hands not been so filthy, I think he might have patted me on the head.

But instead of bridling and manoeuvring him into a corner, I did the unnatural (to me) and unexpected: I went soft, blinking my eyes at him (and contriving to seem shorter than I was) while admitting that it was silly, I knew, but until I could do just a couple of things, like change tyres and fix a starter that wouldn't catch, the aged grandmother I lived with far at the end of a country lane would be vulnerable and might even have to move into town . . .

He relented, patently amused at the idea of a girl changing a tyre, much less cleaning the points of a carburettor, but since the forecourt was empty of other cars – and, perhaps more importantly, other men – he walked around to the bonnet and opened it to demonstrate the key architecture.

Two hours later, having passed from amusement through bemusement to astonishment, he had taught me all the main parts of the motor and what to do in any event short of a broken axle.

Dr X was most taken aback by my appearance, and my aunt filled with outrage, but I shall purchase my own set of coveralls and keep them in the motor, against my next exploration of the guts of the machine.

30th March

IN THE PAST WEEK, <u>The Times</u> has continued to shrink in pages, and expand in its messages of desperation. Letters from the Front speak of <u>A DOCTOR IN THE BATTLE LINE</u> and his <u>AMBULANCE WORK UNDER FIRE</u>, from Neuve Chapelle:

> It has been quite impossible to write lately, as there has been a tremendous battle going on, the earlier part of which was a great success . . . Life has been absolute Hell; there is no other word for it . . . Getting the wounded away was the worst. I had only four stretcher-bearers out of sixteen, and only two stretchers; and the shellfire was so great that it was impossible to carry them to the ambulance a mile and a half away.

Boys at home are being encouraged to respond to the thrill of War, that they might be encouraged to volunteer for service in the Red Cross, to raise War funds, and to dig potatoes for desperate farmers. In the meantime, <u>THE CALL TO WOMEN</u> includes <u>TO WORK IN ARMAMENT FACTORIES</u> doing shell-making, and to shore up the nation's defences by <u>FARMING</u>.

Under this relentless barrage of War news, the headline <u>BRIDES DROWNED IN BATHS</u>, concerning one George Smith of Shepherd's Bush, accused of killing a series of three wives by drowning each of them in a bath, seems positively droll and homely by comparison. As does the description of <u>NEW PROFESSIONS FOR WOMEN</u> that includes <u>POSSIBILITIES OF MUSIC ENGRAVING</u> and <u>WOMEN TRAM CONDUCTORS</u>.

I do not know that music engraving fills a tremendous Wartime need, although I suppose even the boys on the Front would appreciate sheet music from time to time. Driving a tram would at least free a man to carry a gun – as my own driving frees the doctor to concentrate on his work, allowing him to doze on the roads instead of hunching bleary-eyed over them. It may be a sign of his cumulative fatigue (the district's other practitioners are all in France), but either my driving has improved or he is too tired to object. The other night, the sound of a fence post scraping against the side of the motor only caused his snores to briefly pause, and fortunately the post missed the headlamp.

I fear, however, that the good doctor will have to make use of another chauffeur before too long. I am determined to make a more active service to this, my mother's homeland and the land of my birth: driving an ambulance at the Front. This decision has come, I realise now, from a methodical series of lessons, although I did not see the sequence until I looked back: last December, I learnt the skills of appearing older than my years. In January, I perfected the means of getting my way through calm and implacable will. In past weeks, I have learnt to drive: day and night, sun and hard rain, on roads or over uneven ground. I can even perform simple motor repairs. My nerves are steady, my stamina vastly improved, and my wits sharp: England needs such as me. I know my vision of coming to the rescue of Thomas Saunders is but a figment of imagination, but surely any number of other young men could stand in his stead.

I have heard of a local widow-woman who is not only well skilled behind a wheel, but whose sons are now out of her house, leaving her at loose ends for employment. To make matters even more interesting, the lady is of an age appropriate to my Dr X, whose wife died four or five years ago. I have arranged the use of the motor this afternoon, while the doctor holds surgery hours, to go and see if she might be willing to step into my place. If so, I shall forge identity papers and leave for the Front. If a schoolboy with ten shillings of choir money can work his way to France, I shall have no trouble at all slipping into a driver's position amidst the chaos of a field hospital. By the time I am discovered, I will have made myself indispensable.

WOUNDED BRITISH SOLDIERS BY THE HUNDRED RECEIVING WHAT SLIGHT AID CAN BE GIVEN THEM BEFORE THE
AMBULANCES COME TO TAKE THEM BACK TO THE BASE HOSPITAL
(© British Official Photo.)

HOSPITAL EXPRESS TRAIN OF THE BRITISH RED CROSS PROVIDED WITH NURSES, DOCTORS, AND EVERY COM-
FORT, SPEEDING TOWARD THE COAST WHERE THE WOUNDED WERE TO BE TAKEN TO ENGLAND.
(© British Official Photo., from Underwood & Underwood.)

149

6th April 1915

A SLIGHT HITCH IN PLANS has occurred, with the discovery that identity papers are not readily forged by a person with naught but an amateur's workshop. However, by asking around among the village troublemakers, I discovered a man in Eastbourne who can provide the necessary documents, and I have paid him the first instalment of the price. Unfortunately, it will take him some days to finish. My peripatetic reading on the Downs resumes.

I admit to a brief reconsideration of plans following some Times articles this last week, which suggest that the government may be starting to take seriously the potential that lies in the female half of the nation. The government wishes to induce women to come to the aid of agriculturists by doing dairy work, milking, and other 'light' employment. In the meantime, Patrick will be troubled in the coming year by the same article's description of 'the scarcity of farm labour and the requisitioning of hay by the War Office . . .' My two strong arms will be missed, when it comes to this year's harvest. Or perhaps not – with any luck, the War will be over by then. In any event, Thursday's news then trumpeted THE ARMY OF WOMEN with OVER 20,000 APPLICANTS FOR WAR WORK, so perhaps he and my aunt will manage without me.

I suppose it is understandable that Sunday's celebration of the Easter holiday made for a wistful pursuit of normality, with a number of news pieces such as one about the EASTER HARE AND EASTER EGGS. (It asked: what is the connexion of the hare with eggs, and of both with Easter? In reply, the writer claimed that as a Christian symbol, the hare is as old as the catacombs, where it is the emblem of the repentant sinner. This seems a dubious bit of theology to me; I wonder what Mother would make of it?)

Similarly, an earnest gentleman urged the use of HONEY FOR SOLDIERS, in a letter to the editor that began, 'May I bring to notice the value of honey for our warriors? It is an especial nutrient for them when they have lost body heat on deck or in trench . . .'

Lacking Easter eggs, or even pots of honey (which personally I'd have thought unsuitable as a gift for the Front, being both heavy and breakable), I shall divert myself with my former reading material, the Latin text of Virgil. The <u>Georgics</u>, by odd coincidence, contain a section on bees: <u>'First, seek a settled home for your bees, where the winds</u> [. . . of War, perhaps?] <u>may find no access . . .</u>'

I write this in the still hours of the morning, sleep having been banished by a heavy heart. For yesterday, just before tea,

Patrick came to the door with a look on his face such as I had never seen there before. I knew immediately what it meant, and yes: Second Lieutenant Thomas Saunders died of wounds, three days ago.

It was a shock, and a huge sadness, yet I cannot say it was unexpected. I think I knew the moment Thomas planted his shy salute on my cheek that I would never see him again. Just as I know that this War will not be over until it has ripped the heart from every person on earth.

My friend's passing has firmed my own thoughts. The Meteorological Office predicts rain tomorrow, making it a good day to spend in the stables with my thoughts and a review of this journal. When I started it thirty-six weeks ago, I was the daughter of two parents, the sister to a younger brother, resident in a country far from war. A child, with no more pressing concern than my right to visit a friend. So much change, such misery in the world.

When I have finished meditating on the past months, I shall close this book my mother gave to me, and send it to a place where it shall be safe. Then I shall do my best to forget it.

Thursday's forecast is for fair skies. So on that day when the sun rises, before my aunt is astir (her unreasonable behaviour having reached absurd heights, most recently over the purchase of shoes!), I shall pocket the Georgics and a bread roll, to set out for a last day's rambling. Only this time, instead of turning north to the forested Weald, I shall walk towards those distant guns and that ominous stretch of sea, that I might confront them face-to-face.

I do not know when, if ever, I will read the final instalments of The Valley of Fear, a story that has taken up so much of my interest in recent months, a tale that – shallow as I feel to admit it – helped to pull me from the state I was in after the accident.

Stories do not matter, not really. Like the hay harvest, this one may have to go on without me. I shall do what I can, and do it with all my strength, wanting only to feel that my parents, and my brother, would be proud of me.

Mary Judith Russell
Sussex, England

THUS ENDS MARY RUSSELL'S War Journal. Her Memoirs continue in *The Beekeeper's Apprentice*, which opens on that Thursday morning, 8th April 1915, with the words:

> I was fifteen when I first met Sherlock Holmes, fifteen years old with my nose in a book as I walked the Sussex Downs, and nearly stepped on him. In my defence I must say it was an engrossing book, and it was very rare to come across another person in that particular part of the world in that War year of 1915. In my seven weeks of peripatetic reading amongst the sheep (which tended to move out of my way) and the gorse bushes (to which I had painfully developed an instinctive awareness) I had never before stepped on a person.
>
> It was a cool, sunny day in early April, and the book was by Virgil. I had set out at dawn from the silent farmhouse, chosen a different direction from my usual – in this case south-easterly, towards the sea – and had spent the intervening hours wrestling with Latin verbs, climbing unconsciously over stone walls, and unthinkingly circling hedge rows, and would probably not have noticed the sea until I stepped off one of the chalk cliffs into it.

As it was, my first awareness that there was another soul in the universe was when a male throat cleared itself loudly not four feet from me. The Latin text flew into the air, followed closely by an Anglo-Saxon oath. Heart pounding, I hastily pulled together what dignity I could and glared down through my spectacles at this figure hunched up at my feet: a gaunt, greying man in his fifties wearing a cloth cap, ancient tweed greatcoat, and decent shoes, with a threadbare army rucksack on the ground beside him. A tramp perhaps, who had left the rest of his possessions stashed beneath a bush. Or an Eccentric. Certainly no shepherd.

He said nothing. Very sarcastically. I snatched up my book and brushed it off.

'What on earth are you doing?' I demanded. 'Lying in wait for someone?'

He raised one eyebrow at that, smiled in a singularly condescending and irritating manner, and opened his mouth to speak in that precise drawl which is the trademark of the overly educated upper-class English gentleman. A high voice; a biting one: definitely an Eccentric . . .[5]

ADDENDUM: ATTRIBUTIONS

NEWSPAPER QUOTES ARE TAKEN verbatim from *The San Francisco Chronicle* and *The Times of London*. The erratic spelling of newspapers, noted by Miss Russell herself, is preserved

[5] Long excerpts from *The Beekeeper's Apprentice* and other Russell Memoirs are at www. laurierking.com/books. For the momentous meeting from Sherlock Holmes's point of view, see 'Beekeeping for Beginners', below.

in her excerpts: Nurnberg is elsewhere Nuernberg, Leipzig appears as Leipsic, Alcatraz ends in an 's', Asilomar is given as Asilmar, etc.

Photographs used without attribution are my own, or were scanned from original newspapers, magazines, and postcards in my possession. Other images include:

August 4th: Polaris; Irene Adler, 'A Scandal in Bohemia' by Arthur Conan Doyle. *11th*: Library of Congress; Library of Congress. *18th*: Uncle Sam by James Montgomery Flagg, courtesy of Wikimedia; map from *San Francisco and Oakland, a Visitor's Guide* by Rand McNally, 1923. *25th*: Leipzig, courtesy of Wikipedia; *Raffles, the Amateur Cracksman*, courtesy of Wikipedia; *Kroonland* in Panama Canal, 1915, courtesy of Wikipedia.

September 1st: Plane over Paris, courtesy of Wikipedia; Rudyard Kipling, courtesy of Wikipedia. *8th*: Pilot dropping bomb, courtesy of Wikimedia; German cruiser *Nurnburg* in the San Francisco Bay, courtesy of Wikipedia. *15th*: *The Valley of Fear* cover, courtesy of Wikipedia; Toy vendor, Chinatown, San Francisco (circa 1900), courtesy of Library of Congress. *22nd*: *Will You Stand for This*, courtesy of the Imperial War Museum. *29th*: Kitchener poster, courtesy of Wikipedia; Submarine fleet, courtesy of Photos of the Great War.

October 27th: Submarine fleet, courtesy Photos of the Great War

November 17th: *Sunday Magazine*, courtesy of Wikipedia.

24th: Holmes inspecting a moat from *The Valley of Fear*, by Arthur Conan Doyle.

December 1st: Grant Ave & Market, courtesy of Wikipedia. *8th*: Cambrai trench, courtesy of Wikipedia. *22nd*: Holmes with candlestick from *The Valley of Fear*, by Arthur Conan Doyle.

January 5th: Wheeled stretchers, courtesy of Photos of the Great War.

February 2nd: British Army Victoria Station, courtesy of Imperial War Museum; Submarine surfacing, from Photos of the Great War; Artillery barrage, courtesy of Wikipedia. *9th*: Land girl, courtesy of Imperial War Museum. *16th*: Sky lanterns, courtesy of Wikipedia. *23rd*: Queen Mary, courtesy of Wikipedia; Army cycle poster, courtesy Wikipedia.

March 2nd: Ship explosion, courtesy of Wikipedia. *9th*: National Doughnut Day, courtesy of Wikipedia. *16th*: Vickers gun, courtesy of Wikipedia; Trenches, courtesy of Photos of the Great War; Women ambulance drivers, courtesy of Photos of the Great War. *30th*: Women tram drivers, courtesy of Wikipedia; *The Toll of War*, courtesy of Library of Congress.

April 6th: Women's Land Army, courtesy of Wikipedia.

Photos of the Great War: www.gwpda.org/photos
Library of Congress War of the Nations: www.flickr.com/photos/library_of_congress

BEEKEEPING FOR BEGINNERS

The first Russell Memoir, *The Beekeepers Apprentice*, opens with Russell's description of meeting Sherlock Holmes on the Sussex Downs by nearly stepping on him. But what about Holmes? What on earth did a middle-aged, semi-retired detective make of this smart-mouthed, fifteen-year-old girl confronting him over his bees? And did those early weeks perhaps have another interpretation from the one young Mary had, the view that stands in her Memoirs? Well . . .

ONE

A NY REASONABLE MAN MAY reach a point in his life where self-destruction becomes a door worthy of consideration. A point at which it seems that the least a walking anachronism can do for the world is to remove himself from cluttering the landscape.

It was a cool, sunny day in April 1915. I had set out at dawn from the silent villa to which I had retreated out of the London fogs some years before, carrying with me both the impedimenta of my avocation, and the means to end my life.

Do not imagine that I was unaware of the multiple ironies: my beekeeping task required a clear, warm day, while the other was more suited to a bleak and inhospitable sky; my acts were concerned with the populous community of a hive, while my thoughts were at their most solitary; my rucksack carried both restoration and death.

My mind was not entirely made up. However, a lifetime dedicated to the science of thought has taught me that focusing the mind's eye on one matter encourages greater clarity of vision along the periphery of the mental gaze. I should proceed with my surface task, while permitting the deeper machinery of my mind to turn.

In any event, off I walked onto the Downs that morning with a trio of bottles. Two contained paint, red and blue: with these I might track a wild – or rather, feral – colony for one of my empty Langstroth hives, to restore the apiary to full strength. (In a curious parallel, the designer of those hives had himself felt the grim attraction of a voluntary end.) The third vial held a small amount of nearly clear liquid: it would transform me into a mere problem of disposal and a pang of sorrow for those few individuals who held me in affection.

That it might also bring a sense of rejoicing to those who wished the world ill was one of the main reasons I had not made use of the bottle before that day.

I was in my fifty-fifth year on this earth. For nearly forty of those years, my life had been my work. Even during the dozen years of my ostensible retirement to Sussex, I had remained active – indeed, eight months previous, a lengthy case had led to the destruction of a major spy ring, my contribution to the nation's security. Then during the autumn, while the guns of France drew into place and plans were made for what the deluded imagined would be a brief war, I managed to keep myself in a position of usefulness.

But in January, one of my little victories, and its accompanying minor injury, had come to the attention of the powers-that-be. Rather than gratitude, their response had been one of alarm, that a person of my eminence might have been snuffed out by a stray bullet – or worse, taken captive and used as a hostage. One might have thought I was the young Prince of Wales.

My head had been patted, my protests ignored, I had been sent home to Sussex. To my bees, my studies, and the services of my long-time housekeeper, Mrs Hudson. To a soul-grinding boredom and a pervading sense of uselessness.

All my life I have battled grey tedium. The challenges of mental work and physical exertion, the escape of music and the occasional dose of drugs have aided me, but always I could reassure myself that the ennui was temporary, that it would not be long before some criminal laid his scent before me, and I would be off.

Now my so-called friends had conspired against me, coddling me for my own good.

Fifty-four is not old.

I found tedium mentally trying, but physically agonising. As winter turned to spring, it became apparent that the world had finished with me; the only thing required of me was a decision to agree.

So: that absurdly sunshiny April day, with the throb of distant guns an ominous basso beneath the rhythm of waves against chalk cliffs, and a small, clear bottle in the old rucksack at my feet as my hands used the fine camel-hair brush to daub paint on individual honeybees, and my colour-assisted eyes tracked their subsequent flight, and my mind circled ever closer to a decision.

To be interrupted by slow footsteps, approaching across open ground.

After twelve years in Sussex, I was well accustomed to busybodies. Everyone in the county knew who I was, and although they took care to protect me from the intrusion of outsiders, they felt no compunction to offer the same protection from their own attentions. Stepping into the village shop for Mrs Hudson would bring a knowing wink and a heavy-handed jest about *investigating* the choices of soap powder. If I paused to examine an unfamiliar variety of shoe-print on the ground, a short time later I would look back to find a knot of villagers gazing down to see what had drawn my attention. One time, a casual remark to a passing farmer about the sky – that a storm would arrive by midnight – led to a near-panic throughout the Downland community, until the farmer's wife had the sense to ring Mrs Hudson and ask if I'd actually intended to warn him that the Kaiser's troops were lying offshore, waiting for dark.

Only the pub had proved safe ground: when an Englishman orders a pint, his privacy is sacrosanct.

Every so often, perhaps once a year, I would become aware of what is known as a 'fan'. These were generally village lads with too much time on their hands and too many penny-dreadful novels on their shelves. Trial and error had shown that a terse lecture on personal rights coupled with a threat to speak to their fathers would send them on their way.

Now, it seemed, I had another one.

I turned to watch the owner of the slow footsteps approach. The lad was wearing an old and too-large suit, a jersey in place of shirt and waistcoat (it had been cold that morning when I – and, it appeared, he – had set out), and a badly knitted scarf, with a cloth cap pulled down to his ears and shoes that, despite being new, pinched his toes. His nose was buried in a book, as if to demonstrate his noble oblivion to any world-famous detectives who might be hunkered on the ground.

But he had misjudged either his path or his speed, because he was aimed right at me. I waited, but when he neither shifted course nor launched into a performance of astonishment, I cleared my throat.

The astonishment that resulted was, I had to admit, no act. The child was furious – embarrassment has that effect on the young, I have noticed – both at my throat-clearing and at the involuntary epithet it had startled out of him.

He snatched up his dropped Virgil – the *Georgics*, as one might expect – and demanded, 'What on earth are you doing? Lying in wait for someone?'

It being, I presumed, the eternal task of a detective, to be lying in wait at all times and in all places.

'I should think that I can hardly be accused of "lying" anywhere, as I am seated openly, on an uncluttered hillside, minding my own business. When, that is, I am not required to fend off those who propose to crush me underfoot.' And I turned back to my task of bee-watching, unaware that my mild (if condescending) remark had triggered an inexplicable response of fury in the young person.

He planted those ill-fitting shoes into the turf and snarled, 'You have not answered my question, sir.'

I sighed to myself. *Be gone, child*, I thought; *I'm trying to commit a nice, dignified suicide.* 'What am I doing here, do you mean?'

'Exactly.'

'I am watching bees. Now, go away.'

To my relief, I heard him move off – then ten feet away he dropped to his heels to perform the gaggle-of-villagers-solemnly-examining-the-ground routine. Demonstrating that he, too, could be a detective.

I tipped back my head, closed my eyes, clenched my jaws, and stifled the urge to leap to my feet and physically drive away this boorish child with my rucksack. *Patience, Holmes; you've outwaited better men than this displaced London adolescent in ill-fitting garments.*

And so it proved: within three or four minutes, the subtle clues and demands of surveillance proved too much for my 'fan', and he got to his feet and walked away.

The footsteps retreated. In a moment, I heard the patter of startled sheep moving across the spring turf. The rumours of the sea a mile away and the cannon two hundred miles farther off crept back into consciousness, counterpoint to the soothing hum of working bees. I looked down at the rucksack. Should I wait, until dark perhaps, lest some busybody rescue me? Or would it be better—?

But the sound of returning footsteps intruded. My hand tightened on the canvas straps: I could just imagine the newspaper article:

LAST KNOWN ACT OF SHERLOCK HOLMES

In a vicious attack on a visiting lad, whom he beat about the head and shoulders with a rucksack, the retired detective—

'I'd say the blue spots are a better bet,' came a voice, 'if you're trying for another hive. The ones you've only marked with red are probably from Mr Warner's orchard. The blue spots are further away, but they're almost sure to be wild ones.'

As this speech unfolded from the child's lips, I turned to look at him. More than that, I rose, that I might see more closely the expression on this unlikely intruder's face. Hairless cheeks confirmed his youth; blue eyes behind wire-rimmed spectacles displayed alarm, but no triumph; the voice was more complex than I had noticed at first, a mixture of London and America (both coasts). The child even looked vaguely intelligent – though that last was probably an effect of the spectacles. One could only wonder who had wound him up and set him upon me.

'*What* did you say?'

'I beg your pardon, are you hard of hearing? I said, if you want a new hive of bees, you should follow the blue spots, because the reds are sure to be Tom Warner's.'

'I am *not* hard of hearing, although I am short of credulity. How do you know what I am after?'

'Is it not obvious?' I came perilously close to catching up the rucksack and pummelling him, at this mockery of my speech patterns – rather, of the speech patterns that Watson and Doyle between them inflicted upon me: in truth, I rarely descend to open rudeness. However, the lad was still speaking: 'I see paint on your pocket-handkerchief, and traces on your fingers where you wiped it away. The only reason for marking bees that I can think of is to follow them to their hive.' He went on, his words delineating an actual thought process: that I marked bees to follow them; I wished to follow them either to harvest the honey or to claim their queen; since it was not harvest time but it had been a cold winter in which wildlife suffered, I must be in need of another colony. Simple, clean, and utterly unexpected logic.

Far too sophisticated for an adolescent boy. Someone had put him up to it.

Very well: I cranked the gun of open rudeness into position and let fly. 'My God,' I drawled. 'It can think.'

A jolt of startlingly adult fury brought the child's smooth chin up, made the blue eyes blaze behind the scratched glass. 'My God, "it" can recognise another human being when "it" is hit over the head with one. And to think that I was raised to believe that *old* people had decent manners.'

It was clever. I was almost tempted to respond – on another day, I might have lingered to trace this mild puzzle to its source. But if an enemy had sent the lad, it was an enemy who would soon be beyond my personal concern; if a newspaperman (assuming there was a difference between the two categories), then he would soon have a new and unexpected story for his front page.

I bent to retrieve my rucksack, hearing the bottles trill their delicate siren song as I raised them up. The third bottle would have to come into play somewhere else. Which was rather a pity: this would have been a pleasant site for a last view of the world.

'Young man,' I began tiredly—

But I was to get no further. Had the child pulled out a revolver and fired it at me, he could have silenced me no more effectively.

'*Young man?*' he raged. 'Young man! It's a damned good thing you did retire, if that's all that remains of the great detective's mind!' And with that he snatched off his oversized cap. A pair of long blonde plaits slithered down the woollen garments, turning him into a her.

Thus, my first meeting with Mary Russell.

TWO

'I TELL YOU, WATSON,' SHERLOCK Holmes said, 'I haven't laughed like that in months. Years, even.'

Dr Watson's hand, wrapped around the glass, remained suspended in the air for quite a long time before it slowly lowered to the arm of his chair. 'A *girl*?'

Holmes gave a wry shake to his head. 'I will freely admit, it surprised me no end. I'm getting old and blind and feeble, Watson.'

'Well, you sound remarkably cheerful at the prospect.'

'I do, don't I? Ah, old friend, you of all people know how I chafe for lack of a puzzle in life. And here's one, ready-made.'

'She walked up, dressed in her father's old suit, trod on you, insulted you, and made you feel an idiot. And you laugh?'

'Remarkable, isn't it?'

The doctor carefully moved his glass to the table, and leant forward. 'Er, Holmes. I know you . . . That is, we've never discussed . . . That is to say . . .'

'Oh, for heaven's sake, Watson, don't be absurd. I may be old and foolish, but I'm not an old fool. The child has *brains*, Watson. Do you know how rare that is?'

'So I've been made to understand,' the doctor replied, a touch grimly.

Holmes went blithely on. 'She's an orphan, under the care – if one can describe it as such – of an aunt, although the house and land belong to Russell, not to the aunt.'

'Sussex is far from the centre of things, for a young girl.'

'Not altogether a bad thing, considering the vulnerability of London.'

'You're not suggesting that the Kaiser will send troops up the Thames?'

'He doesn't have to, with Zeppelins at his command.'

'Holmes, a schoolboy with a sling could bring down a Zeppelin! Southend was caught unprepared; it won't happen again. It's no reason to keep a bright young girl from London.'

'May I remind you that I warned the government about U-boats years ago? And the *Lusitania* won't be the last civilian vessel they go after.'

The name was sobering. Dr Watson reflected sadly, 'I sailed on her once, you know?'

'Yes.' Both men pondered the awful fate of the ship, and twelve hundred of its passengers, the previous week. Holmes stirred.

'Still, it isn't London that interests the child. She has her eye on University.'

'Girls do that, these days,' Watson reflected. It kept the older lecturers occupied, until the boys came back from war.

'Oxford. Which only gives me two or three years to work with her.'

'What do you mean, "work with her"?'

'Before she gets sucked into the grind of pointless examinations and useless tutorials. For some peculiar reason, she's set on theology. Can you imagine?'

'No. But Holmes, what do you mean—?'

'By working with her. Yes, I heard you. You'd be amazed at how quickly she picks things up. Her mother's doing, I'd imagine – the mother was a rabbi's daughter, and she applied the same rigorous pedagogy to the child. Discipline and creativity are seldom found in the same mind, Watson.'

'Am I to understand that you are *teaching* this child, Holmes?'

'Of course, Watson. What did you imagine I'd do with her?'

The doctor shot the remainder of his drink down his throat, and got up to refill his glass. The tray of drinks was under the window, and he paused for a moment to look out across the Downs, going green with the spring. Lovely place, this. Though he still wished Holmes hadn't moved so far away.

When he returned with the decanter, Watson was surprised to find his companion's glass barely touched. After a moment's thought, he bent to add a splash, regardless – shooting a casual glance at the state of his old friend's eyes as he did so.

Holmes was not deceived. 'No, Watson,' he said, 'any elevation of spirits you may perceive does not have a chemical source. Not today.'

'I'm glad to hear that,' Watson remarked. Glad, but puzzled. The doctor tossed a small log onto the low-burning fire, then settled back in his chair. 'So, you are teaching this stray girl. I can't imagine what subjects a budding theologian would find your tutorials helpful for.'

'I told you, I'm getting my instruction in before she falls under the sway of the dons. Chemistry first, naturally.'

'Oh, naturally.'

'It's useful both in analysis and when it comes to reactions. There's nothing quite so handy as a nice, controlled explosive device.'

'How the devil would explosives be of use to a theologian, Holmes?'

'Watson, what on earth is wrong with you? I'm not interested in training a theologian. I intend to make a detective out of her.'

The doctor's jerk came near to upending the glass. 'A detective? Holmes, are you telling me that after all these years, you've taken an apprentice? A *girl* apprentice?'

'Extraordinary, isn't it?'

But Dr Watson was beyond answering.

THREE

A T DUSK, HOLMES WENT to check on his hives, leaving his glass nearly untouched. Dr Watson stepped into the kitchen, grateful that tonight Mrs Hudson had no assistant.

'Lovely bit of honey cake that was, Mrs Hudson.'

'I've made one for you to take with you, Doctor. It's getting to the time of year that we'll have so much honey, I could bathe in the stuff.'

The image made him blink. 'Er, Holmes tells me he's taken an apprentice. A girl.'

'Can you believe it? A sweet thing, gawky and bright as a penny, though she could do something about the way she dresses. I think she wears her father's old suits.'

The War was not a year old, but shortages had begun to result in eccentric forms of dress. However, a girl in men's clothing was, he agreed, odder than most.

'Is she . . . ? I mean to say, do you think her intentions . . . ?'

'Dr Watson, what a question! I don't know that she has any intentions, other than helping Mr Holmes. In the month he's known her, he's cheered considerably. You've no doubt seen that for yourself.'

'He's put on a few pounds, and he is hardly drinking. Or using other, er . . .'

'Quite.'

'So, the child is no problem? He says she's an orphan. A wealthy one.'

'A motor car accident, as I understand it. In California. There may have been a brother, too – she doesn't care to talk about it.'

'She's American?'

'Her father was. Her mother was a Londoner. It's the mother's sister that Mary is living with now. Unfortunately.'

'Why? What's wrong with the woman?'

'I'll not repeat village gossip, Dr Watson. Leave it to say that Mary's aunt hasn't made a lot of friends for herself here. Now, I hope you'll be stopping with us for a few days?'

'Alas, I sail for America tomorrow,' he began, but Mrs Hudson nearly dropped the pan she was carrying.

'Sail! Oh, no, Doctor, you can't sail! They're saying the Zeppelins will come along the coast next – and even if you get away safely, there's the U-boats!'

'Oh, dear, dear Mrs Hudson, I shouldn't have told you. Please don't worry, the docks are being guarded now, our planes are up, any Hun Zeppelin will be shot down the moment it sticks its head over the Channel. And I've been assured that the Navy is assembling a convoy for the crossing, with warships to guard us.'

'But those U-boats, they're going after passenger ships now! And a person doesn't even know they're there until they shoot their torpedoes!'

'That's precisely why I have to go now. The sinking of the *Lusitania* has shocked America to her core. I had already been asked to go over to help raise support for the War effort, but this will make my job that much easier. And if I sail now, I'll appear such a brave fellow.'

'Dr Watson, don't make jokes about it!'

'I'm sorry, Mrs Hudson, I promised the Prime Minister. I even had a letter from the King.'

At that, the housekeeper admitted defeat. She shook her head, and turned mournfully back to her stove. She had no faith in her final card, but played it anyway. '*He'll* miss you.'

'I can't say that I've been much of a friend this winter. I've only managed to get down here a handful of times, and my visits never seem to distract him much.'

'He enjoys seeing you,' Mrs Hudson protested loyally, her voice lacking utter conviction.

'He'd enjoy me more if I brought him a nice murder to solve,' Watson replied. 'Still, he seems to have found a hobby, just in time for my absence. Perhaps I shall have an opportunity to meet this mysterious young lady before I go.'

But Dr Watson left the house the following afternoon without having laid eyes upon her. In the end, the detective's apprentice did not appear until several mornings later.

Bearing a split lip and amateurish repairs to her spectacles.

FOUR

IT WAS THE THIRD week of May, and the sun was out after a too-long stretch of cold and rain. Holmes was in the garden when Russell arrived, his beekeeper's hat tucked under his arm, smoke dribbling from a small spouted vessel on the ground nearby. When he heard her footsteps, he knocked his pipe against the nearby tree trunk and dropped it into his pocket, then turned to hold out the netted hat, betraying only the briefest hesitation at the sight of her fading bruises. She took the object, examining it with curiosity.

'Put it on,' he said. 'Tuck it under your collar, tuck your trouser legs into your stockings, and get a pair of gloves from the shed.'

'What about you?' she protested.

'The bees know me, but you haven't been properly introduced. One or two stings are nothing to worry about, but too many can stop a heart. Even a young one.'

She dressed as he'd told her, and stood back as he picked up the smoker. 'The Reverend Lorenzo Langstroth, an American, was the first truly scientific beekeeper. He combined the theory of "bee space" – three-eighths of an inch; any other gap, the bees will fill – with the accessibility of moveable frames. His first axiom was, "Bees gorged with honey are not inclined to sting." Such as these.'

He paused, expectantly; she inched slightly nearer.

'I, however, take as my own First Rule of Beekeeping the dictum: remain calm. Smoke makes bees drowsy, plentiful food makes them content, but even if they are hungry and even if one doesn't have a smoker, they will not turn aggressive if one's movements are slow and deliberate. If you appear calm, they won't see you as the source of blame for their roof being ripped off, their lives threatened. If you're calm, you're invisible.'

During the speech, he had finished with the smoker and lifted off the top of the hive. Russell was torn by conflicting impulses: to step forward, or to move well away.

'May I talk?' she asked.

'Yes, if your voice remains even.'

'Does the smoke harm them?'

'Just makes them slow and stupid.'

'They're insects – they must be fairly stupid to begin with.'

'Individually perhaps, but taken as a communal mind, they are quite efficient.'

'Why are you opening up the hive?'

'I am re-queening it. The most vigorous hive is one with a young queen. This one has been laying for thirteen months now. It's time for her to go.'

The top layers of the hive were on the ground. He now began gently to prise up the frames, setting them aside, one at a time. And as he'd predicted, although the bees seemed puzzled as raw sunlight poured into their dark, warm, snug quarters, they did not appear outraged, or even much taken aback. The beekeeper's naked fingers moved among the blanket of insects; not one of the creatures protested.

'How long do queens live?'

'As long as two, even three years.'

'So wouldn't this one be in her prime?'

'Yes.'

'But, you're going to take a queen who's happily doing her job, and just . . . kill her?'

'Rule Two of beekeeping: one must be cruel, only to be kind.'

'Hamlet. Act three. You must be their scourge and minister?'

'Precisely. Ah, here she is.'

As Russell had seen in the glass-sided observation hive built into the corner of Holmes's sitting room, the queen stood out, by her size and by her attendants' attitude. It was an exercise in observation: wherever Regina Apis moved, the others formed a circle around her, drawing the eye in.

Drawing, too, the beekeeper's hand. Cruel steel forceps closed on her, snatching her from her tens of thousands of children; in an instant, the hive was bereft.

But before they could react, Holmes slid a hand into his pocket and drew out a tiny wire cage. He held it up to his apprentice. 'If I were simply to drop this foreigner inside, the others would attack her. However, their memories are short. There is a small, edible plug keeping the new queen in her cage. In the day or two it takes them to chew through it, they will grow accustomed to her presence. When they do free her, it will be to welcome her, not to rip her apart.'

'The queen is dead, long live the queen.'

'Precisely.' He hooked the queen cage inside, then slid the missing frames into place, pushing their tops snugly together.

'Do you have to do this to every hive?'

'Most often the workers perform regicide on their own, either directly or by raising new queens to challenge the old one. On the other hand, it is sometimes necessary to replace the queen for other reasons. That hive there?' He gestured with his chin. 'A month ago, I could not permit you this close. Their new queen is considerably less aggressive.'

'Bees have personalities?' Russell asked in surprise.

'They do, and the colonies reflect their queen.'

With the last frame in place but still uncovered, he squatted next to the box, watching his charges. Then he looked up. 'Would you like to feel them?'

'What, put my *hand* in there?'

By way of demonstration, he inserted his fingers – gently, calmly – into the mass of bees flowing over and around the wooden strips. In seconds, his hand was engulfed by furry bodies. Russell swallowed, then squatted down beside him, pulling off a glove.

'Wait.' He raised his arm, permitting the bees to pour back down into the hive. He gently shook off the stragglers, then reached for her hand with both of his, rubbing her fingers and palms briskly between his long, dry, callused hands until his scent was hers. When he was satisfied, he extended his left hand, palm down, and had her lay her hand atop it. Then he slowly lowered the paired hands to the hive.

In a moment, the tiny prickle of insect feet explored the side of the apprentice's hand, moving up and across its back. She barely noticed when Holmes eased his arm away, leaving her hand engulfed in a warm, pulsating, fragrant glove of bees.

He studied the expression on her bruised face. 'Rule Three of beekeeping,' he remarked in a quiet voice. 'Never cease to feel wonder.'

FIVE

ONE OF THE THINGS Mary Russell liked about the man Holmes was his disinclination to fuss.

He was a most demanding friend, no question about that. Even their informal tutorials tended to veer into the realm of examinations – although she was never certain if he was testing her knowledge, or something more complex. Yesterday, for example, when he had her thrust a hand into the beehive: was that simply a lesson in beekeeping? Or a test of her courage? Her dexterity? Her willingness to obey?

The entire bee episode had been enlightening, and disturbing. Holmes had revealed an unexpected pocket of softness – *Never cease to feel wonder* – atop the ruthlessness of regicide. She supposed *being cruel to be kind* was inevitable in the realm of animal husbandry, like culling the rooster-chicks or slaughtering the meat lambs: she lived on a farm, but she would never make a farmer. Still, the image of the steel forceps snapping down on that glossy full body lingered in her mind. And although she told herself she was being melodramatic, the act brought to mind those of his old cases where he'd demonstrated a god-like willingness to act as judge and jury, and even (by failing to interfere) executioner.

She looked down at the current issue of *The Strand* she had brought out here to read, containing the somewhat disappointing final episode of the story Dr Watson had called *The Valley of Fear*. It left a person with more questions than answers – but asking Holmes about them would be pointless, as he invariably claimed that the chronicler had rewritten them to his own purposes. Someday, she would meet the good doctor, and ask him directly.

Somehow, she suspected that Dr Watson would be something of a fusser, filling the air with protests and queries. Unlike Holmes, who, once he'd presented his test or question, and once it had been answered to his satisfaction, let it be.

Of course, Sherlock Holmes had no need to fill the air with questions. The man could construct a complex theory out of minuscule scraps of data – as Dr Watson had put it in an early story, 'by momentary expression, a twitch of a muscle or a glance of an eye, to fathom a man's inmost thoughts'. She'd known this since their first afternoon together, when he read her entire uncomfortable situation out of one brief phrase and a twist of the mouth: large inheritance; greedy aunt. His subsequent delicate (for Holmes) enquiry – that he tended towards a dim view of human nature, but had she written a will? – had required her to reassure him that, yes, she had a will, and no, her aunt would not benefit enormously from her niece's death.

That settled, they had gone on to other matters.

Then, five weeks later – last Tuesday – she learnt that she had not, in fact, spoken the complete truth. Her lie had been inadvertent, but because she thought it was the truth, it had satisfied him. He might never have had reason to readdress the question of wills and problematical relations.

Until she greeted him with an injured face.

To her gratitude, he took in the facial bruising with one quick twitch of an eyebrow – no exclamations or questions, just that raking glance and a return to the hive of bees.

But she was not surprised when later that afternoon, in a minor diversion to the flow of conversation, he'd brought the topic back around to dangerous relatives.

She knew him well enough already to anticipate the question, and to give him what he wanted without argument.

'When I asked you last month—' he began.

'The papers went down on the *Lusitania.*' She adjusted the small Bunsen flame and held the beaker over it. 'You were about to ask about the will, is that right?'

'By way of confirmation.'

'Well, I signed all kinds of papers in February, including a will, and I thought that was that. But some of my father's properties were in France and America, and it turns out that with the War, paperwork takes longer than the solicitor anticipated. He wrote to me last week to say that some of the key documents were on the *Lusitania.* Which means that my will isn't quite as complete as I'd thought. However, I have an appointment in two weeks – June 1st – to sign another set.'

'Good,' he said, and that was the end of that.

Mrs Hudson, on the other hand, did make a fuss over the split lip, but then, that was Mrs Hudson.

Now the sun was going down. With a sigh, Russell rolled the magazine into her pocket and trudged across the darkening Downs towards home. At least her cousin would not be there. Her aunt's only son did not visit often. He was at University, up in Edinburgh, and found the long trek to the south coast beyond tedious. He was a bully and a bore, and it was no surprise at all that after nine months of war, he had not enlisted.

She would, in an instant, if women were allowed to fight. Back in February, she had tried to enlist in the VAD, having her eye on an ambulance at the Front, but she was turned down as being too young. In the weeks that followed, she'd been compiling a false identity in order to apply again – but then she met Sherlock Holmes. And it didn't take long to realise that if she were to disappear into VAD training, he would find her, and she would be dragged back to Sussex in ignominy. Still, working with him, it no longer seemed so vitally important to get to France.

Her cousin displayed no such urge to serve anything or anyone outside his own interests.

It had been a mistake, to voice the thought aloud when he showed up unexpectedly on Saturday morning. She had managed to retain her self-respect (if not her sense of inviolability) by neither backing down nor giving him the usual subservience; however, it was just as well that her aunt had intervened. She'd been eyeing the fireplace poker, and it probably wouldn't be easy for a girl of fifteen to explain away a battered cousin or claim self-defence, not with the victim's mother there to call it murder.

But her aunt had intervened – by 'accidentally' treading on the spectacles where they lay on the hearth rug – and her cousin had returned to Scotland, leaving behind him an atmosphere of even greater tension than before.

Impossible to explain any of this to Holmes or Mrs Hudson. Instead, Russell wired together her glasses, dressed in long sleeves for a few days, and comforted herself with the knowledge that in two weeks, neither relative would be able to lay hands on the inheritance.

'**M**RS HUDSON? MRS HUDSON! Where has the woman—?'
'I'm just here, Mr Holmes, no need to bellow.'

'Ah, there you are. Have you had word from Russell? She said she'd be here this morning. This is Saturday, is it not? The experiment is only half finished.'

'She probably decided she couldn't face the stench.'

'What was that? Don't mutter, Mrs Hudson.'

'I said,' the housekeeper called from the bottom of the stairs, 'no, I haven't heard from her.'

'Very well, if she arrives, she will find me in the laboratory.'

Half an hour later, the telephone sounded. Mrs Hudson answered, and after a brief conversation, walked up the stairs to rap on the door. A stifled oath and a tinkle of broken glass joined the sulphurous miasma that trickled into the hallway. She made haste to speak at the closed door.

'That was Mary's aunt ringing, to say the child's under the weather and won't be coming today.'

The housekeeper made it as far as the half landing when the door came open. Yellow smoke billowed outward. 'Don't tell me she's fallen yet again? We must buy the girl some proper footwear.'

'I gather she's ill.'

'Ill? Russell?'

'Perhaps it was the idea of breathing the air in your laboratory.'

'Pardon? Mrs Hudson, you mustn't mutter like that.'

This time, the housekeeper did not reply: she had spoken quite loudly enough for him to hear.

As she anticipated, her silence brought him out to the top of the stairs. But instead of a demand that she repeat her statement, or a query as to the symptoms of his apprentice, he frowned, and asked one of his favourite sort of questions, enigmatic and to all appearances trivial.

'Tell me, Mrs Hudson, would you consider naiveté a flaw in intelligence, or merely in experience?'

'Mr Holmes! Naiveté is in no sense a flaw. Innocence is a charming and fragile virtue. We should all be much better off if we could preserve it through life's tribulations.'

His grey eyes looked at her without seeing her: a familiar sensation. 'Hmm. Fragile. Yes.'

'Why do you ask? Are you calling *me* naive? Or is this about Mary?' But her employer merely retreated into the reeking laboratory.

Mrs Hudson shook her head and went to prop open the front door, in hopes the additional ventilation might save the upstairs wallpaper.

When Mary returned the next day, neither of the people in the house thought she looked at all well.

Mrs Hudson's response was to cook for her. Holmes's interest took a more circuitous route.

SEVEN

THE MAY NIGHT WAS quiet. Sherlock Holmes sat nursing his pipe, long legs stretched out on the ground, surrounded by his hives. Two hundred and ninety-nine days since War was declared. Fifty-four days since Mary Russell had come across him on the hillside, watching bees and considering suicide.

It would be difficult to say whether War or Russell was having the greater impact on his life.

The air was warm and still – the poor wretches huddled in the trenches seemed to be having a Sunday night's respite from the guns. The hives gave out a pleasing hum as the night watch laboured to cool their charges within. The new queen Russell had helped him install had made a successful maiden flight and looked to prove herself fruitful; he'd check the frames in a day or two, to see how soon he might think about a harvest.

The colony never showed the slightest mistrust of their replacement queen, delivered by his own Almighty Hand. A beekeeper's success often rested on the imperceptibility of his meddling.

Perhaps that should be Rule Four of beekeeping.

People wondered why the Great Detective kept bees. The question should have been, why didn't everyone keep bees? Endlessly entertaining, intellectually satisfying, beekeeping was philosophy made manifest, theories about behaviour (human and bee) given concrete shape. The study of bees – the triumvirate of queen, drone, and worker – was a study of mankind. It provided a continuation of his life's work of keeping the country running smoothly, free of crime and disruption.

Both tasks required an attention to detail, a willingness to get one's hands dirty – and an acceptance that sometimes one got hurt.

He put away his pipe. As he climbed to his feet, brushing off his trousers, the odd thought occurred to him that Maurice Maeterlinck, that greatest of literary beekeepers, had also met a youthful muse in his later years.

One might assume, however, that Maeterlinck did not then set off across his French countryside at midnight carrying a burglar's bag, and dressed in black clothing.

EIGHT

I KNEW WHERE MY APPRENTICE lived, of course. By then I knew a great deal about young Miss Russell, and not merely the workings of her singular, if untutored, mind. I knew of her family, the events surrounding their death, the situation in which they left her, including the financial. I knew who was living in her house and in the others on her estate. I knew her house would contain one canary and two human beings – they had no dog, the servants slept elsewhere, and the cats lived in the barn. I knew that both Russell and her aunt slept up on the first floor.

What I did not know, however, made for key gaps in my plans. I did not know if my one-sided view of the aunt was a true picture. I did not know what other elements might contribute to Russell's situation. I did not know – not with absolute certainty – how Russell would react were she to learn that I had been here.

Nonetheless, when confronted by ignorance, I generally decide that if I cannot have knowledge, wisdom shall have to suffice.

And I was wise enough to know that Russell must not know of my meddling. I was also wise enough to suspect that for a healthy (and, more to the point, wealthy) young girl, ill-fitting shoes or no, to have a fall, a brawl, and an illness within the space of six weeks took some looking into.

I paused inside the kitchen, senses open.

The air smelt of dull cooking, and even by the moonlight spilling in the windows, I could see the shortcomings of the cleaning staff. Money had been spent here, and recently – the gas-burning cooker was an enamel showpiece that provided the only gleaming surface in the room. I did not for a moment imagine that the aunt's purse had paid for it.

Three doors opened off the kitchen: the one behind me, with a mud-room and two time-bowed stone steps to the yard beyond; one directly ahead, on swinging hinges; and a narrow one to the right.

I stepped to the right, into the pantry, eased the door shut, and turned on my hand-torch.

The door was sufficiently snug that a kitchen towel along the bottom would block most of the light. I pushed one into place, then thumbed the electrical light switch to On.

By and large, criminals are pulled by conflicting impulses: the wish to keep the tools of their crime close at hand, and the need to push them far enough away that they might readily be denied. A woman poisoning her rich niece would be torn between carrying the poison in her pocket at all times, and hiding it at the farthest reaches of the estate.

However, any relative of Russell's was unlikely to be stupid. She would consider a hiding place with care, seeking a place where others did not venture. And although it was true that Russell was no cook, and thus nearly any location within the kitchen would be safe from her, a rational knowledge of this would not win out over an emotional need for concealment.

To say nothing of the servants, who were apt to burrow anywhere. Except . . . inside an object that evoked the worst parts of any housemaid's employment.

At the back of a collection of cleaning supplies stood a tin of stove blacking. It gave me a moment's hope – one might have expected the blacking to be discarded once an enamelled cook-stove was installed – but prising open the top revealed nothing but a near-empty tin of blacking, an overlooked survivor of the former inhabitants.

I went on with my search. A methodical hour later, I admitted that I had been wrong about where the aunt had stored her poison.

Either that, or I had been wrong about poison in the first place.

Perhaps girls of fifteen habitually injured themselves, and took ill? Russell appeared to be growing in fits and starts – hence her new but ill-fitting shoes – and no doubt a changing physique brought its own problems. Still, I had not noticed any particular clumsiness in her, and she had always seemed robust of health.

Or perhaps being thin myself, and hearty, I attributed that combination to the child? I admit, apart from my Irregulars – the street boys I'd hired as eyes on the streets of London – I'd never had much to do with young people.

Over the next hour, I discovered the aunt's stash of banknotes and a handful of valuable jewellery beneath a floorboard, a packet of Veronal sleeping powder in a downstairs medicine cabinet, and indications that a letter had recently been burnt in the sitting-room fireplace – which would have been of little interest, except it had then been battered into powder with the fireplace poker.

I learnt that Russell's mother had an eclectic and sophisticated taste in reading material, although I suspected that some of the books had belonged to the father.

I found that the comfortable chair before the fire had been claimed by the aunt, and that Russell spent little time in the sitting room, or, indeed, in the entire downstairs. The aunt's choice of reading matter was firmly in the realm of ladies' fiction; her needlework was clumsy and suggested a problem distinguishing green from red; the new recording disks beside the expensive gramophone reflected music-hall taste.

The paintings on the walls were a similar mix of old and beautiful interspersed with new and jarring.

Also, the aunt snored.

After an hour in the ground floor, I had found nothing

suggesting attempted murder. The stairs I eyed with suspicion: they were old enough that creaks would come with the slightest pressure, and I am not a small man.

The house had two full stories and a partial attic, which suggested that this was the flight of stairs Russell had fallen down, eleven days after we'd met. 'Three steps from the bottom,' she'd told me ruefully as I'd strapped her wrist, that we might finish Friday's experiment. At the time, I'd thought little of it – after all, a fall of three steps was hardly a life-threatening event, not for a young girl.

However, two accidents and a sudden illness were thought-provoking. That all three had struck on weekends was beyond coincidence.

I lowered my knees with care onto the bottom step (resulting in, as I'd anticipated, a faint creak from the wood) and took out my high-powered lens and the torch. I found a faint line at the base of one of the third-step balusters. Which signified little in itself – except that there was a similar line in the haze of unwiped polish on the brass stair-rail near the wall. A faint line, and an infinitesimal wisp of silken floss, that a less experienced eye would have dismissed as a hair.

Even if Russell thought to look at the time, it might have appeared that a length of the aunt's embroidery floss had accidentally become wrapped across the stairs.

Had she thought to look. But I suspected that the child, humiliated by a display of adolescent clumsiness before her trim, generally disapproving, and self-contained aunt – plus, if my growing hypothesis was correct, the woman's bully of a son – had not thought to investigate. Or if she had, it was after she returned home, when the thread had been cleared away.

I was tempted to risk the stairs, to gain a closer look at this so-called guardian of my new – my only – my utterly unanticipated – young apprentice. But that would risk coming face-to-face with the young woman herself. And that, I feared, might be a form of humiliation she would find impossible to forgive.

I paused in the sitting room to study the framed photographs, then left the house for good.

The rest of the night I spent before the fire with a pipe and a tin of shag tobacco.

NINE

IT WAS RAINING THE next morning when the London train left Eastbourne.

I arrived at the station early, not having dared enquire which train Russell intended to take – clients unaware they were clients always made for a tricky investigation, but with one as clever as Miss Mary Russell, the situation promised to be truly challenging. Her spectacles might be cracked, and their frames bent, but her vision remained startlingly acute.

Fortunately, I have friends in many odd corners of the world, including Eastbourne. I had been in place a little over three hours when a motor pulled up and out she climbed.

She gave a small wave to the man at the wheel – her farm manager, Patrick – and went straight inside, carrying a small valise. I peeled myself off the wall of the tiny storage closet of the office across the street and hobbled on half-asleep feet down the stairs and onto the street.

With her tight budget, and this trip being a mere two and a

half hours (assuming the schedule was not interrupted by troop movement), I did not think she would indulge in a seventeen shilling first-class return. Nine shillings and fourpence would be quite enough of a drain on her purse.

Thus, I bought a ticket for first. I had taken care with my disguise that morning, and my last act before stepping onto the street had been the insertion of the scleral lenses over my eyes, to change their colour from clear grey to muddy brown. The lenses had the unfortunate side effect of making one's tear ducts water ferociously, and would have me in agony by the time we reached Victoria. Still, as a finishing touch, they were far more effective than spectacles. And since our lessons had yet to cover surveillance techniques, chances were good that Russell had never heard of such things.

I pulled the raccoon-skin collar of the alpaca overcoat around my chin, settled my fedora at a rakish angle, and swanned my way towards first class. Even if Russell had been looking directly out of her window at me, I did not believe she had the experience to see through that particular costume and the way I moved inside of it.

It was actually rather amusing: Sherlock Holmes forced to muster all his skills to outwit a child of fifteen years.

The train left on time, then alternated its normal speed with odd pauses in empty countryside, coming to London less than an hour late. I took care to lose a glove amongst my draperies, allowing the other passengers to leave the carriage. Once Russell's head had gone past the windows, I put on the glove, tugged up the wretched collar, and stepped down to the platform.

She did not look back once.

Nor, in this city of soldiers, did she take any note of the young man in uniform who leant against the outer wall. He had one arm in a sling; the other hand held a cigarette.

I stopped beside him, watching intently as my apprentice crossed the busy forecourt towards the street. By now my eyes were burning like fury, but I could see well enough to be certain that no one dropped in behind her, no one broke into a trot to join her omnibus queue.

She should be safe until the afternoon.

'Billy wrote me that you'd been wounded,' I said to the young man. 'Do you require that sling?'

'Er, Mr Holmes?' The young soldier took his eyes off her figure, just for a moment, not at all certain of this person who addressed him.

'Must you wear that sling?' I asked again, more urgently. Injured soldiers might be commonplace in London, but she would notice if the same injury was following her about.

'No, it's not a home-to-Blighty, I'm just filling in at the agency until I can pass my medical boards. I can do without it.' His gaze had returned to the assigned object of his surveillance.

'Good. You see her?'

'Tall girl with yellow hair and a brown hat?'

'That's right. I'll catch you up in an hour.'

The soldier did not ask how, simply heeled out his cigarette and trotted to a parked motorcycle. As he kicked it into life, a young woman stepped out of the crowd and slid on behind him. The two Irregulars eased into traffic in the wake of the bus.

I knew where Russell's optometrist's was; the bus she'd boarded confirmed that her first goal would be to have her spectacles repaired. And since one of her favourite booksellers was just two streets from the shop, she was liable to linger in the vicinity before making her way to her mother's club, which she used when she had to be in Town overnight. That gave me sufficient time for a more deliberate change of persona than just stuffing the loathsome overcoat (the fur had been poorly cured, and stank) and the blinding lenses into the nearest dustbin.

One of the boltholes I had retained across London's great sprawl was concealed as a room in the Grosvenor Hotel, mere steps away. There I flung off the wretched alpaca-and-raccoon, then hurried to ease free the slivers of tinted glass. While the kettle came to a boil over the little room's gas ring, I held a damp flannel to my swollen eyes, mentally composing a letter to Herr Muller with detailed suggestions as to improvements in the corneal lens. When the tears had abated, I brewed coffee and picked out some alternative garments, gluing onto myself the appropriate tufts of hair.

Had I been even ten years younger, a military uniform would have rendered me instantly invisible. But thus far, the armed forces were not interested in men past their fifth decade.

So I became a woman.

I rinsed the cup and hung the extreme overcoat in the wardrobe, then picked up my handbag and went in search of my apprentice.

TEN

I'D HAD SOME SAY in the training of these two Irregulars, and was pleased to find them sufficiently competent to evade the eye of an untutored adolescent. In fact, they were better than competent, they were good: having left Victoria together on a motorbike, they were now apart and on foot. The soldier had no sling, no cigarette, different badges on his uniform, and was so straight-spined, one could not imagine him lounging against the wall of a train station. The girl was nowhere in sight.

I paused to buy a newspaper from the vendor near the cafe by whose door the lad was standing, and murmured his name.

A slight widening of the eyes betrayed the young man's reaction to the dowdy schoolteacher in the sagging skirt, sensible shoes, and worn gloves. That, and the brief delay before he responded reassured me that my costume might suffice.

'Mr – that is, sorry. She left the optometrist's and is in the bookshop.'

'Your friend is with her?'

'She took over twelve minutes ago.'

'Good. Step inside to change your coat, then come back.'

Russell's appointment with the solicitor was for tomorrow, June 1st. I had to assume that her aunt knew not only the time and place of that appointment, but also where Russell would stay in Town, and even more or less where she would go today. I could not afford to let the child range free and unguarded.

The War had stolen away my usual source of Irregulars, including the man who employed these two – Billy Mudd, who had learnt his skills from me long ago. Still, reasonably skilled agents were available, and if more of them were women than men, at this point the streets (and the jobs) of London held a higher percentage of women as well. For my purposes today, women were just fine.

Prolonged surveillance is a task nearly as wearisome to describe as it is to conduct, so I shall not go into close detail. Suffice it to say we did not lose her, and my companions were replaced every two or three hours. As for my appearance, it is extraordinary how much a ladies' handbag may contain in the way of concealment. I felt quite bereft when I transformed at last into a man.

I even managed a quick meal, my first of the day, while the agency's

189

two women – one young, one old – kept their eyes on the inexpensive little bistro where Russell was eking out her meagre allowance.

I joined the older one as she followed my apprentice down the ill-lit street. The wartime ban on street lamps and outdoor lights made it necessary to follow rather more closely than I might have wished, but Russell merely made for the ladies' club. I heard her voice greeting the doorman; the door closed behind her.

'Give me five minutes,' I told the agent. 'Then you can go home.'

The empty building across from The Vicissitude (what a name for a club!) was a block of flats in the process of renovation. My picklocks made fast work of the padlock, and I arranged the chains to appear fastened, should the beat constable give them a glance. Debris-littered stairs led to windows that were not entirely boarded over. I even found a sort of chair in one of the rubbish heaps, its three surviving legs ensuring that, tired as I was, I would not doze off too deeply. I positioned it before the window, and was rewarded with a second piece of luck: the curtains in a room across from me went bright, betraying a gap between them. In that gap my apprentice appeared. She looked down at the motor cars and pedestrians for a moment, then tugged the curtains more completely together. The glow behind them remained on.

Six minutes later, I heard the door below me scrape open and shut; a minute after, the door behind me did the same.

'Do you want me to watch the back of the club?' my companion asked. 'She's given no indication that she's aware of us, and that alleyway has no windows overlooking the back door. I think we'll be safe enough.

'There are rooftops. Or I could take up a position amongst the club's dustbins. Either way, with the blackout, she won't see me.'

Good woman: not only a willing volunteer, but she'd done her homework. Still, I could see no reason to inflict a miserable night on her: Russell had neither the clothes nor the money – nor even, I would have thought, the inclination – to be planning an evening out. If I knew the child at all, she was over there wallowing in her new books.

'That won't be necessary. Just have someone join me here before dawn. A flask of coffee would be appreciated.'

'Have a good evening,' she said, and left me alone with my thoughts, my pipe, and the curtains across the street.

I sat down to my balancing act shortly after nine o'clock. The glow across the way did not vary for two hours. At ten minutes past eleven, faint shadows moved behind the curtains; a tall, slim silhouette passed left to right, then back again. A few minutes later, the room went dark.

I stood, taking care that my three-legged chair did not crash over, and waited at the window for a time. No one emerged from the club door, and I suppressed the inevitable glimmer of doubt – that she had felt her tail, that I should have put someone at the back – to return to the chair.

I stopped. Some odd sound had penetrated the night. I walked to the adjoining window, where more of the glass was missing, and listened to the bells and bellows of a fire engine. It was not near, and it was moving farther away. However, the noise was repeated as another engine hurried across London. Then another.

Some series of catastrophes were afoot. And although I knew it was hubris to assume that distant city fires might be in any way my responsibility, nonetheless, I felt an interest greater than mere curiosity. I studied the dark facade of The Vicissitude, knowing that the sound was unlikely to disturb the sleeper within, yet hating to abandon my watch even briefly.

But I did. I pulled out my torch and trotted up the decrepit stairs to the rooftop, battering the flimsy door open with my shoulder in the interest of speed. Outside, I pocketed my torch, the rooftop being sufficiently lit by the near-round moon and the probing beams of London's dozen or so acetylene searchlights. The fire brigade engines had been to the north, but a flicker to my right drew the eye: fires, several of them, over the East End – alarmingly near the docks and Tower Bridge. After a moment, I lifted my gaze. The night sky held nothing but the beams and the moon – but there! An almost imperceptible motion where there should be none, high up and three, perhaps four, miles distant: a Zeppelin? None of the searchlights lit upon it, but a faint flash from below lent it a momentary trace of substance; seconds later, the sound of a small explosion reached my ears.

Then the oval ghost was gone, turning for home, delivered of its load of incendiary destruction.

Grimly, I returned downstairs. Indeed, it was no business of mine. And as I'd opined to Watson, it would not be the last such attack.

The room opposite remained dark. If Russell had slipped away in my absence, I did not know how I would look my young associates in the face, come morning. I settled to my chair and my pipe, and spent the next hours teetering gently to and fro, to and fro.

Just before three o'clock in the morning, the downstairs door betrayed a slow open, then a slow close. I moved silently behind the inner door, one arm raised to prevent its wood from crashing into me, but from the corridor outside came a familiar voice.

'Mr Holmes, I thought you might like a couple hours' sleep.'

It was the younger of the two women from the evening before, bearing an ancient and bulging Gladstone bag.

'Do you know what the Zeppelin hit?' I demanded.

'Is that what it was? They've been warning us about the Zeppelin menace for months now, I think we'd all but decided they were a myth. All I heard was, there's been a series of fires and explosions in Shoreditch and Whitechapel.'

'No myth. I saw it.' My eyes went to the bag. She dropped it to the floor and drew out the paraphernalia of an angel of mercy: sandwiches, two flasks, some apples, and an old but thick travelling rug. She held out one flask and the rug.

'Tea?'

'What is your name?' I asked.

'Marilyn White.'

'Miss White, I thank you.'

There was sufficient light in the room for me to see the look of apprehension on her features give way to one of pleasure. I unwrapped a sandwich and poured some tea into the flask's beaker while she settled on my inadequate perch before the half-boarded window. I then pointed out the window behind which my apprentice (I hoped) slept, told Miss White to wake me before dawn, and wrapped myself in the rug on the floor.

No need to mention that I had abandoned my post for nearly twenty minutes.

I slept. But when the wake-up call came, it was rather more urgent than a proffered flask of coffee.

ELEVEN

'MR HOLMES — HER LIGHT'S come on!'
I was on my feet and free of the rug in an instant. The glimpse of sky between the boards was not much brighter than it had been: not yet six.

'A lad came to the club's door a few minutes ago, knocked on it, and handed over a note. When her window went light, I thought I should tell you.'

'Good work.' I began to fling on garments. 'When we get down to the street, you go right, I'll go left – I spotted one of the post office's telephone boxes there, I'll ring for reinforcements.'

'Do you want me to ask in the club, after she leaves? They may have seen what the note said.'

'If your colleagues reach us, then yes, but I'd rather have more than one person on her than know what summoned her.'

When Russell came out, she turned in my direction. She went past the telephone kiosk, on the opposite side of the street. I finished my call and fell in behind her.

Rule One of surveillance is the same as that for beekeeping: remain calm. Attitude is all, when it comes to disguise. If one does not emanate tension – rather, if one only emanates the diffuse tension of any ordinary city dweller – even a suspicious eye will not snag upon one's figure. I kept pace with my apprentice, a street's width apart, my slumping shoulders not only serving to reduce my distinctive height, but telegraphing the message that here was but a tired night worker on his way to a hot meal and bed.

I had two distinct advantages. First, I was at home here: apart from the odd newcomer, such as the telephone kiosk, I knew London in the way my tongue knew my teeth, automatically, easily, and without hesitation. And second, my quarry was not only an infrequent visitor to the city, she was all but untutored in the ways of surveillance.

I was grateful for my neglect of her skills, because it meant that she made the mistakes of an amateur. When she glanced back, it was to her own side of the street first, permitting me a split second to slow or speed my gait. She made for a major road, where the buses plied – and where other pedestrians offered concealment, even at that hour. She took a direct route, which not only enabled my telephonically summoned Irregulars to locate me, but allowed me to jog-trot through an ill-marked alley, over a low wall, and around a newsagent's shed to rejoin the hunt in a different position. She waited for a bus, rather than summon a taxi and force me – us – into risking a giveaway leap to do the same.

That last might have had to do with finances rather than inexperience.

When her bus pulled to the kerb, I was down the street in a taxicab, strengthened by two Irregulars. A third hurried to join the queue behind Russell. None of them was Miss White – she had remained with me until the laden taxicab found us, then went back to question the Vicissitude staff.

Our cab driver was – a sight to which my eyes had not grown accustomed – a woman. This was no phlegmatic member of London's usual cab-driving fraternity. Indeed, she was finding it hard to maintain a simulacrum of insouciance; she had the taxicab's clutch poised to leap.

'Do not start until I tell you,' I reminded our modern Boadicea. 'And when you do, drive at a normal speed.'

I was pleased that my apprentice had not chosen to travel via the Underground, although I was not certain why. Her route also seemed to be taking us towards the source of the previous night's devastation – which might explain it, that she had been warned of a possible disruption to the trains. In any event, the smell came first, the reek of burning homes, followed soon after by the sight of filthy, exhausted rescue crews and fire brigade equipment, returning from a terrible night's work. And, unusually enough, the farther east we went, the thicker the pedestrian traffic grew.

'Gawkers,' our driver commented in disapproval.

The young man at my side responded with a question as to the disaster, to which she readily gave answer, although before the end of the first sentence, I could see that she did not actually know what had happened here, but was merely repeating rumours.

She was right about the sightseers, though. A few of those shoving along the pavements betrayed the eagerness of desperate family members; most were merely eager.

In no time, traffic was at a stand-still. Three black rooftops lay between us and Russell's bus; heads began to crane to ascertain what lay ahead.

When Russell came down from the bus, our driver was alone in her taxicab, marooned and bereft of the day's excitement.

My three Irregulars and I worked as a team, taking turns walking close behind her, then falling back to change hat, spectacles, or outer garment before moving up again. She had a goal, that much was clear. At first, I thought it might be Liverpool Street Station, but she kept to the north of it.

The rooftops of Spitalfields Market came into view – an entire city block, where brick buildings along three of the streets created a squared horseshoe, its centre a glass-roofed market hall packed with stalls of many degrees of size and permanence. Despite the proximity of the night's fires – the source could not have been more than a few streets to the east – the market was open for business. The usual Spitalfields odours of citrus and cabbage and onion were all but imperceptible beneath the reek of smoke, just as its usual populace of market porters, costermongers, deliverymen, and shopkeepers struggled to move around the influx of police constables, newsmen, and curious onlookers. Six members of a fire brigade were quenching their thirst outside a public house; an ambulance inched along Lamb Street. As far as the eye could see, the market pulsated like an exposed brood comb. The pavements were solid, the lanes worse, the market hall itself all but impenetrable.

I was, to put it mildly, apprehensive. I pushed forward, so close that Russell could not have failed to recognise me, had she turned. Anyone at all could come up to the child, then be away in an instant, leaving her bleeding into the paving stones.

In addition to the open west side, the market hall had five entrances – one each through the three-storey buildings on the north and south, and three on the long eastern face. At the northern, Lamb Street entrance, Russell paused to speak to a constable whose ash-streaked face made it clear where he had spent the night. He ducked his head to hear against the din, then straightened to point forward, directly across the market hall. What on earth had brought her here? What did she imagine she was going to find, two streets from a bombing site?

I made up my mind: no matter the repercussions, I could not risk her further freedom. I should have to elbow my way forward and take her under my wing. I braced my shoulders, permitted my spine to straighten to my full height – and saw over the heads the familiar visage of Miss White, searching the crowd from atop a box on the southernmost Brushfield Street side. The passageway leading to that entrance was partially blocked by a piece of what appeared to be fire brigade equipment, and a handwritten sign, illegible at this distance, had been put up where the passage opened onto the hall itself. My sight of the Irregular was blocked for a moment by a porter threading his way through the crowd with a load of baskets on his head, then she was back.

Russell had worked her way halfway across the hall, and was

now closer to Miss White than she was to me. I rose up on a display of potatoes (ignoring the protests of the vegetables' owner) and waved my arm widely. The young agent saw my gesture, and lifted a hand by way of response. I jabbed my forefinger at Russell, then swept my arm forcibly to the side, stating a clear order to remove Russell from this place, immediately, by whatever means necessary.

Miss White craned for a moment until she spotted the brown hat coming towards her, and gave me a quick nod before hopping down from her perch.

It was then that I saw the shadowy figure.

TWELVE

A PERSON STOOD AMONG THE shadows atop the framework of a closed stall, half hidden by one of the iron stanchions, under a dark portion of the glass roof that had been covered by tarpaulins, a stone's throw from the Brushfield entrance. The stall beneath him was a rag-tag structure, appearing to be little more than drapes and wood scraps, although clearly it was substantial enough to hold his weight.

I did not need to see the figure's face to know it would match the framed photographs on the aunt's desk; nor did I need to examine closely what he held between both of his hands to know that it mustn't land upon the head of a passer-by, particularly one who was of value to me. He was forty feet away and ten feet from the ground; Miss White was twenty feet on the other side and had not seen him; Russell was working her way around the less-crowded edges of the hall, closing inexorably on the waiting trap.

I jumped from my perch and sprang beneath the beefy arm of a drayman hauling at his horse's bridle, then scrambled around three sightseeing shop girls and a messenger boy pushing his bicycle, knocked into a vendor of roasted peanuts, and aimed myself at my goal: a market porter with a stack of nine fully laden wicker baskets balanced atop his cloth cap.

I hit the poor fellow with the sort of rugby tackle I hadn't attempted in forty years. Baskets exploded in all directions, raining the market with fresh peas ripe for shelling. Women shrieked, men shouted, horses shied, constables whistled, the local wags that afternoon jested that peas had broken out in Spitalfields – and more to the point, Mary Russell leapt away in surprise, stopping with her back against a wall.

I tucked my head down and scuttled like an orangutan through and around the turmoil, dodging legs and skirts, hooves and wheels.

I knew precisely where I was going: the markets of London had not changed appreciably in my lifetime, and Spitalfields had the same shape (and, for all I could see, the same personnel) it had when Robert Horner built it three decades before. I rounded the stall of a seller of lettuces and passed through a tidy booth mixing blooms and strawberries before leaping over a pyramid of new potatoes, throwing myself at the rough ladder that had been wired to this particular stanchion since 1901.

His back was to me. At his side was a boxful of some dark round objects the size of doubled fists: cocoanuts. He was holding one between his hands, poised at the edge of the makeshift booth. The rugby tackle would not do – I did not wish to send us both tumbling in front of Russell's boots – but the hall was so noisy, the sound of my approaching feet was swallowed up. His first hint that I was there was my hand in his collar, yanking him backwards.

The cocoanut flew, cracking harmlessly on the ground but attracting the attention of Miss White. She stared up at me, then glanced at the crowd before looking back with an urgent question writ large on her face.

I shook my head and made a gesture of pushing her away, a signal that she was to stand down from the need to evacuate Russell, then returned my attention to the young man at my feet. He was cursing and beginning to rise, so I gave his supporting wrist a gentle kick and he collapsed again. This time, I seized his wrist and put it into a hold in the Oriental martial art I had long practised, which froze him into place, if not into silence.

I peered over the edge of the stall, and saw Russell walk up, read the shop signs in the passageway, and stop beneath one. She pulled back the sleeve of her coat to glance at her watch. I dropped my head to speak into my captive's ear.

'If you wish a chance to avoid a charge of attempted murder, you will lie absolutely still until your cousin leaves the market.' He struggled, so I moved his wrist to a position of both pain and incipient damage. I changed my threat. 'If you wish your cousin not to know that you were trying to kill her, you will lie still.'

He lay still.

'Why here?' I said into his ear, too low to be heard past the top of the stall. 'Why did you arrange for her to come here?'

There was no response, but then, I had not expected one. I used often to conduct with Watson what appeared to be discussions but were, in fact, monologues to assist the thought process. I had been known to do the same with villains.

'You knew where she was staying. You must know where her solicitor's office is, and the time of their appointment. You could

200

have come after her in either of those places, and yet you go to the effort of bringing her across town. With your Jewish heritage, you may have relations in this parish, but I cannot believe you feel at home in this market, not a person of your background. Which means some quality other than sheer familiarity brought you here.'

He tested my grip, until I moved his arm half an inch; he subsided.

'I am not the police,' I told him. 'I have no interest in prosecuting you.'

'I was up here minding my own business, and you attacked me,' he blustered – but keeping his voice low enough that he might as well have made an admission.

'True. Why bring her here? Has it to do with last night's aerial attack?'

His twitch was a yes. I removed my hat and raised my head far enough to see Russell. Her new lenses flashed as she studied the shopfronts, the passers-by, the fire brigade equipment half blocking the end of the passage. When she looked back into the market hall, I suppressed the urge to duck: I was in a dark place and would appear as nothing but a round shape, and in any event, her vision would be dazzled after looking at the light. She checked her wristwatch again. If her appointment with the solicitor was the first of his day – which would be the most convenient choice for a girl needing to make her way back to Sussex by dark – she would need to leave soon.

If the cocoanut had come down on that brown hat, two pounds propelled by both gravity and muscle, what would have happened? Even a glancing blow would have stunned her; a direct hit might well have fractured her skull. One way or the other, she would have collapsed, beside this empty stall that was mostly tarpaulin, in the only sparsely inhabited corner of a crowded marketplace. In Spitalfields. *Think*, Holmes! Spital Field; one-time Roman cemetery; site of St Mary's Hospital Without Bishopsgate; a centre of the silk industry, and later for Jewish refugees, tailors, and weavers. A parish with one of the darkest histories in London: three hundred feet from where Russell stood, checking her wristwatch, Mary Kelly had died, fifth victim of the Ripper. Twenty-seven years later, a site containing smoking devastation.

Smoke. Incendiary bombs. Market.

And tarpaulins.

'Your original plan was an attack on the streets between her club and the solicitor's office. Since I am forced to assume that you have some iota of the family intelligence about you, I shall take it as a given that you arranged an alibi to cover the time. But last night you heard news of the aerial bombing – perhaps you even have relations here in Spitalfields, from the days when the Jewish community took their refuge here – and it occurred to you that here was an ideal alternative: far enough from the solicitor's office that the death and the change of her will would be separated by half the city, yet in a neighbourhood about which you had some knowledge. If you could entice her out to the East End, conceal her body, then arrange for her to be found amongst the rubble, she would appear to be one of the victims. And even if she were discovered today in the market, to all appearances she would be the victim of a freak accident, a falling cocoanut.

'Am I correct?'

The silence he gave me was answer enough.

I fished a length of twine from my pocket – I always carry twine, it is the most useful substance in the world – and bound his wrists. Then I turned him onto his back.

He was older than I'd anticipated, perhaps twenty-three or -four, and with the softness that suggests obesity by fifty. The struggle and tension brought no symptoms of weak heart or lungs to the fore. His eyes were angry, but behind the anger was fear.

I considered the tools available to me. He was half my age, and a coward – a dangerous coward, but not an uncontrollable one.

'You know who I am.'

'You're the man who attacked me.'

'The name is Sherlock Holmes.'

His eyes went wide. 'I thought . . .'

'You thought the rumours were a rural Sussex myth. No.'

Before he could consider the wider meaning in being confronted by a legend, I put to him the key question in the future safety of my apprentice.

'How much did your mother have to do with this?' I could see him begin to speculate: better to lay the blame elsewhere, or to protest her innocence?

'What did your cousin ingest on Friday night that made her ill?'

'Oh, that? That was just a joke. To teach her a lesson – she sneaks down and steals food from the pantry. I mixed something in with the leftover soup.'

'It is Miss Russell's food, Miss Russell's pantry, and you would poison her for making use of it?'

'Not poison! Well, not really.'

'And the sprained wrist, and the fall on the stairs, and the split lip?'

'Those, it was only – the child is so irritating, so . . . condescending! To both of us, even Mother, who has given over her life to Mary.'

'Do not speak her name.'

The command, which slipped out of me without thought, silenced him. Half my age, and a coward, I reminded myself: very well.

'Your mother had nothing to do with the outright attacks on Miss Russell?' Slowly, his head went back and forth. Still, I needed to have this same conversation with the aunt, and soon.

'I shall for the moment believe you. And since I do not wish the young lady to be aware that you tried to murder her' – or, indeed, to know how I had come to stand guard over her – 'I will not turn you over to the police. Inside of two hours, her new will shall go into effect, and her inheritance will be beyond your reach. You may be tempted to take a petty revenge upon her, but let us be clear: if anything happens to her, anything at all, I will find you and I will punish you. Do you understand?'

He swallowed, and the sweat on his forehead declared his belief.

'You will not go to Sussex again. Instead, before today is out, you will go to a recruiter's office and you will enlist in the army. You will go into uniform, and you will serve your country, and you will be grateful that I do not leave your body here, atop a deserted stall in the Spitalfields Market.' And because he was the sort of blustering young man who requires an illustration to make a threat real, I drew out my folding knife, opened it, and let him look at it for a time. Then I folded it away.

'Now, you will lie quietly until she leaves,' I told him. I moved away, to a place where I could watch my apprentice, and closed my mind to the loathsome creature at my feet.

Rule One: remain calm. I had done so, and solved the problem while preserving the naiveté – that *charming and fragile virtue* – of my young client. I hadn't even needed to kill a man to do it.

Rule Two: one must occasionally be cruel to be kind. To force this young man into uniform might, possibly, give him some backbone, turning him from the path of greed and cowardice. If nothing else, it would provide another rifle-bearer for the King.

Rule Four: success often rests on the imperceptibility of one's meddling. If that was so, I might judge myself successful, indeed, for the head beneath the brown hat consulted the watch yet again, gave a small shake, and turned towards the street outside.

But not without first giving a quick glance in the direction of Miss White, whose out-of-place clothing and too-casual loitering had raised the suspicions of an untutored, inexperienced girl ten years her junior.

I watched my apprentice move towards Brushfield Street, the very slight tilt to her head telegraphing a roused awareness, making it clear – to me, at least – that no one else would follow her unawares this day. I felt my face relax into a smile of distinct pleasure – nay, call it by name: pure joy.

For of all the rules of beekeeping, Rule Three is prime: never, ever, cease to feel wonder.

THE MARRIAGE OF MARY RUSSELL

The second Russell Memoir, *A Monstrous Regiment of Women*, ends with a momentous decision: Russell and Holmes will marry. When the third Memoir starts up (*A Letter of Mary*), years have passed and the rough edges have worn off – but this story is set at the very beginning. Here, Mary Russell and Sherlock Holmes embark upon the riskiest adventure of their partnership: their wedding.

MARRIAGE IS A CONTRACT, a formal acknowledgement that two individuals – and their families – are legally bound together. Yes, for some (particularly the young and impressionable) marriage is also the end point of wild infatuation, romantic fantasies, and physical urges, but when the two people in question are undeniably mature and constitutionally level-headed, they keep matters rational.

At least, they try to.

It was February 1921.[6] I had known Sherlock Holmes for the best part

---

[6] Events referred to are either in *The Beekeeper's Apprentice* or, for the Margery Childe case, *A Monstrous Regiment of Women*.

of six years, during which time he had gone from unexpected neighbour to demanding tutor to surprisingly co-operative partner-in-detecting. I had recently turned twenty-one and stepped into the responsibilities of my inheritance, but even before that, I found myself deliberating the benefits, and disadvantages, of the married state in general and to one specific male person in particular.

This was, remember, a time when the Great War still loomed. A quarter of my generation was dead. Those who remained were often physical and emotional shadows of the men they had once been. Being unsuited to nursing, and unwilling to lower my demands, I was left looking at the man I had met during the War, the Baker-Street-detective-turned-Sussex-Downs beekeeper, who had taken me on as his apprentice, his equal, and finally, his partner.

On the one hand, the very idea was absurd. Marriage, to Sherlock Holmes? He was the least marriageable man I knew. On the other hand, we were already partners. And having that piece of paper – that otherwise meaningless piece of paper – would undoubtedly ease such matters as border crossings, hotel rooms, and claiming one another's body in the event of a fatal mishap. Marriage would also keep me from the temptations of pure academia, a world that, especially for a woman, could become terribly enclosed.

Marriage – *this* marriage – would ensure that I was never bored.

So, it was a rational decision, a sensible choice for two intelligent and level-headed people, the obvious next step in our partnership.

Ironic, really, that it would be Holmes who complicated matters with the emotional. And I am fairly certain that the mild concussion I was suffering at the time of the proposal had little to do with it.

One might imagine that, given his devoutly Bohemian nature and my own youthful disdain for societal mores – and considering how little family either of us had – marriage might not have been high on our list of necessities. This was, after all, the modern age, when the exhilaration of those who had survived the War looked to be ushering in an era of high spirits: even at its early stages, the Twenties showed little interest in Victorian, or even Edwardian, niceties.

As for the concerns of *The Book of Common Prayer* (our society's guide to the rituals of life): neither of us had any intention that the procreation of children enter into matters. Nor did we anticipate being tempted by the sin of fornication – *that such persons as have not the gift of continency might marry, and keep themselves undefiled* – since defilement seemed a Medieval sort of concern, easily dealt with by a solemn vow not to pull the other aside into a nearby *fornix* for the purpose of gratification. If anything, the Prayer Book's third concern came closest to defining our choice: *for the mutual society, help, and comfort, that the one ought to have of the other, both in prosperity and adversity.*

Experience had already proved that adversity was inevitable. And as the Anglican rites agree, there's nothing like a signed contract to make one stick to one's commitments.

Still, we would have been just as happy to spend the rest of our lives in a state of amiable sin, regardless of the ease with which we might be abandoned and the risk to our immortal souls – except that we each had one person whose disapproval filled us with dread. In Holmes's case, this was Dr John Watson. The two men had met in 1881, going from flat-sharing to friendship over the years, until Watson became as much a brother as Holmes's actual blood relation. (As for Mycroft Holmes himself, Holmes's older brother did not factor into our debate: it went without saying that Mycroft's concerns would be less the state of our souls than how my presence might affect his brother's continued availability.) And although Holmes appeared to have spent much of the last forty years actively thwarting Watson's expectations, in fact, he was always aware of his friend's opinions on matters. The thought of that sadly reproving gaze would have been trying even for Holmes.

As for me, I had neither judgemental friend nor family pressures. What I did have was a housekeeper.

A housekeeper may not be a young woman's usual conscience, but I had been orphaned at fourteen. From that time, my life was far too complicated for the easy intimacies of close friendship. As for extended family, my American grandparents lived on the other side of an ocean – literally as well as figuratively – while my English mother's relations were either dead or estranged from me. I had come into the Holmes household as a fifteen-year-old girl, overtly proud and internally empty. Mrs Hudson had instantly sensed the aching void and stepped in, offering her ears, her arms, and all the forms of nourishment an orphan could need.

If I had any family, it was she.

The actual marriage proposal had come when my head was spinning (I having been knocked unconscious, deliberately – by Holmes) and his head was dripping wet, grease-clotted, and thoroughly scorched from the fiery, mid Thames boat wreck that claimed the life of our most recent villainous opponent. Miraculous survival, one's own and of one's most significant attachment, has a way of adding its own spin to the head. Or perhaps it was just, as I mentioned, the concussion. In any case, when Holmes emerged from the filthy surface of the Thames, there followed an astonishing, unexpected, and remarkably . . . stimulating physical encounter, right there on the docks. Namely, we kissed.

I believe this reminder of the physical surprised Holmes as much as it did me. Certainly, both of us took care, over the next days, to maintain a cool and distinctly Victorian degree of propriety, even – particularly – when we were alone. Although we had addressed the primary negotiations of the marriage contract then and there (Holmes: *I promise not to knock you unconscious again, unless it's absolutely necessary.* Me: *I promise to obey you, if it's something I'd planned on doing anyway.*), the next stages were somewhat less straightforward.

Fortunately, we had other matters into which we could retreat, saving ourselves from awkward silences and intense contemplations of the view out of the window. We returned to Sussex a few days after the Margery Childe case finished, spending the first half of the trip wrestling with the compartment's heater and the case's more difficult conundra, then the next twenty miles reaching the delicate decision that perhaps we would not tell anyone quite yet about our change of status. I then made some passing and humorous remark about the ceremony itself. A moment of silence descended, before his cautious question:

'You wish an actual . . . wedding?'

He'd have sounded less dubious had I suggested matching tattoos. My first impulse was to laugh it off, but I controlled myself long enough to think it over. 'I don't know that *I* particularly want one, but marriage is said to be a community event. And there are people to take into account.'

'You want my brother to walk you down the aisle?'

'Of course not. Nor do I have any great wish to see Watson standing beside you with a *boutonnière*.'

'You prefer a Jewish ceremony, then.'

I had not even considered the possibility until that moment, and allowed myself a moment to dwell on Holmes, *kippah* on head, standing beside me beneath the *chuppah*, signing the *ketubah*, and stomping on the glass, then me lifted high in a chair—

'I think not.'

'Broomsticks? Handfasting? The anvil at Gretna Green? An arch of sabres?'

'I suppose a registry office would do. Unless you happen to have a family chapel?' I added, as a joke.

'Ah,' he said. 'Well, as a matter of fact . . .'

My gaze snapped away from the passing countryside. 'You don't! Do you?' He had a house in Sussex and half a dozen secret boltholes scattered across London, but . . . could the man actually own a chapel?

'Strictly speaking, it belongs to Mycroft.' *Well*, I thought, *this sounds unusually promising.* 'If it's still standing.' *Maybe not so promising.* 'And if we could get at it.' I eyed him warily. 'Although it would have to be a night-time affair. And Mycroft may insist that we transport our witnesses either with masks, or behind blacked-out windows.' I opened my mouth to say that, really, a registry office would do. 'Plus, there's the shotguns to consider.'

I closed my mouth.

If ever I'd imagined that Sherlock Holmes did not know precisely how to snag my interest in a matter, that delusion ended right there.

'Shotguns,' I repeated.

'Yes. You see, there is some disagreement, amongst the wider reaches of the Holmes family, over who inherited the rights to the estate upon my father's death. Since neither Mycroft nor I care to bury ourselves in the depths of the Midlands, we rarely assert our claim. However, nor have we given the place over to our cousin entirely. The name Jarndyce comes to mind.'

'And your . . . cousin who lives there would turn a gun on you?'

'It has been known to happen.'

'Do I want to ask why you don't press matters?'

'Probably not.'

'Do you – or Mycroft – *want* the house?'

'Not really.'

'Then why even mention it?'

'Because you asked if I owned a chapel. And . . .' He stretched out a hand for his pipe, which even at my young age I well knew was a man's way of hiding emotion. When he got it going, he finished his sentence. '. . . my ancestors have been baptised, wed, and buried in the family chapel since the days of Bolingbroke. It would be mildly irritating for the usurper to keep me from my rights.'

Sherlock Holmes was the least sentimental person I had ever encountered. If he was admitting to mild irritation, it meant that the longing for his home chapel went bone deep. It mattered not that we had no right to it, or that I was Jewish, or that armed men stood ready to repel us.

He had my attention.

Still: 'Night-time, under the threat of imminent attack, and with our guests literally in the dark as to its location. Would the bride wear black? Paint her face?'

'A dark blue overcoat should be sufficient.'

'With a revolver tucked into my bouquet. Holmes, this all sounds a bit . . .'

'Piquant?'

'Memorable.'

'It needn't be. Two witnesses and a priest – I'm sure Mycroft could come up with three experienced soldiers to fill the two categories. Twenty minutes, in and out. Even if the family are wakened by dogs, it would take that long for them to rouse the butler.'

'Holmes, I think—'

'I wonder if they have changed the locks. Perhaps we should allow twenty-five minutes.'

'Holmes, what about—?'

'Or we could seize an opportunity to solve the problem once and for all by setting fire to the opposite wing. That would distract them nicely.'

'Holmes, unless you're planning on keeping our married state a secret for the rest of our lives, or having another ceremony in your sitting room, the repercussions of a clandestine wedding would be considerable.'

'And illegal,' he mused. 'Since 1754.'

'Sorry?'

'Clandestine marriages. Illegal since Lord Hardwicke's 1753 Marriage Act. Is that not what you were talking about?'

'I'm talking about our friends. Being left out would break Dr Watson's heart. Mrs Hudson would finally hand in her notice, and your brother . . . well, I can't imagine what your brother would do.'

'Retreat to the Diogenes Club, as usual.'

'Either that or manipulate two colonies into declaring war on each other, in a way that would require your presence for the next five years.'

'You suggest we make a community ceremony out of it?'

'Unless you plan on moving permanently to Tibet or West Africa.'

'You may be right,' he allowed. 'However, I don't know that I'd want to put Watson under fire. He's not as fast on his feet as he once was.'

'What about Mycroft? Or Mrs Hudson?'

'Nothing can kill Mycroft.'

'But you don't mind someone taking potshots at your landlady? For heaven's sake, Holmes, she must be seventy!'

'Mrs Hudson is sixty-five, and there may be more to her than you realise. However,' he went on before I could object further, 'I do see your point. A registry office it is.'

Reluctantly, I agreed.

But I could not get his regretful tone out of my mind. If he had let me see the longing – if he had gone so far as to let *himself* see it – then that family chapel represented something important to him.

It was, of course, ridiculous. A marriage is a contractual arrangement, formalising the bonds between two individuals, their families, and the generations to come. However, given our circumstances – no family, no shame, no children – a piece of paper was less an essential component of life than a convenience, for deferring certain minor nuisances that might occur down the line.

No: when it came to family chapels and putting those we loved in danger, a registry office would do just fine.

And yet . . .

I could not shake the feeling that to accept a cold and utilitarian setting for this signing of contracts would begin an already challenging enterprise on a note – however faint – of failure. Surely, if there was to be any romance whatsoever in this relationship, it ought to be there at the start?

This man Sherlock Holmes, nearly three times my age and with long decades of history behind him, had spent the past six years rearranging his entire life around first an apprentice, then a partner-in-crime. He now, with no hesitation – no visible hesitation – proposed to change himself even further, sacrificing his independence to become half of a whole. There was nothing I could do about my youth, or about the coach and horses that marriage was going to drive through his orderly existence. Both those things meant that I should have to be even more sensitive than most wives about what parts of our life I could impress control over.

Such as, taking note of his look of regret at being denied the chapel.

Monday morning was cold, the sky lowering with the threat of snow, but I laced on my boots and trudged across the Downs to hunt down my . . . fiancé?

As I approached his old flint house, close enough to the coastline that one could hear the waves at Birling Gap, I was surprised to see all the windows flung open wide. I went in the back door, gingerly venturing a head inside the kitchen.

'Mrs Hudson?'

I did not need to go any farther to know why the Downs air was being invited inside. I hastily dug out a handkerchief to clap across my face. The door to Mrs Hudson's quarters, which had been firmly shut, opened a crack. One brown eye gazed out at me: brown, but bloodshot.

'An experiment gone awry?' I asked her.

'The man will kill us all,' she declared.

'Any idea how long . . . ?'

'He said the worst of it should be gone by noon.'

That seemed optimistic, but there was no need to say that to her. Mrs Hudson had survived two decades as Holmes's Baker Street landlady before – for reasons I still could not fathom but attributed to a deeply pathological need for self-mortification – she had followed him in retirement down to Sussex and become his housekeeper.

Many things I did not understand about Mrs Hudson. However, as I said, when I appeared on her doorstep in 1915, she had opened her arms and her heart to me, and was now as near to a mother as I would ever again have.

No, I thought, as I studied her bloodshot eye: it would not be possible to wed Sherlock Holmes without the participation of Mrs Hudson.

'I don't suppose he's still up there?' I asked.

'In the laboratory? No, he discovered some urgent task elsewhere.'

'Of course he did. Any idea what direction?'

'He put on his Wellingtons.'

That meant either towards the sea, or up the Cuckmere. I thanked her, and beat a hasty retreat from the noxious fumes.

A few snowflakes danced around me at the Birling Gap cottages, where I followed the sound of a hatchet to ask the young man – the son of one of the lighthouse keepers – if he had seen Holmes go past. He said no, and pointed out (with patience, as if to a sweet but stupid child) that in any event he'd not have got far, since the tide was in.

Not the lighthouse, then.

Walking back up the silent lane, I decided to abandon my tracking of Holmes across Sussex to Alfriston or Seaford – or wherever he had gone. All I wanted was to deliver an apology, that my presence in his life promised not only to complicate matters, but to do so without even such benefits as doing open battle for his ancestral manor. Perhaps if I offered to accompany him on his next tedious and uncomfortable investigation, by way of recompense?

Both apology and offer could wait until he was restored to his aired-out home.

However, it had been a long cold walk across frost-crisp Downland, with an equally long and frigid way back again. I could always throw myself on Mrs Hudson's hospitality and thaw out my toes before her fire, but it might be simpler (and less dangerous, when it came to letting slip Certain Pieces of News) to plant myself before the considerably larger and less socially fraught hearth at the nearby Tiger Inn. The innkeeper might even have a pot of soup on the hob.

Naturally, having decided not to seek after Holmes, The Tiger was where I found him, stockinged heels propped up before the crackling logs, beer in one hand and pipe in the other.

The sight of that ravaged scalp over the back of the chair gave me pause: his barber had made an attempt at tidying the results of the fire, but short of taking a razor to it, ear to ear, only time would restore normality. His head was currently an odd mix of neatly cropped greying hair and frizzed stubble, with traces of nearly bald skin here and there. It looked curiously . . . vulnerable.

With that thought came another – one that would not have crossed my mind for a thousand years, were it not for the events of this past week: should I present my cheek for a demure but affectionate kiss? It was the done thing, between two people on the edge of marriage, but . . . Holmes? I stood there a moment longer, studying that mottled scalp, but in the end, the thought of the reverberations of such a greeting – through Sussex and to the world beyond – swept any faint impulse out the door.

That decision, I would realise a very long time later, both reflected and set the pattern for our future behaviour: affection between us remained a private thing. Private even, occasionally, from one another.

'Hello, Holmes,' I said.

He tipped his head as I came around his chair to the fire; his eyes were still a touch shot with red, which I did not think was from the cold. 'Ah, Russell,' he said. 'I see you have been down to Birling Gap. Did Mrs Hudson tell you where to find me?'

I wavered briefly over how he'd known, then refused the bait. 'Mrs Hudson seemed to think you were headed to the lighthouse – or to the beach, at any rate. She's got all the doors and windows wide open.'

'Yes, I'm not sure what went wrong. I may have added sulphur when I meant to reach for the saltpetre. Nothing seriously wrong, but the air was a touch thick.'

'I'm glad the walls are still standing. No, I was heading for home, but thought I'd have something warm first.'

'Do sit,' he agreed, making no move to fetch me a seat.

I had a word with the innkeeper, returning to the fire with another chair. As I arranged it as close as I could get to the heat without risking combustion, my foot brushed something that clanked. I looked down – noticing first the distinctive black hairs on my trousers that betrayed my encounter with the lighthouse keeper's dog, then the object on the floor.

'What on earth is that?'

'It would appear to be a sterling silver flail.'

Did I want to know? Wellington boots; a peasant's weapon made from an aristocratic metal; its source in the tiny hamlet of

East Dean – the combination bore all the hallmarks of one of his outré cases, and I wished merely to get the matter of the Holmes family chapel off my mind. However, he took my brief pause as an invitation, and launched into an unlikely tale that seemed to involve a well-digger, the restoration of a nearby abbey, a lesser title from an Eastern European country, and strange marks on a stone bridge. Or perhaps it was an aristocratic bridge-restorer and strange digging marks in an abbey: I admit I was not paying much attention.

My bowl of cock-a-leekie soup was half gone before he drew breath, but I did not leap to interrupt him. I was enjoying the sensations of the moment: the fire at my knees felt as if it had been burning for two centuries, the beer in my glass was cool, the soup was a comfort within. The satisfaction made me aware that, once we were married, we could come here anytime, day or night, with no concern for village proprieties.

This startling idea kept my mind well occupied until he leant forward to crack the dottle of his pipe into the fire. I noticed that his glass – and apparently his story – had come to an end, and I cast a quick glance around us to make sure we were not overheard before speaking.

'Look, Holmes, about the . . . the wedding.'

'Have you another regiment of guests we would offend if they went uninvited?'

I opened my mouth to deliver the speech I had so carefully composed, about how sorry I was that we weren't able to use his family chapel, and what we might do instead . . . and yet I heard a very different set of words coming out. A set of words, moreover, that said one thing, but meant another.

'Do you suppose your cousin could be bought out?'

The moment I said it, I knew what the question represented: the bride's gift to her husband. *You've spent your life straightening out the problems of others*, I was telling him, *let me do this for you.*

'It's not his to sell,' he said automatically. 'And if it were, he'd refuse to sell it to me.' Then he paused, his right eyebrow quirking up as he turned his gaze from the fire. 'Do you mean, would he sell to you? Good Lord. Why would you want that old pile?'

'I don't especially want another house. But buying it might simplify matters. For you and Mycroft, that is. Unless – is the property entailed?'

He let out a bark of laughter and sat back, fingers laced across his waistcoat. 'The Holmes family is hardly grand enough to entail a property in the interests of primogeniture. And I assure you, ownership of that house would trade one small and symbolic problem for a cartload of mundane nightmares. No, I for one am perfectly happy to allow my cousin to continue fretting over tax bills and the state of the roofs and the return from the tenant farmers. I merely refuse to withdraw from the field of battle and cede my rights of access and usage.'

'Oh,' I said. 'Well, in that case.'

'Yes?'

I took a deep breath. 'Holmes, if we can keep Mrs Hudson and Dr Watson from being peppered with birdshot, I should be honoured to accompany you in breaking into your family chapel and having the words of marriage recited at speed over our heads.'

However (why is it, I wonder, that my accounts of adventures with Holmes so often employ that word?), our window of opportunity promptly slammed down upon our fingers, a bare two hours later. My first exploratory telephone call was to Dr Watson. He was not at home. His housekeeper informed me that her employer was currently visiting friends in Edinburgh, and although he would return in two days, he would be at home less than seventy-two hours before boarding a ship for New York, where a band of literature lovers (or at any rate, fans of the Doyle tales) were to present him with an honour and – more to the point – a paying lecture series. The dates, unfortunately, were set in stone.

It was now Monday evening; the good doctor would return on Wednesday; his ship sailed at midday on Saturday.

I hung up the telephone earpiece and gazed down at the scrap of paper on which I'd made some quite unnecessary notes. Holmes and I were in my newly painted and partially refurbished house a few miles north of his, where the air smelt not of sulphur but of varnish, paint, the fresh dyes of carpets and curtains, and the eggs I had scorched for our supper. In the current absence of my neighbour and occasional housekeeper, Mrs Mark, the only sound was the whisper from the fire. 'This is not going to work.'

'Don't sound so disappointed, Russell. You were not keen on the venue to begin with.'

'I am now.'

'We could proceed without Watson.'

'We really couldn't. No, Holmes, it's just not practical. Even without posting banns for a church – assuming we could convince a rector that I counted as one of his flock – we'd still need a fifteen-day period for the registrar.'

'When Watson gets back, then.'

I looked sadly at my final note on the page: July 7th. Five whole months. An eternity.

But what did it matter? Holmes and I would go ahead as we were – as we had been before I stood on a London pier and, seeing him resurrected from a fiery death, literally embraced an unexpected future. *Patience, Russell.*

And yet, I was afraid. That real life would intervene. That doubts would chew at our feet, causing one or both of us to edge away from the brink. That neither of us had really meant it, and the memory of those dockside sensations would turn to threat. That my gift to him was nothing but the selfish impulse of an uncertain young girl.

I felt his gaze on me, and put on a look of good cheer before raising my face. 'Of course. July will do nicely – and will give us plenty of time to arrange a distraction, to get your cousin and his shotguns away from the house.'

He did not reply. Under his gaze, my smile faltered a bit. 'It's fine, Holmes. You have commitments in Europe next month; I have much to do in Oxford. I will be here when you get back.'

Abruptly, he jumped to his feet and swept across the room to the door. I watched him thrust his long arms into the sleeves of his overcoat. 'Thursday, Russell,' he said, clapping his hat onto his head. 'Be ready on Thursday.'

'For what?' I asked, but he was gone.

For anything, knowing him.

Tuesday morning dawned. I expected . . . I don't know what I expected. Excited telephone calls from Mrs Hudson, a disapproving telegram from Mycroft. Earthquakes . . .

What happened was precisely nothing. A pallid sun crawled above the horizon, setting the frost to glittering. Patrick, my farm manager, let the horses out and wrestled with the aged tractor for a while, achieving a few moments of roar and a stink of burnt petrol over the landscape. Mrs Mark let herself in and pottered dubiously about the newly equipped kitchen. The children from up the lane hurried by for school. An aeroplane passed overhead.

Normal life, it appeared, was going on.

I dressed and went downstairs, eating the breakfast Mrs Mark cooked for me and drinking her weak coffee without complaint. I tried to settle to a paper I had been working on, back in the days of innocence before I turned twenty-one and reached out to seize my majority, but I could make little sense of it. None of the crisp new novels I had bought in London bore the least interest. Even the newspapers were filled with faraway events and two-dimensional problems.

Another day, I might have taken the train to London, but London was filled with Margery Childe and all the uncomfortable elements of that case, that life. Or Oxford, where normally I would have happily fled at an instant's notice – but its beloved spires seemed awfully . . . far away.

At midday, I found myself staring out of the window wishing I smoked.

With a sound of irritation, I went to find my warm clothes and set off for the sea.

The Downs were thick with gravid ewes, heads down to the close-cropped grass, scarcely bothering to move out of my way. I wandered along the cliffs, watching all manner of ships ply up and down the grey Channel waters. The new owners of the old Belle Tout lighthouse – the one atop the cliff – were out in their windswept garden, hands on hips as they surveyed the exterior. They invited me inside, ushering me up the defunct tower to admire its predictably magnificent view of the new lighthouse, standing with its feet in the water (where it might actually be of some use when the sea mists rose) five hundred feet below and well out from the cliffs. Once we had exhausted the conversational possibilities (the view, the weather, and the sheep), I continued on, greeting shepherds, ramblers, and lighthouse-men as I went, to where the track turned north below the old smugglers' path. The Tiger Inn, perhaps?

No.

Mrs Hudson had the windows snugly shut again. Smoke trickled from the main chimney, but lights burnt in the kitchen, so I circled the house, rapped loudly at the back door, and let myself in.

When I saw her face, I realised that I had been hoping Holmes had told her, so I would have someone to talk to about . . . it. But her face betrayed no sign of excitement, no shared knowledge – not even a faint reproof from her brown eyes, that I had said nothing . . .

She didn't know.

Of course, there were all kinds of things this good woman did not know, even when it came down to the events of one previous week: that Holmes and I had nearly died; that both of us had done violence to the other; that there had been drugs and death and kisses and a startling revelation of Holmes's warbling soprano voice.

Not all weeks were quite that eventful. Still, as with Sherlock Holmes long before I came on the scene, I had grown accustomed to hiding things from Mrs Hudson, lest she be shocked or, worse, disappointed in me. My face gave nothing away now as I greeted her and exclaimed at the aroma from her oven.

She had not seen Holmes since the previous afternoon. As she reached for the flowered teapot, giving a little arthritic wince, she said, 'He was here, though. The house was still cold after I'd finished in the kitchen, so I took to my rooms early, but I heard him come in about eight o'clock – no one else slams the door quite like he does. He was on the telephone for a time, then I heard him crashing about upstairs. And this morning I found half the clothes from his cupboards strewn all about.'

I knew without asking that she'd have put everything away, grumbling all the while. 'Was anything in particular missing?' I asked casually.

She was not fooled, and fixed me with a sharp gaze. 'Mary, what is going on?'

'I don't know,' I told her. 'He was at my house yesterday evening, then put on his hat and said he'd see me in a few days.' It was, strictly, the truth, though hardly the whole of it.

'Well, from what I could see, he either went to Town, or to a cricket match.'

'I beg your pardon?'

'That's right. His silk hat, good suit, and ebony cane are missing. I thought that was it until I got down to the lower levels and found that his cricket whites were gone as well.'

'He owns cricket clothes? I didn't know he played.'

'Near as I can tell, Mr Holmes tries everything at least once,' she pointed out, a voice of long experience. 'Though this being winter, it's more likely to be for a fancy-dress party.'

I tried to envision his head – particularly in its current bedraggled condition – topped by a cricket cap; those piercing grey (and somewhat bloodshot) eyes looking out from under that diminutive little brim. I failed. Worse than the deerstalker with which the public mind had cursed him.

'Ah well,' I said. 'We're sure to find out eventually. Are those scones done yet?'

(In fact, I should note here, we never did – at least, *I* never found out why he needed cricket clothing that day. One of the many unsolved mysteries of Sherlock Holmes.)

When Mrs Hudson had stuffed as many scones into me as she could – to my complete lack of argument, since among other things, this past month had seen me locked in a dark cellar on a bread-and-water diet – I finally pushed away my plate, drained my final cup of tea, and asked if she would like me to carry the last few in the basket home to Patrick.

'Oh, Patrick's away, dear.'

'Away?' One might as well say the roof had gone missing. 'Patrick's never away.'

'Something about a horse. Buying one? Taking one of the mares to one? I can't remember.'

At this last claim, I frankly stared: Mrs Hudson remembered everything. She blushed faintly. 'He caught me when I was washing my hair,' she said. 'We spoke through the bathroom door.'

Modesty, thy name is Hudson – particularly, I thought, if Patrick had said he was putting one of the mares to a stallion. I pushed down a smile. 'I see. But, why didn't he tell me?' He lived a stone's throw from my house, yet several miles away from this one.

'Oh, he'd just decided. Spur of the moment, I'd say. He was here to pick up something I had for Tillie. Are you sure you want those, dear? They've gone quite cold. It'll take no time at all to make a fresh batch, if you'd—'

'Good heavens, no, you mustn't make any more just for me. I can barely walk as it is.' I watched her wrap the remaining three golden treats into an old napkin, and as I put out a hand for it, a belated thought occurred. 'But, that leaves you with none. And you must have been making them for yourself.'

'Make scones for myself? Never. I sometimes bake just because my hands feel like stirring. If you hadn't shown up, I'd have taken them to the rector. His wife means well, but she's a bit absent-minded when it comes to the oven.'

I allowed myself to be convinced, and tucked the still-warm parcel into my pocket, to supplement my supper. But as I arranged my hair beneath my woolly cap (wincing a touch at the still-tender knot on my skull), I saw from the clock that it was barely three: so much of the day left, then another day to get through . . .

'Mrs Hudson, would you like to do something tomorrow? Go to the cinema, perhaps? Tea on the front, in Eastbourne?'

She looked surprised – and something else. Apologetic? Evasive? 'Oh, Mary, I'm sorry, I have things to do. While Mr Holmes is out. You understand.'

'Oh, absolutely,' I hastened to say. 'No, really, I have a hundred tasks myself, what with spending the last month in London, and everything there, and, well . . .' What with recent trauma and abandonment and a loathing of darkness that might have me sleeping with lights on for the rest of my life . . . 'I just thought you might be, that you'd – I'll go now.'

And I did.

When I reached home, the house was dark, the kitchen empty. A lone saucepan stood on the sideboard, with a note propped up against it from Mrs Mark: stern instructions on how to heat up the soup without ruining the pan.

I ate it cold, along with the single scone I had not consumed on my walk home.

Perhaps I should go up to Oxford tomorrow after all.

Habit kept me in place: habit, and a determination not to run from discomforts. Also the knowledge that Thursday was approaching and Holmes was sure to appear at some point to let me know what he was up to. Probably not until five minutes to midnight, but still.

Once the decision was made, I managed to settle into something resembling honest work, and got through Wednesday with an awareness of solitude that was merely pressing, not grinding. I did not look for a reason to delay Mrs Mark when she had finished for the day, nor did I set off to waylay villagers or passing strangers to engage in conversation. In the evening, I only checked all the doors and windows twice, and I shut down the lights in a few of the more distant rooms. When I went to bed, the hallway light alone was sufficient to let me fall asleep. After a time.

Truth to tell, I'd scarcely dropped off when a 3 a.m. clamour of the bell ripped me from my warm slumber. I jerked bolt upright, listening to the fading echoes and wondering if the fire brigade were about to arrive. But silence followed rather than the crash of axes meeting wood: my brain began to order itself, and came up with an alternative meaning.

'Holmes?' I croaked. I threw back the warm covers and shivered my way to the window, sticking my head out into the icy air. This time my voice functioned a bit more clearly. 'Holmes, is that you?'

'Have you another man in the habit of presenting himself at this hour?' rose from the dark below. He sounded revoltingly cheerful. I closed the window, and made him wait on the doorstep until I had replaited my mussed hair, found my glasses, and put on a few more layers of clothing.

'Holmes, what on—?' But I was talking to his back, as he swept past into the house. He was dressed for Town, from his high silk hat to his patent leather shoes, but atop the finery there were indications of a day's harder work: smuts from a train on his white shirt-linen, mustard on his neck-tie, engine grease on one cuff, and Sussex soil up to his ankles.

Then he was gone, the hallway empty. The sound of water running into the kettle came from the kitchen. I became aware that a great deal of cold air was wrapping itself around me, and hastened to shut the door, finding as I did so that there was something in my hand. An envelope. Since I hadn't brought it downstairs with me – I didn't think I had – Holmes must have handed it to me in passing.

Yawning, I followed him to the kitchen, which was lovely and warm from the stove's banked fire. I dropped the envelope and set my chin into my hands, closing my eyes, only dimly aware of the sounds of tea preparation.

I came awake when a cup nudged my elbow. As I reached for it, I noticed the envelope I had let fall on the table. It was large, and of paper so lusciously thick, it tempted the hand. 'What is this?' I asked, at the moment more interested in the toast he had slathered with butter and was now drizzling with some of the honey I had helped him process the previous summer.

'A gift. For the, er, bride.'

I jerked back, nearly upending my laden cup over the pristine rag paper, and eyed first Holmes, then the luxurious rectangle, with equal misgivings.

Holmes stood propped against the sink, grey eyes studying me over the top of his cup. I rubbed my palms down my dressing gown, and gingerly picked up the envelope.

No writing: a red wax seal on the flap. I fetched a knife – one free of butter, honey, or even a fleck of dust – and edged it under the seal.

The paper inside, thrice-folded, was similarly blessed with red: an embossed seal, a strip of meaningless ribbon, a second embossing down below, a formal signature. It began:

Randall Thomas, by Divine Providence, Archbishop of *CANTERBURY*, Prince of all England, and Metropolitan, to our well-beloved in *CHRIST* ~

Sherlock Escott Leslie Holmes *of the Parish of Saint Simon and Saint Jude in the County of Sussex a Bachelor and* Mary Judith Russell *of the Parish of All Saints Oxford a Spinster* ~

GRACE and HEALTH. WHEREAS ye are, as it is alleged, resolved to proceed to the Solemnisation of true and lawful Matrimony and that you greatly desire that the same may be solemnised in the face of the Church: we being willing that these your honest Desires may the more speedily obtain a due Effect, and to the end therefore that this Marriage may be publicly and lawfully solemnised in the ~ Parish ~ Church of

SAINT WULFSTAN'S IN NORTHAMPTONSHIRE ~

by the RECTOR, VICAR, or CURATE thereof, without the Publication or Proclamation of the Banns of Matrimony, provided there shall appear no Impediment of Kindred or Alliance, or of any other lawful Cause, nor any suit commenced in any Ecclesiastical Court, to bar or hinder the Proceeding of the said Matrimony

There was quite a bit more of this sparsely-punctuated prose, with a formal signature at the bottom: + RANDALL CANTAUR.

I blinked. After a moment, I removed my spectacles and rubbed my tired eyes, before resuming the attempt. But it would seem that the problem was less in my vision than in my comprehension.

'The Archbishop of Canterbury?' I said weakly.

'He owed me a favour. Several, come to that.'

'The Parish of All Saints Oxford?'

'He thought it convenient, being the University church. And I imagined you might appreciate the designation.'

The Church often gave the name 'All Saints' to churches built on previous sites of pagan – or occasionally Jewish – importance. Had I told him that? God only knew.

'Saint Wulfstan's?'

'Ah, yes. That ate up two or three of the favours owed, since it's not exactly the correct name for the chapel.'

Or the location – assuming this was his 'family chapel'.

'Holmes, what is this?'

'I should have thought it obvious,' he said in surprise, and leant over me to tap the line that followed the chapel name – or misname. 'No banns; no public notice. And since the family – that is, Mycroft and I – appoint the chapel's rector, we can take whomever we like along for the purpose, and issue the appointment then and there. However, may I draw your attention to the addendum on the side?'

His long fingers swivelled the elaborate form ninety degrees, so I could read aloud the print: 'This Licence to continue in force only Three Months, from the date hereof.' July was five months off, not three.

'And also please note the emendation to the time of day.' The formal hand that had filled in our names, our details, and the chapel designation had also struck through the word 'Forenoon' to replace it with 'Evening'.

'Between the hours of Eight and Twelve in the *Evening*.'

'Mycroft has arranged a special train for six tonight. I've put Billy in charge of finding Watson and delivering him to Euston by a quarter to. I shall somehow get Mrs Hudson there at the same time, although I may need to dose her with laudanum in the process. I shan't be there – I will take an earlier train up, so as to examine the ground before the, er, guests arrive.'

My eyes had fixed on one particular line: . . . *resolved to proceed to the Solemnisation of true and lawful Matrimony.* For some reason, the words wavered in my vision.

'Oh, Holmes,' I whispered. My attempted gift had been returned to me, tenfold.

Three o'clock in the morning may not be the ideal time to embark on a project both abrupt and important, but embark we did. Following much strong coffee and a change of clothing (for me, that is: opening my deceased father's wardrobe to Holmes would have had overtones even a non-Freudian could hardly deny), we got the motor car running and I took him to his villa, then turned my headlamps in the direction of London. Despite his less-than-complimentary assurance that no one cared what I wore so long as I was able to run in it, I refused to be wed in a twice-let-down frock and shoes more suited to a farmyard.

In an odd coincidence of impulse and practicality, I had recently set up an establishment in London composed of a too-large and peculiarly furnished Bloomsbury flat into which I had poured unlikely knick-knacks, expensive clothing, and a pair of servants by the name of Quimby. Before the dust had settled, I realised it was an experiment doomed to failure, but I had yet to break it up; if I had suitable clothing, it would be there.

Under other circumstances, I'd have grumbled that the first

train from Sussex did not reach London until nine o'clock – or gone back to bed entirely and set off for Town at my leisure. However, between the coffee buzzing in my veins and the thoughts whirling through my head, I rather thought I might never feel sleepy again. Motoring through the dark countryside at least kept the whirling thoughts under control.

The flat's brittle and dramatic furnishings were particularly stark by dawn's early light, even when the Quimbys appeared (summoned by the doorman – I'd have let them sleep) bearing newspapers and breakfast. Mrs Q found me in the bedroom, frowning over the clothing I had flung across the huge modernist-sculpture object that passed for a bed.

Even if I'd had until July, I'd have regarded the traditional white satin wedding dress with floor-length veil as an absurdity, suitable for those wed in a cathedral with scores of family and a phalanx of uniformed groomsmen to hand. I did not even wish eggshell silk, since wearing it would instantly bring me into contact with engine grease, fresh blood, or a pool of quicksand. Surely something on this vast bed would serve my purpose? The eau-de-Nil sheath and the black-and-white frock with the dropped waist were both more suited to an afternoon tea than a midnight wedding. The brown-and-scarlet was beautiful, but those colours were a very long way from the traditional. And if I were to take Holmes's caveat seriously (should I?), the magnificent ice-blue evening gown, the burnt-orange frock with the snug skirt, and the green lacy piece with the uneven hemline and train would each render brisk flight impossible. There was one piece with a lot of beads that I liked, but if silence was required in addition to speed, I'd have to strip it off and flee in my camiknickers.

Which left the grey-blue wool skirt-and-jacket with the

Kashmiri embroidery along the front. With a white silk blouse underneath and its matching hat, I would be both presentable and capable of an all-out sprint. I even had a dark overcoat, in the event of rain or skulking in the shadows.

I wondered what the fashion pages might say regarding a throwing knife strapped somewhere about the bride's person. Better than a revolver in the handbag, I decided, and told Mrs Quimby that I would have three eggs for my breakfast, and a lot of toast.

I got through the day somehow. In the afternoon, I did nearly fall asleep in the bath, but when Mrs Q then took charge of my hair, leaving me with nothing to do but envision the next few hours, my stomach began to feel the approach of nerves, that strange physiological reaction of icy hands and over-warm body. It was all I could do not to wrench away from her – or, worse, blurt out why I was in such a state – but I managed to submit to her attentions, allowing her chatter to wash over my head and across the crystal fittings on the glass-and-mirrored dressing table.

I remember little about that endless afternoon. Time seemed to stretch and contract like the pulling of taffy – until eventually a glance at the clock snipped it off and swept me out the door in a panic, convinced that I would miss the 4:15 from Euston. (Holmes would not take the 3:05, since that train arrived by daylight, and the 4:00 was a local, its many stops eating up an extra thirty-two minutes. The 4:15 it would be.)

Holmes no doubt intended for me to be on Mycroft's Special with our priest and witnesses, but the thought of being locked for ninety minutes behind blacked windows with those inquisitive friends was more than I could bear. No: whatever Holmes had in mind, I would stand with him, Kashmiri embroidery or no.

We spotted each other across the crowds at Euston Station. He did not look surprised. Nor did he look like a man dressed for his wedding. I opened my mouth to comment on what looked like a hansom driver's outfit – then I shut it. Today, for once, he would not provoke me. At least he had shaved.

'Good afternoon, Holmes,' I offered primly.

'Russell,' he said with a tip of his disreputable hat.

'Shall we?' I asked.

'Ah,' he said. 'I'm afraid I've a third—' He stopped, looking down at the ticket I was holding out.

'I bought two in first class,' I told him. 'We shall have a compartment by ourselves.'

He submitted with surprisingly good grace, and handed me into the compartment, taking my small valise – the one with the long strap to free one's hands for flight or fight – to place in the rack overhead. He, I noted, had none. I stifled a sigh, and held out to him the smaller parcel I had fetched as my taxi passed through Town.

Champagne with two glasses; pate with biscuits, three wedges of cheese, grapes that had hurried across Europe from some Egyptian hothouse.

His mouth gave a twitch, and he set about decanting our picnic. For the first time that day, I relaxed: whatever lay before us, it would include emotional swordplay, and it would involve Holmes. I raised my glass to him, then sat back against the leather seat. 'Tell me what we are likely to encounter,' I requested. 'Other than dogs, furious cousins, and armed butlers.'

'That may be enough to be going on, considering our hostages to fortune.'

'Mrs Hudson and Dr Watson,' I supplied. 'And Billy?' William Mudd, once the young page on Baker Street, now an investigator in his own right.

'Once he's seen the other two off at Euston, Billy's work is finished. No, just Mycroft.'

I came perilously near to splashing wine on the pale wool. '*Mycroft?* Your brother is removing himself from London?'

'A rare occurrence, it is true.'

Such an event had been described as a planet leaving its orbit.

'Plus his pet Anglican rector,' I said.

'Not . . . exactly.'

I fixed him with a gaze. 'Tell me, Holmes: will anything about this ceremony be recognised in a court of law? I ask because my solicitors are sure to do so.'

'Your solicitors will be quite satisfied with the paperwork,' he said.

'And we won't be required to commit bloodshed in the course of it?'

'I fully intend our presence to go without notice.'

'Then would you hand me the grapes?' I requested. The rest of the journey passed in an amiable silence. I may even have napped.

It was dark when we arrived in . . . not Northamptonshire, but near there. Holmes carried my small valise across the platform and through the station to the street beyond, but rather than summon one of the two taxis at the kerb, he turned right. Around the corner waited a large, shiny motor car, its heavy engine idling a cloud into the frigid air. We climbed in. Without waiting for instructions, the driver switched on the headlamps and put it into gear.

'Friend of yours?' I asked.

'An acquaintance.'

We drove some five or six miles, out of town and up first one country road, then a smaller one, and finally a rough track that had the man pulling himself forward to peer over the wheel.

At the end, he turned into a wide spot and applied the brakes. Headlamps and engine cut off; silence and blackness descended. Holmes addressed our driver. 'It might be best to turn the motor around, the next time.'

'For ease of departure, yes, sir.'

'We shall return here within two hours.'

'I'll keep your friends here until you come.'

'Russell, you're certain you won't hold me to blame for the ruination of your shoes or garments? We have a mile or so of ground to cover.'

'In that case,' I said, 'hold on a moment.'

I knew my . . . intended well enough to have suspected that formal clothing would be doomed, so I now felt around for the valise, opened it, and pulled out a pair of shoes considerably less sleek than those I currently wore. I laced them on by touch, then pushed the good pair inside with the kit for emergency repairs: replacement silk stockings, sponge bag with damp cloth, nail scissors, hairbrush, and pins. I did up the buttons on my overcoat, to preserve the more vulnerable clothing beneath from snags and grime, and dropped the long strap of the valise over my head.

'Ready,' I said.

There was just enough moon to give definition to the land around us. We appeared to be on a bridle path – less pitted and filled with ordure than a farm track – leading through trees, up a low hill, and finally opening onto pasture land. A trickling sound ahead of us gave evidence of a small stream; beyond that, a dark shape took form, soon resolving into the roofline of a considerable building.

Holmes took my elbow, guiding me over a narrow footbridge that crossed the stream, then let me go to lead the way up what felt underfoot like close-mowed lawn. As the silhouette of the building became more precise, he grew alert, then stopped.

'What is it?' I whispered.

'Lights,' he breathed back. 'Around the front of the house.'

'Is that unusual?'

'A bit. My . . . as a boy, I only saw them lit when we had guests.'

'Oh dear.'

'Shouldn't matter. If anything, guests will keep the family occupied.'

I supposed a house party was unlikely to migrate towards a chapel, unless his cousin was particularly religious or intending a Black Mass; still, this evidence of the rightful owners – rather, the residents – brought back the day's clammy nerves.

'Come,' he said, and we continued.

The path grew narrow, between shrubs of some kind. I followed a thin white line – Holmes's shirt collar – with my arms folded across my chest, feeling the pluck of branches at my sleeves. The white line grew less and less conspicuous, until I was forced to give a little *hsst* through my teeth: my eyes were poor at night, but I hadn't thought his were *that* much better.

A white shape hovered into view: his shirt front, rather than back. 'How can you see where you're going, Holmes?'

'My feet learnt these paths as a boy,' he replied, and set off again, leaving me to consider Sherlock Holmes as a bare-kneed lad.

The next time I caught him up was beside a stone wall where the air smelt of horses. He lowered his head to speak into my ear. 'This next bit is complicated. You wait here while I go through to unlatch the door. I'll be two minutes.'

I tugged my coat lapels together against the cold, and felt more than heard him move off.

Now that I was still, I could hear the night: the faintest of breezes through the leaves; the cry of a vixen in the woods; from a window over my head, the snort of a horse reacting to a stranger's scent. No dogs yet, thank God. Then I tensed: voices.

They were far off, possibly near the front of the house where the glow was coming from. I could not make out the words, although I thought there were two men. Still, they came no closer, and soon faded away, leaving me with the fox, a far-off owl, and the tiny shift of pebbles beneath my shoes.

A scraping noise came, and a creak, followed by footsteps, hurrying down a stone stairway as if by daylight. Then Holmes was again touching my elbow, leading me up a flight of deeply worn stone steps in the direction of a dim rectangle.

The warm odour of honey told me where we were before I stepped through the doorway: a tall, fragrant beeswax candle hung over the altar, filling the world with sweetness.

The chapel was small: forty celebrants would have been a crowd, with a small gallery over the back for a choir of at most half a dozen. It was old: those windows might have come from the thirteenth century, and the vaulted ceiling not much later. And it was simple: hand-hewn stone, time-smoothed floors, three tapestries whose colours had faded into abstract patterns, carved wooden pews in need of polish – none of the clutter of statues, memorials, and religious bric-a-brac that family chapels tended to collect over the centuries.

With one modern exception. Beside the door, gazing across the intervening pews at the altar, was the portrait of a woman: thin, grey-eyed, with a nose too aquiline for conventional beauty. Her force of personality dominated the silent room.

And something else: the silver-and-pearl brooch at her throat. My hand rose of its own volition to touch this very necklace, resting against my own skin, a most uncharacteristic present from Holmes on my eighteenth birthday. Inside it was a miniature image of his grandmother, the sister of the artist who had painted it, Horace Vernet. That side of the Holmes family – a family otherwise composed of stolid English country squires – proved to his mind (as he had once mused to Watson) that art in the blood was liable to take the strangest forms: surely only the artistic gift for observation and deduction could explain the marked abilities of both Holmes brothers.

The tiny miniature did not give much scope for the artist's gift of observation, but this portrait manifestly did. She appeared to be about my own age, but even in youth, she shone with the same blazing intelligence and understanding as the man at my side.

'Your mother?' I asked.

'Yes.'

She had died when Holmes was eleven. But for all his reaction now, the portrait might not have been there. When he had closed the door again, Holmes walked past me to the centre of the room and spread out his arms to declaim at the altar:

'My name is Ozymandias, King of Kings.
Look on my works, ye mighty, and despair!'
Nothing beside remains. Round the decay
Of that colossal wreck, boundless and bare,
The lone and level sands stretch far away.

His voice, by nature somewhat high-pitched, was gathered by that vaulted ceiling and ushered back down at us, resonating like a struck G string. When he stopped speaking, the stones continued to murmur the words to themselves. Something like a whispering gallery, only delivering its sounds to all corners simultaneously.

I was struck by a thought. 'You've played the violin in here, haven't you?'

He turned and grinned. 'Only when the vicar was out of earshot. If he caught me, I'd get a beating.'

For a brief fraction of an instant, I saw the boy beneath the greying man. At my startled reaction, his humour faded. 'What?' he asked.

'Oh, Holmes. I wish – I wish we'd met when you were young.'

'You'd have found me priggish, cocksure, and impatient. Just ask Mrs Hudson.'

'Did she . . . ? Oh, of course – you couldn't have been more than, what, twenty, when you let rooms from her on Baker Street.'

'About that. Though we'd met somewhat earlier.'

'Had you? I feel I know so little about your past.'

He snorted. 'Yet the rest of the world seems to think it knows me all too well, thanks to Watson and his friend Doyle.'

'When did you—?'

'Russell, this is hardly the time. I'd like to take a closer look at what's going on at the front of the house, before we bring our "guests" here.'

Meekly, I followed. But as we passed out of the chapel, his gaze rose in a brief, pained, and involuntary glance, telling me beyond doubt that tonight's labours were well justified: this place mattered to him.

We spent an hour exploring first the grounds nearest the

chapel, then what we could see of the house itself. As we stood pressed among the rhododendrons that flanked the entrance drive, my mind trying (and failing) to see any signs of Holmes in this most conventional of English facades, a sudden play of headlamps came from the lane behind us. We ducked down, watching a lorry pass by. To my surprise, it came to a halt at the front entrance. A man in formal dress came out of the door, followed by a footman and maid who, under the other man's direction, helped the lorry's driver unload a number of anonymous crates.

'Odd place for a delivery, isn't it?' I said.

He made a noise suggesting agreement.

'I don't suppose you can make out any marks on those crates?'

This time, his grunt expressed irritation.

As we watched, a second lorry arrived, and the same ritual followed. When both deliveries were received, the lorries drove off and the servants went back inside, leaving the powerful lights burning.

'Is this not also an odd time of day for deliveries?' I asked Holmes.

'Particularly from lorries with no company names on their sides.'

'Was that your cousin, in the high collar?'

'The butler,' he said.

'You think the family are at home?'

'Not many lights burning upstairs,' he pointed out.

'That would be nice,' I said. 'Still, it's odd the servants took a delivery at the front door. Feels rather like drinking the master's port when his back is turned.'

'True, they were none too furtive about it.'

As we waited to see if another lorry would arrive, I played with this little mystery. There could be any number of explanations, from the innocent (a daytime delivery with mechanical breakdown?) to the criminal (a servants' romp? A drugs party? A below-stairs smuggling operation?). I rather liked one of the latter possibilities – although in all fairness, just because Holmes had a disagreement with his cousin, I would not wish a servants' revolt on the man. And I found that, although Holmes might be happy with cutting all ties with the house, I nonetheless felt somewhat protective about it. The house that had shaped the boy deserved better than larcenous caregivers.

'Hard on a household, when the servants can't be trusted,' I reflected. 'Not that I've ever run a house this size, but it's such an oddly intimate relationship. Can you imagine, if Mrs Hudson were getting up to something behind your back?'

At the thought, I had to stifle a guffaw. Holmes, on the other hand, made no reply. In fact, he seemed remarkably silent.

'Wouldn't you agree, Holmes?' I pressed.

He pulled out his watch to check its luminous hands. 'Time we were on our way.'

Ah, I thought: something touchy from his past, involving a servant and trust betrayed. Not the best time to ask, perhaps.

I took another glance at the house, brightly lit but uninformative. These servants, faithless or not, weren't using the chapel for their drugs party or illicit hoard: the minor puzzle of a front-door, after-hours delivery did not affect our own clandestine plans.

We extricated ourselves from the shrubbery and left the front of the house to itself. When we were across the stream and the path had grown wide again, I came up beside him.

'Holmes, are you quite certain?'

'That we will not be discovered? I see no reason to fear it.'

'No – well, that too, I suppose, but I was thinking of the house itself. You know, until I signed all those papers for my coming-of-age last month, I didn't realise how much money I have. It's quite a ridiculous amount. You and I haven't – that is, at some point we'll need to decide how to arrange finances, but I suppose . . .' In truth, I had no idea if Holmes was well off or skirting the edge of penury – one more part of his life where I was in complete ignorance. 'Holmes, are you sure you don't wish to buy this place?'

I could feel his gaze on me, although it was rather too dark to see. 'My dear Russell, are you proposing that you turn your inheritance over to your husband?'

'No! Well, not exactly. But . . . Holmes, we're a partnership. Pooling resources and energies are a part of that. I'm just saying that if you've changed your mind, if you decide that you want this house, I'll back you.'

'Ah. No, thank you, Russell. The occasional visit – once every twenty years or so – should prove quite sufficient. Beyond that, a visitation threatens to become . . . a haunting.'

I wished I could see his face. I wished I knew more, that I understood his past, that I felt certain about . . . Ah, but no: here I was on firm ground. Certainty was the one thing I did have, when it came to this man at my side.

I submitted to an urge and tucked my arm through his, letting his sure feet lead us both through the night.

When the big motor car had come back down the lane and gave up its passengers, I braced myself for emotional excess: exclamations and cries – tears, even. But to my astonishment, our two witnesses appeared to have worn out their enthusiasms on the train up. Mrs

Hudson (showing no signs of laudanum) merely gave me a hard embrace and began deftly rearranging my hair, while Dr Watson harrumphed and shook Holmes's hand with only a degree more emphasis than necessary.

Mycroft drew his brother's attention to a set of clothing on the front seat, then launched his massive form off in the direction of the house. Holmes ripped the top from the box and folded himself into the back of the car, rapidly divesting himself of the hansom driver's raiment (thank goodness!) while I introduced myself to the car's fourth passenger: a small, ginger-haired fellow with a surprisingly firm handclasp and an unexpectedly rich voice that had begun life in Wales. Hearing it, I instantly regretted that the marriage service was not to be sung, since that voice in the chapel would be a thing of beauty.

However, losing that voice in song would rouse the household, if not every other one for miles: best not.

The driver handed me a trio of shaded hand torches, one for each guest. Our progress down the hill was considerably slower and less silent than it had been with just the two of us. Holmes, shiny now from evening shoes to silk hat, caught us up before the stream. Mycroft, despite his bulk, was in the chapel when we arrived.

And there, dear reader, I married the only man who mattered in my life.

Reverently, discreetly, advisedly, soberly, and in the fear of . . . well, perhaps not of God, but certainly of prowling cousins with shotguns, we vowed that we knew of no impediment to our joining; we swore that we would love, comfort, honour, and keep, in sickness and health; and we entered into the state that was ordained for the mutual society, help, and comfort that the one ought to have of the other, both in prosperity and adversity.

(Did I imagine it, that brief glance Holmes shot towards the portrait that hung beside the door, as the vows were being said? I do not think I did.)

Our Welsh friend romped us through a nice brisk service, trimming away any references to obedience, skipping over the part with the rings (we'd both forgot about rings), and glossing over all mentions of children, Christ and the Church, or St Paul (indeed, pretty much the remainder of the service). He fell to the temptation of acoustics and sang his portions of Psalms, although his voice was throttled down considerably from what he so clearly wanted. At the end, Mrs Hudson was in tears, Dr Watson was bright pink, the vicar was beaming, and even Mycroft looked moved as he reached inside his breast pocket for a pen.

We hadn't even been interrupted by gunfire.

The forms were signed, congratulations exchanged, the vicar handed an envelope.

Then Mycroft cleared his throat. 'Er, Sherlock. Mary ought to see the Hall. Just this once.'

There was a solemn but silent exchange between the two brothers. At the end, Holmes said, 'Cousin Rudy is sure to have sealed the doors. Wouldn't you think?'

'One way to know.'

Holmes's gaze slid sideways to where the other three stood. Mycroft, rightly, took this as agreement, and reached for his overcoat. 'I will escort our guests.'

The four of them filed out. Holmes slid the ancient oaken bar across the door, and in the honey-scented silence delivered the traditional salute of the bridegroom. We then passed up the length of the little chapel to the narrow chancel door. Outside, a dim electrical bulb revealed one of those odd collection of angles that result when an ancient house falls victim to a later generation's urge for grandeur: to the right, a long, trim eighteenth-century wall; to the left, a jumble of stones considerably less even and more spotted with lichen. An archway into the darkness was stained at the centre from generations of passing rush-torches.

Under the archway we went, into a narrow passage open on the left like a diminutive cloister. Three doors opened in the right-hand wall, none of which appeared to have been used since gentlemen wore breeches. At the third, Holmes reached up to pat along the ledge created by a long, protruding stone. He located what he was searching for, but had to prise at it with his penknife (which he had kept despite the change to formalwear) before his hand came away with a key so old it had rusted into the stones.

But not, it seemed, quite rusted through: the lock mechanism gave way before the key's shaft did.

The air inside was no warmer; on the other hand, no roomful of servants sitting around a fire looked up at our entrance. Although the space could have concealed any number of servants, since its lack of windows meant it was completely black.

Holmes reached out his hand and, with the eagerness of a boy, led me with sure feet into the house where he had been born.

Along the dusty stones of unused corridor, up some narrow and equally gritty wooden stairs, through a many-windowed room that seemed to contain shrouded furniture, down more stairs, and through another corridor.

By the time we climbed a spiral stairway – the ancient clockwise sort designed to free a swordsman's arm against invaders – I would not have sworn that we weren't on the outskirts of Oxford, if not London. Down the next passage, Holmes let go of my hand. His clothing rustled, then he went still, the only sound his breathing. He had his ear pressed to the wall – or, I realised on perceiving a faint outline in the Stygian dark, to a door.

Perhaps two minutes went by with the sound of our breath and the odours of dust and horse hair and a faint but dangerous mushroom smell of dry rot (one of any old building's 'cart-load of mundane nightmares'). At the end, he straightened, and began to explain.

'Below us lies what was once the Great Hall, although by the time I was born, it was little more than a very cold formal dining room – the tapestries had disintegrated, the dais was levelled, and the screened rooms were turned into a butler's pantry. One could see the bones of the original hall, just, beneath the plaster and modernity. Up here was the minstrel's gallery. Mycroft and I used to stretch out here to analyse the guests, trying to deduce their histories, their medical conditions, and their secrets. Step away a bit,' he suggested, adding, 'We'll see if it's been nailed shut.'

I retreated until my back was against the opposite wall. There came the sound of metal against metal – a noise alarmingly like the cocking of a revolver – and the faint line grew sharper. The door gave way with a sudden *crack*, and we froze, waiting for exclamations from below.

None came.

Radiating embarrassment, Holmes licked his thumb to rub spittle against the hinges, then tried again.

This time, nothing but a mild creak betrayed the door's movement.

Holmes made a quick survey below, then stood back, allowing me to peer around the frame of the door. The electrical lights in the high-ceilinged room were on, but it was empty of people, so I dared to venture out onto the narrow balcony. A pair of long tables had been arranged against the wall below: one had been laid with plates, cutlery, glasses, and an unlit chafing dish, while the other held unidentifiable shapes beneath linen drapes. Late-night party, or preparations for a formal breakfast? This being the Season, it could be either, or both. If the much-despised cousin had daughters – granddaughters? – of coming-out age, they might be bringing home house guests after a nearby dance. Or perhaps they rode with the local hunt, and had a meet scheduled for the morrow. For all I knew, it was a household of Miss Havishams, laying out a banquet for a party that would never come.

Then I noticed what the air was telling me: the room was not only lighted, it was far from cold, and bore all the signs of incipient life: woodsmoke, furniture polish – and food.

These were not preparations for a hunt breakfast, nor were they a madwoman's decaying feast. The servants here were no criminal cabal – the lorries we had seen were delivering food and drink for immediate use. Guests were expected, and soon.

Holmes had reached the same conclusion. His hand came down on my left shoulder, and he began to say, 'Russell, I think we—'

Before he could finish, sudden movement came from the doorway below. Boot heels rang against tile, and instantly he whirled, one arm swinging across my stomach to hurl me backwards through the doorway.

'Ooph!' was my response, followed by 'Ow!' as I slammed against the opposite wall. He shut the door, quick but silent, then grabbed my hand again to haul me down the corridor.

Breathless and somewhat befuddled, it wasn't until the top of the spiral stairs that I balked. 'Holmes, wait!'

'If we don't beat them to the door, the only way out is the roof.'

'Holmes, that was Billy.'

'Don't be absurd.'

'I'm pretty sure.'

After a long moment, the pressure on my hand slacked off.

'Billy?'

I ran the moment back through my mind: yes, I was in the act of being dragged at speed, off my feet and backwards, but that distinctive skin colour, that head of hair, and stocky body. 'Pretty sure,' I repeated.

'Positive?' he demanded.

I did not know Holmes's one-time Irregular and long-time assistant terribly well; it had also been some time since I'd laid eyes on him. 'Eighty . . . -five per cent?'

Eventually, his hand loosed from mine.

'If we have to go off the roof,' my gracious husband informed me, 'I'm not standing below to catch you.'

Back along the narrow corridor to the faint outline; the slide of metal like the gun cocking; a flood of light.

The moment our two heads ventured above the rail, a cheer rose up, an enthusiastic 'Hip, hip, hurray!' that, despite the sparse numbers, had dust sifting from the rafters. Billy, yes – along with Mycroft, Mrs Hudson, and Dr Watson – but others as well. Inspector Lestrade of Scotland Yard stood shoulder to shoulder with my farm manager, Patrick Mason; Old Will, Holmes's gardener with the questionable past, was standing with striking familiarity between two royal princes, while a former prime minister seemed particularly chummy with a mismatched Eton-and-Balliol pair: a duke's younger son, and the reformed cracksman (more or less reformed) who had taught me his skills at the combination dial.

Below us lay our extended and idiosyncratic circle of friends: our family.

Holmes and I looked at each other, then went down to join them.

Mycroft's doing, of course, from a spur-of-the-moment invitation to Balmoral that swept the cousin's family away from home to the special train from Euston (rather fuller than either Holmes or I anticipated). He had made the estimate of precisely how long it would take us to get from chapel to minstrel's gallery. He had summoned all the friends he could lay hands upon and spread them at our feet, beginning the instant he received Mrs Hudson's telephone call.

'Wait,' I interrupted him. 'Mrs *Hudson*?'

That good lady was standing nearby, wearing a remarkably handsome dress, rearranging a platter of her mouth-watering gougeres and directing the maids (who belonged here, and who clearly had no idea that we were from The Family's Other Side – again, Mycroft's doing). When the grey-haired housekeeper heard her name, she looked up. 'Yes, dear?'

'But you didn't know,' I protested. 'Not when I saw you on Tuesday. You must have discovered it after that – but how did you have time for all . . . this?'

Her brown eyes filled with affection and mirth, and she shook her head. 'Oh, the two of you, imagining you can keep anything from me. Mary dearest, I've known Sherlock Holmes since he was a beardless lad in a borrowed top hat. Forty years and more we lived under the same roof: do you imagine the man can keep a secret this momentous from me? And you – why, I could see this was in the works the day you came looking for him, just after Christmas. All it wanted was the date. Then the two of you came back from London last week with the news leaking out of you like steam from a boiler, so I telephoned the doctor and Mr Mycroft, warning them that it would be very soon. Patrick, too, although I had to get him away once he knew: that poor man will never learn to lie. Take some food, my dear. You're looking a bit light-headed.'

I gazed at her, then at the room beyond, and started to laugh helplessly.

I had given Holmes this wedding as a gift – only to have him turn around and hand it back to me tenfold. And now his two oldest friends in all the world had conspired against our plans, casually rendering our feeble attempts at a gift into solid gold.

Really, one could only laugh.

Later, fed and well plied with a champagne far superior to what we had drunk on the train, I found my eyes drawn to the corner where my . . . yes, my *husband* was in conversation with Inspector Lestrade and Mrs Hudson, his long fingers wrapped around a delicate glass. Thoughts and speculations began to stir: nerves, with icy hands and over-warm body—

As if I had said his name, Holmes's grey eyes came up – and as if my hand had brushed an electrical cord, I jerked away, to turn and speak to the swarthy man at my side. I was vaguely aware that Billy had been talking, but rather than try to retrieve the topic, I said merely, and a bit abruptly, 'Mrs Hudson has hidden depths to her.'

'She most definitely does that,' he agreed with an odd fervency, although his face gave away nothing. Some history between the two, no doubt.

I heard Holmes laugh. Lestrade was looking increasingly owlish, and Holmes exchanged an unspoken message with Mrs Hudson. She smiled at him, reaching for a bottle to refill the inspector's glass. More history there.

So many threads of past experience weaving through the room; so many reasons to feel new and untried. Or there would be, were I the usual twenty-one-year-old girl.

Still, I should have to take care, in the years to come, to stand my own ground and practise the art of self-assertion. Beginning, perhaps, now.

'Tell me, Billy. Would you be interested in helping me break a law or two, strictly in the course of justice?'

He shot a quick look across the room – at Holmes, or Lestrade? Or Mrs Hudson, even? – before returning his close attention to the glass in his hand. 'One thing I learnt early from Mr Holmes: the law is not the only path to justice. What did you have in mind?'

'There's a painting,' I said. 'I'd like to give it to my husband.'

MRS HUDSON'S CASE

Sherlock Holmes's long-time Baker Street landlady, Mrs Hudson, was a fixture in the Conan Doyle stories, providing tea, hearty breakfasts, clients' escort to the Holmes rooms, and regular exclamations of horror over the antics of her tenant, his clients, and his street gang of Irregulars. Not until *The Murder of Mary Russell* did Mrs Hudson's true past come out. This story gives Russell a first hint of Mrs Hudson's hidden nature, her observational skills, and her determination.

As HAS BEEN NOTED by a previous biographer, Mrs Hudson was the most long-suffering of landladies. In the years when Sherlock Holmes lived beneath her Baker Street roof, she faced with equanimity his irregular hours, his ill temper, his malodorous and occasionally dangerous chemical experiments, his (again) occasionally malodorous and even dangerous visitors, and all the other demands made on her dwelling and her person. And yet, far from rejoicing when Holmes quit London for the sea-blown expanses of the Sussex Downs, in less than three months she had turned her house over to an estate agent and followed him, to run his household as she had formerly run her own. When once I dared to ask her why, late on a celebratory evening when she had rather more drink taken than was her wont, she answered that the devil himself needed someone to look after him, and it made her fingers itch to know that Mr Holmes was not getting the care to which he was accustomed. Besides, she added under her breath, the new tenants had not been in place for a week before she knew she would go mad with boredom.

Thus, thanks to the willingness of this good woman to continue suffering in the service of genius, Holmes's life went on much as before.

Not that he was grateful, or indeed even aware of her sacrifice. He went on, as I said, much as before, feeling vexed when her tidying had removed some vital item or when her regular market-day absence meant that he had to brew his own coffee. Deep in his misogynistic soul, he was not really convinced that women had minds, rights, or lives of their own.

This may be unfair; he was certainly always more than ready to dismiss members of his own sex. However, there is no doubt that a woman, be she lady or governess, triggered in him an automatic response of polite disinterest coupled with vague impatience: it took a high degree of determination on the part of a prospective client who happened to be female to drag him into a case.

Mrs Hudson, though, was nothing if not determined. On this day in October of 1918 she had pursued him through the house and up the stairs, finally bearding him in his laboratory, where she continued to press upon him the details of her odd experience. However, her bristling Scots implacability made little headway against the carapace of English phlegm that he was turning against her. I stood in the doorway, witness to the meeting of irresistible force and immoveable object.

'No, Mrs Hudson, absolutely not. I am busy.' To prove it (although when I had arrived at his house twenty minutes earlier I had found him moping over the newspapers), he turned to his acid-stained workbench and reached for some beakers and a couple of long glass tubes.

'All I'm asking you to do is rig a wee trap,' she said, her accent growing with her perturbation.

Holmes snorted. 'A bear trap in the kitchen, perhaps? Oh, a capital idea, Mrs Hudson.'

'You're not listening to me, Mister 'Olmes. I told you, I wanted you to fix up a simple camera, so I can see who it is that's been coming in of rights and helping himself to my bits and pieces.'

'Mice, Mrs Hudson. The country is full of them.' He dropped a pipette into a jar and transferred a quantity of liquid into a clean beaker.

'*Mice!*' She was shocked. 'In *my* kitchen? Mr Holmes, *really.*'

Holmes had gone too far, and knew it. 'I do apologise, Mrs Hudson. Perhaps it was the cat?'

'And what call would a cat have for a needle and thread?' she demanded, unplacated. 'Even if the beastie could work the latch on my sewing case.'

'Perhaps Russell . . . ?'

'You know full well that Mary's been away at University these four weeks.'

'Oh, very well. Ask Will to change the locks on the doors.' He turned his back with an optimistic attempt at finality.

'I don't want the locks changed, I want to know who it is.

Things have gone missing from all the neighbours, little things mostly, but it's not nice.'

I had been watching Holmes's movements at first idly, then more closely, and now I took a step into the room and caught at Mrs Hudson's sleeve. 'Mrs Hudson, I'll help you with it. I'm sure I can figure out how to booby trap a camera with a flash. Come, let's go downstairs and decide where to put it.'

'But I thought—'

'Come with me, Mrs Hudson.'

'Mary, are you certain?'

'*Now,* Mrs Hudson.' I tightened my grip on her substantial arm and hauled, just as Holmes removed his finger from the end of the pipette and allowed the substance it held to drop into the already seething mixture in the beaker. He had not been paying attention to his experiment; a cloud of noxious green gas began instantly to billow up from the mouth of the beaker. Mrs Hudson and I went with all haste down the stairs, leaving Holmes to grope his way to the shutters and fling them open, coughing and cursing furiously.

Once in her kitchen, Mrs Hudson's inborn hospitality reasserted itself, and I had to wait until she had stirred up a batch of rock cakes, and questioned me about my progress and my diet up at Oxford in this, my second year there. She then put on the kettle, washed up the bowls, and swept the floor before finally settling in a chair across the soft scrubbed wood table from me.

'You were saying,' I began, 'that you've had a series of break-ins and small thefts.'

'Some food and a bit of milk from time to time. Usually stale things, a heel of bread and a knob of dry cheese. Some wool stockings from the darning basket, two old blankets I'd intended for the church. And as I said, a couple of needles and a spool of black thread from the sewing case.' She nodded at the neat piece of wooden joinery with the padded top that sat in front of her chair by the fire, and I had to agree, no cat could have worked its latch.

'Alcohol?'

'Never. And never have I missed any of the household money I keep in the tea caddy or anything of value. Mrs Prinnings down the road claims she lost a ring to the thief, but she's terribly absent-minded, she is.'

'How is he getting in?'

'I think he must have a key.' Seeing my expression, she hastened to explain. 'There's always one on the hook at the back door, and one day last week when Will needed it, I couldn't find it. I thought he maybe borrowed it earlier and forgot to return it, that's happened before, but it could have been the thief. And I admit I'm not always good at locking up all the windows at night. Which is probably how he got in in the first place.'

'So change the locks.'

'The thing is, Mary, I can't help but feel it's some poor soul who is in need, and although I certainly don't want him to waltz in and out, I do want to know who it is so that I know what to do. Do you follow me?'

I did, actually. There were a handful of ex-soldiers living around the fringes of Oxford, so badly shell-shocked as to be incapable of ordinary social intercourse, who slept rough and survived by what wits were left to them. Tragic figures, and one would not wish to be responsible for their starvation.

'How many people in the area have been broken into?'

'Pretty near everyone when it first started, the end of September. Since then those who have locks use them. The others seem to think it's fairies or absent-mindedness.'

'Fairies?'

'The little people are a curious lot,' she said. I looked closely to be sure that she was joking, but I couldn't tell.

Some invisible signal made her rise and go to the oven, and sure enough, the cakes were perfect and golden brown. We ate them with fresh butter and drank tea (Mrs Hudson carried a tray upstairs, and returned without comment but with watering eyes) and then turned our combined intellects to the problem of photographing intruders.

I returned the next morning, Saturday, with a variety of equipment. Borrowing a hammer, nails, and scraps of wood from old Will, the handyman, and a length of fine fishing twine from his grandson, by trial and error Mrs Hudson and I (interrupted regularly by delivery boys, shouts from upstairs, and telephone calls) succeeded in rigging a trip wire across the kitchen door.

During the final stages of this delicate operation, as I perched on the stepladder adjusting the camera, I was peripherally aware of Holmes's voice raised to shout down the telephone in the library. After a few minutes, silence fell, and shortly thereafter his head appeared at the level of my waist.

He didn't sneer at my efforts. He acted as if I were not there, as if he had found Mrs Hudson rolling out a pie crust rather than holding out a selection of wedges for me to use in my adjustments.

'Mrs Hudson, it appears that I shall be away for a few days. Would you sort me out some clean collars and the like?'

'*Now*, Mr Holmes?'

'Anytime in the next ten minutes will be fine,' he said generously, then turned and left without so much as a glance at me. I bent down to call through the doorway at his retreating back.

'I go back to Oxford tomorrow, Holmes.'

'It was good of you to come by, Russell,' he said, and disappeared up the stairs.

'You can leave the wedges with me, Mrs Hudson,' I told her. 'I'm nearly finished.'

I could see her waver with the contemplation of rebellion, but we both knew full well that Holmes would leave in ten minutes, clean linen or no, and whereas I would have happily sent him on his way grubby, Mrs Hudson's professional pride was at stake. She put the wedges on the top of the stepladder and hurried off.

She and Holmes arrived simultaneously in the central room of the old cottage just as I had alighted from the ladder to examine my handiwork. I turned my gaze to Holmes, and found him dressed for Town, pulling on a pair of black leather gloves. 'A case, Holmes?'

'Merely a consultation, at this point. Scotland Yard has been reflecting on our success with the Jessica Simpson kidnapping, and in their efforts to trawl the bottom of this latest kidnapping have decided to have me review their efforts for possible gaps. Paperwork merely, Russell,' he added. 'Nothing to excite you.'

'This is the Oberdorfer case?' I asked. It was nearly a month since the two children, twelve-year-old Sarah and her seven-year-old brother Louis, had vanished from Hyde Park under the expensive nose of their nurse. They were orphans, the children of a cloth manufacturer with factories in three countries and his independently wealthy French wife. His brother, who had taken refuge in London during the War, had anticipated a huge demand of ransom. He was still waiting.

'Is there news?'

'There is nothing. No ransom note, no sightings, nothing. Scotland Yard is settling to the opinion that it was an outburst of anti-German sentiment that went too far, along the lines of the smashing of German shopkeepers' windows that was so common in the opening months of the War. Lestrade believes the kidnapper was a rank amateur who panicked at his own audacity and killed them, and further thinks their bodies will be found any day, no doubt by some sportsman's dog.' He grimaced, tucked in the ends of his scarf, buttoned his coat against the cool autumnal day, and took the portmanteau from Mrs Hudson's hand.

'Well, good luck, Holmes,' I said.

'Luck,' he said austerely, 'has nothing to do with it.'

When he had left, Mrs Hudson and I stood looking at each other for a long minute, sobered by this reminder of what was almost certainly foul murder, and also by the revealing lack of enthusiasm and optimism in the demeanour of the man who had just driven off. Whatever he might say, our success in the Simpson case two months earlier had been guided by luck, and I had no yearning to join forces in a second kidnap case, particularly one that was patently hopeless.

I sighed, and then we turned to my trap. I explained how the camera worked, told her where to take the film to be developed and printed, and then tidied away my tools and prepared to make my own departure.

'You'll let me know if anything turns up?' I asked. 'I could try to make it back down next weekend, but—'

'No, no, Mary, you mustn't interfere with your studies. I shall write and let you know.'

I stepped cautiously over the taut fishing wire and paused in the doorway. 'And you'll tell me if Holmes seems to need any assistance in this Oberdorfer case?'

'That I will.'

I left, ruefully contemplating the irony of a man who normally avoided children like the plague (aside from those miniature adults he had scraped off the streets to form his 'Irregulars' in the Baker Street days); these days he seemed to have his hands full of them.

I returned to Oxford, and my studies, and truth to tell the first I thought about Mrs Hudson's problem was more than a week later, on a Wednesday, when I realised that for the second week in a row her inevitable Tuesday letter had not come. I had not expected the first one, though she often wrote even if I had seen her the day before, but not to write after eight days was unprecedented.

I telephoned the cottage that evening. Holmes was still away interviewing the Oberdorfer uncle, Mrs Hudson thought. She herself sounded most peculiar, distracted, and said merely that she'd been too busy to write, apologised, and asked if there was anything in particular I was wanting?

Badly taken aback, I stammered out a question concerning our camera trap.

'Oh, yes,' she said, 'the camera. No, no, nothing much has come of that. Still, it was a good idea, Mary. Thank you. Well, I must be gone now, dear, take care.'

The line went dead, and I slowly put up the earpiece. She hadn't even asked if I was eating well.

I was hit by a sudden absurd desire to leave immediately for Sussex. I succeeded in pushing it away, but on Saturday morning I was on the train south, and by Saturday afternoon my hand was on the kitchen door to Holmes's cottage.

A moment later my nose was nearly on the door as well, flattened against it, in fact, because the door did not open. It was locked.

This door was never locked, certainly not in the daytime when there was anyone at home, yet I could have sworn that I had heard a scurry of sound from within. When I tried to look in the window, my eyes were met by a gaily-patterned tea towel, pinned up neatly to all the edges.

'Mrs Hudson?' I called. There was no answer. Perhaps the movement had been the cat. I went around the house, tried the French doors and found them locked as well, and continued around to the front door, only to have it open as I stretched out my hand. Mrs Hudson stood in the narrow opening, her sturdy shoe planted firmly against the door's lower edge.

'Mrs Hudson, there you are! I was beginning to think you'd gone out.'

'Hello there, Mary. I'm surprised to see you back down here so soon. Mr Holmes isn't back from the Continent yet, I'm sorry.'

'Actually, I came to see you.'

'Ah, Mary, such a pity, but I really can't have you in. I'm taking advantage of Mr Holmes's absence to turn out the house, and things are in a dreadful state. You should have checked with me first, dear.'

A brief glance at her tidy, uncovered hair and her clean hand on the door made it obvious that heavy house-cleaning was not her current preoccupation. Yet she did not appear afraid, as if she was being held hostage or something; she seemed merely determined. Still, I had to keep her at the door as long as I could while I searched for a clue to her odd behaviour.

Such was my intention; however, every question was met by a slight edging back into the house and an increment of closure of the door, until eventually it clicked shut before me. I heard the sound of the bolt being shot, and then Mrs Hudson's firm footsteps, retreating towards the kitchen.

I stood, away from the house, frankly astonished. I couldn't even peer in, as the sitting-room windows overlooking the kitchen had had their curtains tightly shut. I considered, and discarded, a full frontal assault, and decided that the only thing for it was stealth.

Mrs Hudson knew me well enough to expect it of me, of that I was fully aware, so I took care to stay away that evening, even ringing her from my own house several miles away to let her know that I was not outside the cottage, watching her curtains. She also knew that I had to take the Sunday night train in order to be at the Monday morning lectures, and would then begin to relax. Sunday night, therefore, was when I took up my position outside the kitchen window.

For a long time all I heard were busy kitchen sounds – a knife on a cutting board, a spoon scraping against the side of a pot, the clatter of a bowl going into the stone sink. Then without warning, at about nine o'clock, Mrs Hudson spoke.

'Hello there, dear. Have a good sleep?'

'I always feel I should say "good morning", but it's night-time,' said a voice in response, and I was so startled I nearly knocked over a pot of herbs. The voice was that of a child, sleep-clogged but high-pitched: a child with a very faint German accent.

Enough of this, I thought. I was tempted to heave the herb pot through the window and just clamber in, but I was not sure of the condition of Mrs Hudson's heart. Instead I went silently around the house, found the door barred to my key, and ended up retrieving the long ladder from the side of the garden shed and propping it up against Holmes's window. Of course the man would have jimmy-proof latches. Finally in frustration I used a rock, and fast as Mrs Hudson was in responding to the sound of breaking glass, I still met her at the foot of the stairs, and slipped past her by feinting to the left and ducking past her on the right. The kitchen was bare.

However, the bolt was still shot, so the owner of the German voice was here somewhere. I ignored the furious Scotswoman at my back and ran my eyes over the scene: the pots of food that she would not have cooked for herself alone, the table laid for three (one of the place settings with a diminutive fork and a china mug decorated with pigs wearing toppers and tails), and two new hairbrushes lying on a towel on the side of the sink.

'Tell them to come out,' I said.

She sighed deeply. 'You don't know what you're doing, Mary.'

'Of course I don't. How can I know anything if you keep me in the dark?'

'Oh, very well. I should have known you'd persist until you found out. I was going to move them, but—' She paused, and raised her voice. 'Sarah, Louis, come out here.'

They came, not, as I had expected, from the pantry, but crawling out of the tiny cupboard in the corner. When they were standing in the room, eyeing me warily, Mrs Hudson made the introductions.

'Sarah and Louis Oberdorfer, Miss Mary Russell. Don't worry, she's a friend. A very nosy friend.' She sniffed, and turned to take another place setting from the sideboard and lay it out – at the far end of the table from the three places already there.

'The Oberdorfers,' I said. 'How on earth did they get here? Did Holmes bring them? Don't you know that the police in two countries are looking for them?'

Twelve-year-old Sarah glowered at me. Her seven-year-old brother edged behind her fearfully. Mrs Hudson set the kettle down forcefully on the hob.

'Of course I do. And no, Mr Holmes is not aware that they are here.'

'But he's actually working on the case. How could you—?'

She cut me off. Chin raised, grey hair quivering, she turned on me with a porridge spoon in her hand. 'Now, don't you go accusing me of being a traitor, Mary Russell, not until you know what I know.'

We faced off across the kitchen table, the stout, ageing Scots housekeeper and the lanky Oxford undergraduate, until I realised simultaneously that whatever she was cooking smelt superb, and that perhaps I ought indeed to know what she knew. A truce was called, and we sat down at the table to break bread together.

It took a long time for the various threads of the story to trickle out, narrated by Mrs Hudson (telling how, in Holmes's absence, she could nap in the afternoons so as to sit up night after night until the door had finally been opened by the thief) and by Sarah Oberdorfer (who coolly recited how she had schemed and prepared, with map and warm clothes and enough money to get them started, and only seemed troubled at the telling of how she had been forced to take to a life of crime), with the occasional contribution by young Louis (who thought the whole thing a great lark, from the adventure of hiding among the baggage in the train from London to the thrill of wandering the Downs, unsupervised, in the moonlight). It took longer still for the entire thing to become clear in my mind. Until midnight, in fact, when the two children, who had from the beginning been sleeping days and active at night to help prevent discovery, were stretched out on the carpet in front of the fire in the next room, colouring pictures.

'Just to make sure I have this all straight,' I said to Mrs Hudson, feeling rather tired, 'let me go over it again. First, they say they were not kidnapped, they fled under their own power, from their uncle, James Oberdorfer, because they believed he was trying to kill them in order to inherit his late brother's, their father's, property.'

'You can see Sarah believes it.'

I sighed. 'Oh, yes, I admit she does. Nobody would run away from a comfortable house, hide in a baggage car, and live in a cave for three weeks on stolen food if she didn't believe it. And yes, I admit that there seems to have been a very odd series of accidents.'

Mrs Hudson's own investigative machinery, though not as smooth as that of her employer, was both robust and labyrinthine: she had found through the servant sister of another landlady who had a friend who – and so forth.

There was a great deal of money involved, with factories not only here and in France, but also in Germany, where the War seemed on the verge of coming to its bloody end. These were two very wealthy orphans, their only family left the one uncle. An uncle who, according to below-the-stairs rumour collected by Mrs Hudson's network of informants, exhibited a smarmy, shallow affection to his charges. I put my head into my hands.

It all rested on Sarah. A different child I might have dismissed as being prone to imaginative stories, but those steady brown eyes of hers, daring me to disbelieve – I could see why Mrs Hudson, by no means an easy mark for a sad story, had taken them under her wing.

'And you say the footman witnessed the near-drowning?' I said without looking up.

'If he hadn't happened upon them they'd have been lost, he said. And the maid who ate some of the special pudding their uncle brought them was indeed very ill.'

'But there's no proof.'

'No.' She wasn't making this any easier for me. We both knew that Holmes, with his attitudes towards children, and particularly girl children, would hand these two back to their uncle. Oh, he would issue the man a stern warning that he, Holmes, would in the future take a close personal interest in the safety of the Oberdorfer heirs, but, after all, accidents were unpredictable things, particularly if Oberdorfer chose to return to the chaos of war-ravaged Germany. If he decided the inheritance was worth the risk, and took care that no proof was available . . .

No proof here either, one way or the other, and this was one case I could *not* discuss with Holmes.

'And you were planning on sending them to your cousin in Wiltshire?'

'It's a nice healthy farm near a good school, and who would question two more children orphaned by Zeppelin bombs?'

'But only until Sarah is sixteen?'

'Three years and a bit. She'd be a young lady then – not legally, of course, but lawyers would listen to her.'

I was only eighteen myself, and could well believe that authorities who would dismiss a twelve-year-old's wild accusations would prick their ears at a self-contained sixteen-year-old. Why, even Holmes . . .

'All right, Mrs Hudson, you win. I'll help you get them to Wiltshire.'

I was not there when Holmes returned a week later, drained and irritable at his failure to enlighten Scotland Yard. Mrs Hudson said nothing, just served him his dinner and his newspapers and went about her business. She said nothing then, and she said nothing later that evening when Holmes, who had carried his collection of papers to the basket chair in front of the fire and prepared to settle in, leapt wildly to his feet, bent over to dig among the cushions for a moment, then turned in accusation to his housekeeper with the gnawed stub of a coloured pencil in his outstretched palm.

She never did say anything, not even three years later when the young heir and his older sister (her hair piled carefully on top of her head, wearing a grown woman's hat and a dress a bit too old for her slim young frame) miraculously materialised in a solicitor's office in London, creating a stir in three countries. However, several times over the years, whenever Holmes was making some particularly irksome demand on her patience, I saw this most long-suffering of landladies take a deep breath, focus on something far away, and nod briefly, before going on her placid way with a tiny, satisfied smile on her face.

A VENOMOUS DEATH

The association of Sherlock Holmes with bees dates back to Arthur Conan Doyle, who continued a long tradition linking aged philosophers with beekeeping. Sometimes, however, honeybees are a source not of musings, but of death. This tale began with a letter from printmaker Mark Lavendier, asking if there might by any chance be a brief – very brief – Russell and Holmes story that woodcut artist Katie Wynne could illustrate for a broadsheet. And what do you know? There was.

I GINGERLY PUSHED MY HEAD through the doorway of the stone cottage to ask my husband, 'The constable wants to know if it's safe yet.'

'Oh, quite.' Sherlock Holmes was squatting beside the small wooden crate into which he had knocked the swarm of bees five minutes earlier, holding its lid open a crack for the last stragglers.

I stepped in, keeping a wary eye on the crate. PC Harris, who had summoned Holmes an hour before – as a convenient beekeeper, not a consulting detective – ventured a look in, then retreated briskly into the pale October sunshine. Holmes, however, wasn't even wearing a beekeeper's net: swarming bees were generally not aggressive. Which made this death a puzzle.

'I've heard of swarms following a queen into odd places, but never through the open window of a man's bedroom.'

'They did not. This was murder.'

'Holmes,' I protested, 'I'd have thought bee-sting a somewhat roundabout method of homicide.'

'Russell, Russell, bees swarm in summer. And the entire village knew the professor was deathly allergic to bee venom.' He absently scraped a stinger from the back of his hand.

'So a retired professor of philosophy had a mortal enemy who decided to chuck a hive of bees through his window?'

'You of all people should know how vituperative academics can be.'

'For heaven's sake, Holmes, this was an expert on Aristotelian hermeneutics!'

'Ah, but his housekeeper told his gardener, who told Old Will over a pint in The Tiger, who in turn told me over the potato patch this very morning, that one of the professor's oldest rivals in academia came to call recently, and their conversation ended in shouting.'

'About Aristotelian hermeneutics?'

'The housekeeper did not say.' The last of the bees had crept with relief into the wooden chest. Holmes shut the lid and took out a ball of twine. 'But you are right, I should look to something less elevated for the cause of this death. Such as the boundary dispute that has sprung up with the professor's neighbour, Josiah Warner. The little Standish lad overheard an exchange of threats between the two men concerning the wall that separates the professor's lane from Mr Warner's orchard – young Master Standish was up an apple tree in said orchard at the time, intent on plunder. He informed his mother, who told the postmistress, who mentioned it to our own Mrs Hudson two days ago when she went in to purchase stamps.'

'And Josiah Warner keeps bees,' I noted. I had wondered why the PC did not ask Warner to remove the bees: a long-time dispute explained that.

'What is more, Mr Warner had the stonemasons in yesterday morning to talk about repairing the wall. As if already aware that the dispute was moot.'

I interrupted before he could recount how this tale reached his ears. 'Still, that will be hard to prove.'

'Yes, but this should not.' He had manoeuvred his way out of the door with the box (causing PC Harris to backpedal down the walk) and now set it down, holding out a narrow splinter of wood some three inches long with blue paint up one side. 'I found this on the bedroom windowsill. Sycamore, I should say. Warner uses a blue box made of sycamore to transport his swarms. Take it, Harris – you will find a matching gap in one corner of Warner's box, where he hit the window frame as he poured the bees inside.'

Harris studied the sliver of wood in bemusement, taking no notice when Holmes retrieved the furiously protesting crate and tucked it under one arm.

'Country life,' Holmes mused happily as we turned for home. 'The city has nothing on it for sheer viciousness. Now, Russell, where shall we install our newest community of Apis mellifera?'

I opened my mouth to protest, then subsided. Perhaps a hive of man-killing bees was just what our household needed.

Birth of a Green Man

The Green Man is a widespread figure in British folk mythology, a pagan spirit of spring growth, joyous and inexorable (appropriately, it is a common name of British pubs). The figure appears in the Russell Memoir *The God of the Hive*, in the person of one Robert Goodman. This brief story takes place after Goodman left Craiglockhart Hospital in Edinburgh, where he was being treated for shell shock, and before Mary Russell dropped out of the sky on him in 1924.

A GOD IS BORN WHERE need and torment meet. A god is born when dark and light are one and the same. A god is born, and the earth is given voice in which to sing its joy and its terror. And where a god is born – have no doubt about this – there is blood.

He died when the god named War ripped open his skull and thundered confusion inside. He died, until one spring day he left the hospital, creeping away to a place of childhood quiet and innocence, among the Cumbrian lakes. A place where all deaths were meant to be and the only thunder lay in the rain.

There, green air washed him, wood and soil touched him, fur and feather healed him. He shunned a mansion; he built a cave in the green. He went days, weeks without speech.

The greens-man heard the child first, a gulping, choking noise pressing through the summer-thick trees and troubling the birds. He thought it a creature caught in a poacher's cruel trap; he was not altogether wrong.

A boy, thin and brown and years from a razor's touch. He'd seen him before in his woodland rovings, noticed the way the woodland creatures did not mind the boy's presence, did not feel that this was a lad who turned restlessness into cruelty.

The boy was hunched beneath a tree, and although he cradled his left arm with exquisite tenderness, the tears were those of a still-child's impotent rage.

Pain was a thing the greens-man could deal with.

He stepped from the trees, permitting a branch to whisper against his sleeve. The startled boy gaped at this figure born of the woods: a man with too-long hair and untidy beard, whose clothes might have been woven from the branches behind him, who waited, at a distance, palms outstretched, saying nothing. The boy dashed the moisture from his cheeks, and his sharp fear subsided into wariness.

The man came forward. He dropped to his heels, holding the boy's eyes, and stretched out his hands in invitation. Hesitant, the boy's supporting hand loosened, then fell away. The man's fingers took a moment to confirm what his eyes had told him, and he sat back on his heels to talk the boy calm.

'It's dislocated. I can fix it for you, but it'll hurt like the devil for a moment. Afterwards it will be just sore. I knew a man during the War who had a shoulder just like yours. He drove a team of horses at the Front, hauling shells, wire, equipment. A German shell landed while he was unloading the wagon. The horses panicked and he reached out for them as they bolted. Yanked his shoulder right out its socket.'

The man went on for a time, embroidering a thread of heroism into the story, while the boy tried to wrap his mind around the idea of further pain. But he was a brave lad, and trusting, and eventually he gave his permission by saying, 'He didn't mean to do it. My da.'

The man kept his eyes from the raw swollen mouth, and rose to do what had to be done.

When it was over, when fresh tears were stinging their way into the half-sealed scabs on his face, the boy's face wore the same look that the driver's had: wonder, relief, and gratitude, a mix indistinguishable from joy.

He sent the boy on his way, and followed, silent this time as a woodland pool. The boy paused at the edge of a walled pasture, then trudged manfully towards the unkempt farmyard below. The woodsman watched as the farmer came out of the cowshed, crowded up to the boy, cuffed him to the ground, and went inside. He watched the boy pick himself from the ground, and follow.

At dawn the next day, the farmer went to milk his cow. When the farmer's wife went to see what was keeping her husband, she found him on the muck-strewn floor, his head stove in by a tidy bash the size of a cow's hoof. The milking stool stood upright, a full pail of milk beside it, a silver coin on its top.

From then on, every so often a silver coin was found, here and there around the farm.

A god is born at the intersection of need and torment, and brings joy where he can.

MY STORY

or The Case of the Ravening Sherlockians

Among the great mysteries of the Mary Russell Memoirs is the question, Why is Laurie R. King listed as their author? Who is this person to take credit for Russell's work? The first few Memoirs give details of a trunk of manuscripts that Ms King received, transcribed, and published, although she declares herself as puzzled as anyone as to why she was sent them in the first place – or even by whom. Fortunately, 'My Story' and its sequel, 'A Case in Correspondence', explore Miss Russell's motivations, with events of a considerably more recent past than her usual world of the Twenties.

ONE

HARD AS IT IS to believe, fifteen years have passed since Ms Laurie King published – under her name – the first volume of the Mary Russell Memoirs. She recounts (in her Editor's

Preface to that volume, which was given the title *The Beekeeper's Apprentice*) her puzzlement as to what these manuscripts were and why she was the recipient of these multiple volumes of handwritten (for the most part) manuscripts recounting the life of a stranger, and, moreover, a stranger who claims to have been married to one Sherlock Holmes.

Now, the fifteenth anniversary of the publication of *The Beekeeper's Apprentice*, may be as good a time as any to answer that puzzle.

It began in the winter of 1989, when a bout with a troublesome although ultimately meaningless illness left me with an awareness that, in my ninetieth year, I was perhaps not to be immortal. It was time to gather my thoughts for posterity and make some arrangement for their preservation.

I might have done it long before, truth to tell, but for the identity of my husband. When one is married to a person of considerable fame, one tends to choose invisibility over all else. And since any memoirs I was to pass on would be of occasionally inflammatory nature, I needed to choose my literary agent with care.

TWO

ANY LITERARY AGENT WHOM I put in charge of my memoirs needed to be, first of all, a woman. She needed to be strong-minded enough to resist the blandishments and threats unleashed upon her once the nature of these manuscripts came to light. And since I thought it best to begin with someone whose links to Mary Russell stood above any links to Sherlock Holmes, I cast my mind over my relatives: cousins of various stripe abound, but search as I might, I could find no combination of literary interest and common sense.

Next, I sought out the descendants of my University friend, Veronica Beaconsfield, only to find that the current generation lacked the wit of their grandparents. So I went further back, to my childhood in San Francisco, and there, in the early weeks of 1992, I found the person I sought. The granddaughter of a childhood friend, she was in the early stages of a literary career – her first novel had been accepted at a New York publisher – but she was also sensible enough to balance the demands of children, travel, a husband with his own career, and a complex household. And an untold benefit: she had a background in Old Testament theology!

Without delay, I began to assemble the manuscripts and prepared to send them off to Ms King in California. Before I could do so, catastrophe struck.

THREE

I DOUBT IT WILL COME as a surprise to the reader when I say that my husband's popularity in the world of letters approximates that of a lesser divinity. More than a century ago, when Sir Arthur Conan Doyle had an attack of pique and sent Holmes to his 'death' over the Reichenbach Falls, readers protested with black armbands, cancelled subscriptions to *The Strand*, and outrage to Conan Doyle's face. Were that story to be published now, I should expect Molotov cocktails to be thrown.

This degree of renown brings, as you might expect, considerable problems. The cooperation of our neighbours is essential, and elaborate ploys are occasionally necessary to turn would-be visitors from our door in Sussex – although we have found that the most effective of these is encouraging the world to think of us as fictional characters. This weeds out all but the overly whimsical and the truly insane and, until one cool spring morning in April of 1992, permitted us to maintain our privacy.

I was in the downstairs sitting room finishing the task of assembling and sealing together the pages of my various memoirs, when my eye was attracted by motion at the window. I looked up, and saw to my horror that our rural home was being invaded, by none other than a ravening pack of Sherlockians.

FOUR

SEEING THE PRESS OF eager faces at my window, I knew in an instant that I was in mortal danger – or if not mortal, then certainly our sanity was to be challenged. At least ten of them, Americans all, each wearing one or several lapel decorations depicting a bee or a calabash pipe or the address 221B. They were unmistakable, and unstoppable.

I raised my voice in alarm, and scurried as fast as a woman of ninety-two can to check the locks on the doors. The cook came to see and, being a woman of wit as well as culinary ability, joined instantly in battening down our defences. While she went around the perimeter, closing the curtains, I picked up the telephone and summoned assistance: the stout, and stout-hearted, grandson of my old farm manager, both of the generations named Patrick.

In minutes, young Patrick was roaring over the paddocks

in his Land Rover, dog and shotgun to hand. The Sherlockians made a hasty retreat, first to the road and then, when Patrick took up a position mid drive with his shotgun over his arm, up the road in the direction of the village. I was tempted to telephone the inn and request that they deny these invaders entrance, or at least make certain their beer was overly warmed, but on second thought, an open declaration of war might only stir these Americans' dander.

Still, a declaration of war it had become.

FIVE

HOLMES EVENTUALLY CAME TO a safe place to pause in his ongoing chemical experiment and toddled down the stairs to see what the uproar was. The cook set before us a pot of powerful tea and a plate of scones flavoured with outrage; Patrick leant his gun inside the door and joined us, trusting to his dogs to raise an alarm; we sat around the kitchen table for a council of war.

Holmes and I had long been prepared for this day when his past came to roost on our heads. In fact, given a mere thirty seconds' warning, we were equipped to walk out with the essentials of life on our persons, and disappear permanently.

This, we thought, would not require such extreme measures. Instead, we planned how best to instigate our second defence, which we had come up with some years earlier when the local amateur Eastbourne Dramatic Society put on a production of *The Hound of the Baskervilles*. The gentleman playing the lead, a local solicitor of barely forty, did a competent (if somewhat flamboyant) job of acting Holmes; later, we invited him to the house and arranged with him a smaller-scale dramatic rendition of the Great Detective. The thought of acting a pseudo-Holmes in place of the actual Holmes appealed to his droll, Sussex-born sense of humour, and he agreed to be available, if and when we called on him.

It was time to raise the curtain on our idiosyncratic one-man show.

SIX

BY GOOD FORTUNE, OUR solicitor-actor would be available for several days, to play the part of a genial if rather befuddled elderly farmer who, indeed, happened to bear a resemblance to one Sherlock Holmes. With him in place, the Americans could batter themselves against our doors until they were convinced that their information was faulty, at which time they might go back to the plains or prairies whence they had come.

Behind our drawn curtains, Holmes returned to his experiment and I to my manuscripts. Before padlocking the trunk, however, I went through the house and collected an armful of treasured memorabilia that called to mind our cases and adventures over the years. They were, with certain exceptions, items of little commercial value – a friend's trademark monocle, one of Holmes's more disreputable pipes, some newspaper clippings – but were they to be spotted by any sharp-witted Sherlockian (if that be not an oxymoron), they could not only give lie to our ruse, they would be themselves vulnerable to the predations of the horde outside: Sherlockians are inveterate collectors.

I arranged them atop my memoirs, and padlocked the lid.

When I had more leisure, I should write a letter of explanation to the recipient of the trunk, but today, I had much to do.

SEVEN

WITH THE TRUNK OF manuscripts and memorabilia securely packed, I went upstairs and assembled a pair of valises for us, that we might at least keep dry and comfortable in exile during the American siege. I doubted that they had found my own house in Oxford – I would have heard, had there been strangers climbing over the walls and loitering out front – but Holmes and I have not made it to our respective ages by making easy assumptions.

Night came. Mrs Hudson – our latest Mrs Hudson – did the washing-up and grumbled her way towards bed. The downstairs lights were turned off, then those in the laboratory, and finally the bedroom went dark. All this time, Patrick sat prominently behind the wheel of the Land Rover while the dogs prowled the grounds.

Except that shortly after dark, Patrick's outline in the car was, in fact, a scarecrow made of stuffed shirts and a hat. Leaving the more obedient of his two dogs to guard the dummy and the car, and the less obedient one inside the house to bark warningly, the three of us set off across the dark landscape.

One advantage of having walked the Downs for the better part of a century – daylight and dark, rain and snow – is that one's feet know the way when one's eyes do not. We strolled in easy silence over the cropped grass, keeping to the sheep tracks to reduce the sound of crackling frost. In half an hour, we came out in the roadside car park near the road to Eastbourne, and Patrick went forward to tap at the window of the Mercedes sedan that waited there.

EIGHT

THE DOOR OF THE waiting car clicked open and the gravel crunched. Our actor greeted us in low whispers as we handed over Holmes's outer garments (which the Americans might recognise, if they had been keeping watch for some days) in exchange for his keys. In under two minutes, we were in the car and Patrick was leading the actor back the way we had come.

He was, I thought, already dressed and made up for his role, although anyone paying attention to his gait would know his middle-aged strength – he was a competitive runner, which gave him the necessary thinness to enact Holmes. In fact, I learnt later, this fleetness of foot came in useful the very next afternoon, when the waiting Sherlockians saw 'Holmes' set out for a walk along the cliffs, and went baying after him, only to be utterly confounded when Sherlock Holmes broke into a brisk sprint and left them panting in his wake.

(The following day, Patrick withdrew his guard, and within the hour, a knock came on the door. The actor was suitably taken aback by these Americans who imagined his stone cottage was inhabited by Sherlock Holmes. With exquisite rural politeness he asked, Were they not aware that Sherlock Holmes was a fictional character?)

By the time the confused and downhearted pack walked back up the drive, we had been gone for three days.

NINE

THE HOUSE IN OXFORD to which we retreated was in the northern district of the town, a tree-studded neighbourhood of large brick houses inhabited by dons and their families. It is close enough to town that a stroll to the Bodleian and Radcliffe libraries, even with an arm full of books, is a pleasant interlude; it is far enough from the centre that the wrangle of bells of a Sunday morning is amusing, not headache-inducing.

My house is like its fellows from the outside, with high walls on all sides, a spacious gravel drive at the front, and a narrow turret glued onto one corner. The house and its garden are too nondescript for any passer-by to bother with a second glance, and as far as the neighbours are concerned, the owner is an independent older woman who spends much of her life travelling and working on her academic studies, which (it being Oxford) could be Romanian campanology or liver flukes of the upper Nile.

Once upon a time, Holmes had arrived at my student flat through an upper window, setting off an elaborate and circuitous traverse of Oxford's rooftops in the snow. Fortunately for us, this time I was permitted to drive through the elaborate and circuitous city roads in the actor's Mercedes.

TEN

MY OXFORD HOUSE HAS a self-contained apartment at the front, in which I habitually install a series of graduate students, mostly women, whose only rent is an agreement to keep the rooms aired and the car's battery charged, to pick me up at the train station if I ring, and to tell the neighbours nothing about me. The resident that year was a small, wide girl with adenoids and a brilliant medical mind, who greeted our 6 a.m. arrival in a startling pink dressing gown, a cup of tea in one hand, and the current copy of *Lancet* in the other.

I greeted her, and asked if she was aware of any stray Americans asking about me, or if she had received any odd telephone calls. 'No calls, no questions,' she said. 'Shall I bring a bottle of milk through to your kitchen?'

I thanked her for her thoughtfulness, blessed her for her preoccupation, and left luggage and husband in the house while I drove the Mercedes over to the train station for retrieval.

I thought we were safe.

ELEVEN

I RANG PATRICK THE FOLLOWING evening – trusting that our Sherlockian pursuers lacked the wherewithal to tap lines and trace telephone calls – to ask him to stow the trunk of memoirs with a third party for the time being. He told me of the pack's confounding by the actor's cross-country sprint, and said he would spend another night sleeping in the Land Rover at our door. On the morrow, he would load up our trunks and valuables and abandon his post, leaving the actor to his play.

We spent a pleasant three days in my second home of Oxford, visiting with old friends, pursuing our varied studies, and worrying not in the least that we would be discovered – the ancient city is generously endowed with ancient academics, and even the closing days of April are cool enough to justify hats and the occasional scarf.

On the fourth day, my medical student greeted our return with the news that a couple of rather odd Americans had come to the door while we were out. With sinking heart, I asked if they had worn lapel pins with pipes, deerstalker caps, or 221B.

No, she replied – they were hounds. 'Holmes,' I shouted up the stairs, 'time to be off.' But when I went to get out the car, they were lying in wait.

TWELVE

Y OU NEED TO REMEMBER, this was 1992, and the number of people who knew that Sherlock Holmes had a wife was relatively small. No doubt our pursuing Sherlockians thought I was a housekeeper, or a nurse – they were standing watch outside of the gate, and began to bay wildly when first I set foot out of the house. I feigned great age – admittedly not a difficult act, at ninety-two years – and hobbled to the car, back bent with apparent arthritis and a large straw hat pulled down, not so much to hide my features as to explain why I wasn't seeing ten jumping figures thirty feet away. I got the door open with my ancient hands, bent slowly – slowly, to retrieve some small object from the door pocket – then inadequately closed the door and, crouching low, crept back into the house.

Thus, before dawn the next morning, the three who had been set to watch overnight from their hire car recognised the hatted old lady behind the wheel of the motor that pulled out of the gate, and hastened to follow – it being too dark to see that the person at the wheel was a foot shorter and seventy years younger. Nor did they notice that the brisk young man closing the gate was, in fact, the old woman they thought they were following.

Whistling, I went to finish my coffee and leave the house, on what promised to be a perfectly lovely May Day morn.

THIRTEEN

MAY DAY IN OXFORD IS an ancient ritual, practised with such enthusiasm that it has been suspended at various times over the centuries due to excessive unruliness. The celebration begins well before dawn, when from all directions people trickle into the high street, making their way in the direction of the Magdalen College tower.

At dawn, choirboys raise their voices to the day, their sweet, high chorus trailing down over the packed street of families and homeless men, passing tradesmen and beer-sodden undergraduates, antiquarians, and tourists. Participants of the previous night's college balls, held upright by the press of the throng, pass around half-empty bottles of cheap champagne, most of them bedraggled, tieless, sometimes shoeless, and often sodden from the puzzling ritual of leaping out of punts or off of bridges in their evening dress. When the snatches of song finish drifting down from on high, the crowd shakes off its attentive silence, gives a noisy pulse, and reverses its progress, out from Magdalen College. Morris dancers bounce and rattle on the paving stones surrounding the Radcliffe Camera, hobbyhorses give the kiss of fertility to doomed young women, odd foodstuffs are sold, the manifold clergy of the town looks on fondly at the pagan frenzy, and the rites of spring are officially ushered in.

When the sky was still dark overhead, Holmes and I let ourselves out of the gate and joined the trickle, soon stream, of May Day celebrants. Before the Magdalen choir had finished, we were spotted.

FOURTEEN

I DO NOT KNOW IF our American pursuers were actively watching for us, or if they had decided to make the best of their visit and take in the May Day festivities while waiting for us to emerge, but at the corner of the Botanic Garden, where Rose Lane comes into the High, the music drifting from on high was shattered by loud American accents: 'Hey! There he is!' And the hunt was on again.

I spoke in Holmes's ear, ordering him to abandon me. He hesitated, being neither cowardly nor disloyal, but even he could see the logic in my suggestion. He bent down enough to vanish in the crowd, while I appropriated a nearby furled umbrella (in any English crowd, there will always be a man who doubts the clear sky overhead) and tripped one attacker, jabbed the second in the stomach, and nudged the third into the large, intoxicated rugby player beside him.

With that trio temporarily disposed of, and making certain they had seen me, their unlikely assailant, I pushed into the crowd, crossing to the Magdalen side of the High and making for Magdalen Bridge.

Halfway across, I ducked down to make my way back up the human stream, ducking into the grounds of the Botanic Garden and making for the river.

Holmes had located a punt, worked its anchoring pole out of

the bottom, and was waiting for me. I heard a shout behind me – English, not American – and tumbled into the boat. He pushed off, and I turned to face the boat's irate owners.

'Terribly sorry,' I called to them. 'There's a trio of Americans just behind you who said they'd be happy to repay you for the hire cost. You take it up with them, there's a good lad.'

A sweet old lady in a boat; how could he argue with me?

FIFTEEN

HAD OUR PURSUERS BEEN familiar with Oxford, they could have caught us up several times over. As it was, by the time they extricated themselves from the young man whose boat we had stolen, then consulted their maps, we were away from the riverside path in Christ Church Meadow – by this time, I was punting – and down the new cut to the Isis proper.

By the time they had located the Thames path, gone back up to Folly Bridge, and crossed the river to get to the towpath, the current had moved us briskly downstream. The fleet-footed leaders nearly caught us up at Iffley, when the lock-keeper protested about working the locks for one solitary punt, but a few coins changed his mind, and we were away.

The day was warm, the cushions were comfortable, and the merest touch of the pole kept us moving in the right direction. We stopped from time to time to take refreshment. And at one such stop, I bought an antique postcard, thinking to amuse Ms King in California.

When evening came upon us, I changed into raiment that would draw less notice than trousers on a woman my age, and we abandoned our vessel. In a fit of whimsy, I left the day's clothing folded in the boat, with my secondary pair of spectacles, since every reader of crime fiction knows that suicides always remove their spectacles.

Thus, the explanation of how Ms King came to possess my memoirs. I may at a later time recount the story of our subsequent communications: what I meant by the antique postcard that she read as, More to follow; why we were in Utrecht when I sent it; and why, most puzzling of all, *The Times* did not publish its account of the punt found in central London for an entire three years.

Is it not satisfying to know that there is always more to any tale?

A Case in Correspondence

The exploration of events leading Mary Russell to send her manuscripts to Laurie R. King continues with a series of postcards and written communications. Interestingly, the political issues at the centre of the tenth Memoir, *The God of the Hive*, surface here as well, with an official protest oddly similar to what Miss Russell faced then – and which troubles her no more in 1992 than it did in 1924.

DOCUMENT ONE: POSTCARD FROM MARY RUSSELL
TO SHERLOCK HOLMES

POST CARD

3 May 1992

Holmes—I trust you reached home without difficulty, following my crass abandonment of you on the banks of the Thames. As I expected, I had no problem creating the façade of aged and infirm old woman—one of my rescuers even insisted on pressing a £5 note into the cabbie's hand. I will be here at the Vicissitude for two or three days, completing that research the Americans interrupted. If you wish anything from Town, a note will reach me in the usual way. R

PS. I discovered a box of ancient postal cards behind the shot-gun shells in the Brompton Road bolt-hole, which I am appropriating for the purpose. Do you never clear anything out?

3rd May 1992

Holmes – I trust you reached home without difficulty, following my crass abandonment of you on the banks of the Thames. As I expected, I had no problem creating the facade of aged and infirm old woman – one of my rescuers even insisted on pressing a £5 note into the cabbie's hand. I will be here at the Vicissitude for two or three days, completing that research the Americans interrupted. If you wish anything from Town, a note will reach me in the usual way. R

PS. I discovered a box of ancient postal cards behind the shotgun shells in the Brompton Road bolt-hole, which I am appropriating for the purpose. Do you never clear anything out?

4 Nov 1992

Dear Mrs Holmes, I opened the envelope containing your post-card, but I regret to say that Mr Holmes has not returned. Could he have gone to his brother's old flat? Quiet has returned to the farm, following the excitements of the previous week. The wireless reports that we are to expect rain, so when you find Mr Holmes, kindly remind him to carry his umbrella.

Yours, Emma Hudson

Mrs Mary Russell-Holmes
The Vicarstitude Hotel for Ladies
Altamont Close
London W2

Mrs Mary Russell-Holmes
The Vicissitude Hotel for Ladies
Altamont Close
London W2

4th May 1992

Dear Mrs Holmes, I opened the envelope containing your postcard, but I regret to say that Mr Holmes has not returned. Could he have gone to his brother's old flat? Quiet has returned to the farm, following the excitements of the previous week. The wireless reports that we are to expect rain, so when you find Mr Holmes, kindly remind him to carry his umbrella.

Yours, Emma Hudson

The Refreshment Pavilion, Kew Gardens.

POST CARD.
For Address Only

5 May
Hello Billy, I hope you and the family are well? I've lost Holmes again—I don't suppose you have seen him since Friday? I put him into a taxi that afternoon at Kew, having a punt to dispose of (long story), and I expected him to return to Sussex. However, I have just learned that Mrs Hudson has not seen him. Ring me at Mycroft's old number if you have news.

Russell

P.S. The last time I looked in, your namesake grandfather seemed much better. We had a long chat about the Robert Goodman case—one which no doubt you have heard about in endless detail, due to its repercussions.

Printed in England.

5th May

Hello Billy, I hope you and the family are well? I've lost Holmes again – I don't suppose you have seen him since Friday? I put him into a taxi that afternoon at Kew, having a punt to dispose of (long story), and I expected him to return to Sussex. However, I have just learnt that Mrs Hudson has not seen him. Ring me at Mycroft's old number if you have news.

Russell

P. S. The last time I looked in, your namesake grandfather seemed much better. We had a long chat about the Robert Goodman case – one which no doubt you have heard about in endless detail, due to its repercussions.

DOCUMENT FOUR: POSTCARD FROM MARY RUSSELL
TO MRS HUDSON

POST CARD.

THIS SPACE MAY BE USED FOR PRINTED
OR WRITTEN MATTER.

ONLY THE ADDRESS TO BE
WRITTEN HERE

5 May

Dear Ms H, (It is amusing how, even though we've had you as THE Mrs Hudson in our lives for a decade now, there persists a moment of astonishment as my mind's eye attempts to link your name with the face of your husband's great-grandmother!)

I am glad to hear that the American invasion of Sussex has ceased—no doubt they are still quartering Oxford in hopes of finding our scent. If they reappear, do not hesitate to call on Patrick for assistance. About Holmes, please don't concern yourself, no doubt he thought of some urgent business in Town, I shall let you know when I find him.

—M.R.

5th May

Dear Ms H (It is amusing how, even though we've had you as THE Mrs Hudson in our lives for a decade now, there persists a moment of astonishment as my mind's eye attempts to link your name with the face of your husband's great-grandmother!), I am glad to hear that the American invasion of Sussex has ceased – no doubt they are still quartering Oxford in hopes of finding our scent. If they reappear, do not hesitate to call on Patrick for assistance. About Holmes, please don't concern yourself, no doubt he thought of some urgent business in Town, I shall let you know when I find him.

– MR

WILLIAM MUDD INVESTIGATIONS

5 May (though only just)
Miss R, Sorry, haven't seen Mr Holmes since Easter.
Neither has Granddad. If you wish me to stir up
an enquiry first thing in the morning, just say
the word.
Billy (III)
PS. The wife sends her regards and says that you
are to come to dinner soon, now that Billy-the-Fourth
is now quite house-trained, or enough that there will
be no more accidents onto visiting laps.
P.P.S. Were you aware that The Cracker is in Town?

WILLIAM MUDD INVESTIGATIONS

5th May (though only just)

Miss R, Sorry, haven't seen Mr Holmes since Easter. Neither has Granddad. If you wish me to stir up an enquiry first thing in the morning, just say the word.

Billy (III)

PS. The wife sends her regards and says that you are to come to dinner soon, now that Billy-the-Fourth is now quite house-trained, or enough that there will be no more accidents onto visiting laps.

P. P. S. Were you aware that The Cracker is in Town?

DOCUMENT SIX: LETTER FROM MARY RUSSELL TO DR WATSON-SCOPES

6 May

Dear Dr Watson-Scopes,

I read of your honour recently, my heartiest congratulations. Your grandfather would burst his waistcoat buttons with pride.

I wonder if I might ask a favour of you? Six days ago (Friday) I dropped my husband at Kew expecting him to make his way to Sussex, only to discover on Tuesday that he did not. I have begun the usual enquiries at hospitals and through friends and associates, but with your medical network, might you also put out the word that an aged and no doubt querulous individual has gone missing? I shall be moving about a great deal, but messages at the Vicissitude or at your "Uncle" Mycroft's old flat will reach me.

Mary Russell

6th May

Dear Dr Watson-Scopes,

I read of your honour recently, my heartiest congratulations. Your grandfather would burst his waistcoat buttons with pride.

I wonder if I might ask a favour of you? Six days ago (Friday) I dropped my husband at Kew expecting him to make his way to Sussex, only to discover on Tuesday that he did not. I have begun the usual enquiries at hospitals and through friends and associates, but with your medical network, might you also put out the word that an aged and no doubt querulous individual has gone missing? I shall be moving about a great deal, but messages at the Vicissitude or at your 'Uncle' Mycroft's old flat will reach me.

Mary Russell

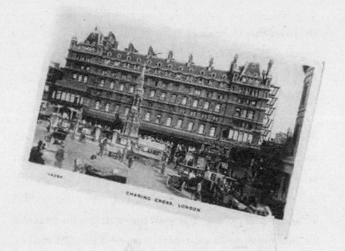

CHARING CROSS, LONDON

Billy- No doubt he'll be extremely cross when he finds out, but yes, I'd appreciate it if you would kindly spread the word that we've looking for Holmes. A week without a word, at his age, is not to be taken lightly.

MR

PS. If I haven't heard from him by tomorrow, I'll get into touch with the current 'M', who won't be happy with me either, for different reasons.

PPS. I wrote to ask Watson's granddaughter—another Dr Watson—to enquire after him amongst her medical colleagues, however I have since heard that she is away in New York for another week.

PPPS. Get word to The Cracker that if he does not scuttle back under his Glaswegian rock posthaste, he should expect a broken nose from the walking-stick of a 92 year-old woman. And if Holmes catches him first, the nose will be the least of it.

Billy – No doubt he'll be extremely cross when he finds out, but yes, I'd appreciate it if you would kindly spread the word that we're looking for Holmes. A week without a word, at his age, is not to be taken lightly.

MR

PS. If I haven't heard from him by tomorrow, I'll get into touch with the current 'M'. Who won't be happy with me either, for different reasons.

PPS. I wrote to ask Watson's granddaughter – another Dr Watson – to enquire after him amongst her medical colleagues, however, I have since heard that she is away in New York for another week.

PPPS. Get word to The Cracker that if he does not scuttle back under his Glaswegian rock post-haste, he should expect a broken nose from the walking-stick of a 92-year-old woman. And if Holmes catches him first, the nose will be the least of it.

DOCUMENT EIGHT: LETTER FROM
MARY RUSSELL TO 'M'

7 May 1992

Dear 'M',

I write for a reason unrelated to our most recent series of communications, namely, that my husband seems to have gone missing. Holmes was last seen a week ago, on the afternoon of the first, at Kew Gardens. Telephone calls to hospitals and police stations have led to nothing, and I spent much of yesterday at Kew with a photograph, but the only response was from one attendant who thought he recalled a tall old man talking with a sturdy blond man in his thirties—an individual who may even have had green eyes.

This ironic resemblance to Robert Goodman is so striking as to be XXXX unavoidable, but surely bears no significance apart from stirring up the recent conflict between us. I have no intention of removing the document related to Goodman from the memoirs I am sending to my American agent.

In any event, recent newspaper articles suggest that the government are already moving forward with the requisite public revelations.

If you receive news of Holmes, I would appreciate it if you would pass it on to me.

Yours,

MRH

Mary Russell Holmes

7th May 1992

Dear 'M',

I write for a reason unrelated to our most recent series of communications, namely, that my husband seems to have gone missing. Holmes was last seen a week ago, on the afternoon of the first, at Kew Gardens. Telephone calls to hospitals and police stations have led to nothing, and I spent much of yesterday at Kew with a photograph, but the only response was from one attendant who thought he recalled a tall old man talking with a sturdy blond man in his thirties – an individual who may even have had green eyes.

This ironic resemblance to Robert Goodman is so striking as to be ~~susp~~ unavoidable, but surely bears no significance apart from stirring up the recent conflict between us. I have no intention of removing the document related to Goodman from the memoirs I am sending to my American agent.

In any event, recent newspaper articles suggest that the government are already moving forward with the requisite public revelations.

If you receive news of Holmes, I would appreciate it if you would pass it on to me.

Yours,
MRH
Mary Russell Holmes

DOCUMENT NINE: POSTCARD FROM
WILLIAM MUDD TO MARY RUSSELL

277 LONDON. — Westminster Bridge. — LL.

POST CARD.

The Cracker's scarpered, so quick he all but left his shoes behind.
I'm working to track back a rumour putting Mr Holmes in a shiny
black car Friday tea-time crossing Westminster Bridge. Funnily enough,
I'd just been working a case involving a lost kiddie near the same
bridge—calling to mind the Goodman affair for about the third time
in three days. If I was your husband, I'd be hunting for hidden
meaning, but me? I'd say it's coincidence. Just like coming across
this postcard in the wife's desk was a coincidence.
   I'll let you know if anything comes of the black-car rumour, so far it's
just a third-hand mention of a resemblance.
Bill

The Cracker's scarpered, so quick he all but left his shoes behind.

I'm working to track back a rumour putting Mr Holmes in a shiny black car Friday teatime crossing Westminster Bridge. Funnly enough, I'd just been working a case involving a lost kiddie near the same bridge – calling to mind the Goodman affair for about the third time in three days. If I was your husband, I'd be hunting for hidden meaning, but me? I'd say it's coincidence. Just like coming across this post-card in the wife's desk was a coincidence.

I'll let you know if anything comes of the black-car rumour, so far it's just a third-hand mention of a resemblance.

Bill

DOCUMENT TEN: POSTCARD FROM
MARY RUSSELL TO WILLIAM MUDD

B 11847. VICTORIA STATION, S.E. & C.RLY. CONTINENTAL AND MAIN LINE DEPARTURE PLATFORM

POST CARD.

THIS SPACE MAY BE USED FOR PRINTED
OR WRITTEN MATTER.

ONLY THE ADDRESS TO BE
WRITTEN HERE.

7th

Just to let you know, Billy, I've just posted a somewhat incendiary letter to the man currently heading Mycroft's organisation. (I was tempted to pile on the alphabet soup of my degrees and honours, but in the end chose dignity over delivering a kick to the poor fellow's pride. That his father was a barrow-boy may have been one of the reasons Mycroft picked him from the crowd.) And as fate would have it, my letter too brought to mind l'ffaire Goodman. To say nothing of this stash of old postal cards, which for some reason are dominated by places from that case.

For a drop of insurance, I wanted to mention to you that I had riled the poor fellow, so that if I disappear from view along with Holmes, you should not only know where to look, but you would know to watch your back.

R.

7th

Just to let you know, Billy, I've just posted a somewhat incendiary letter to the man currently heading Mycroft's organisation. (I was tempted to pile on the alphabet soup of my degrees and honours, but in the end chose dignity over delivering a kick to the poor fellow's pride. That his father was a barrow-boy may have been one of the reasons Mycroft picked him from the crowd.) And as fate would have it, my letter, too, brought to mind *l'affaire* Goodman. To say nothing of this stash of old postal cards, which for some reason are dominated by places from that case.

For a drop of insurance, I wanted to mention to you that I had riled the poor fellow, so that if I disappear from view along with Holmes, you should not only know where to look, but you would know to watch your back.

R.

DOCUMENT ELEVEN: LETTER FROM
'M' TO MARY RUSSELL

8 May 1992
HM Treasury
Whitehall

Dear Mrs Holmes,

The 'recent conflict between us,' which you would
present as a mild disagreement between individuals,
has on the contrary developed into a major political
consideration to the new government. As you no doubt
saw in yesterday's *Times*. The Prime Minister has been
forced to address those 'requisite public revelations'
at a time that will have severe repercussions. My own
recommendation would have been to arrest the two of
you, but Mr Major and █████ do not agree. Personally, I'd have thought your husband would care something for the life's work of his own brother, but
clearly his wife's memoirs take precedence over
matters of national security such as the history of
certain ██████████████████.

                                          M

8th May 1992

Dear Mrs Holmes,

The 'recent conflict between us', which you would present as a mild disagreement between individuals, has on the contrary developed into a major political consideration to the new government. As you no doubt saw in yesterday's Times, the Prime Minister has been forced to address those 'requisite public revelations' at a time that will have severe repercussions. My own recommendation would have been to arrest the two of you, but Mr Major and ███████ do not agree. Personally, I'd have thought your husband would care something for the life's work of his own brother, but clearly his wife's memoirs take precedence over matters of national security such as the history of certain ████████████████████.

M.

POST CARD

THE ADDRESS TO BE WRITTEN HERE

8 May '92

M—I have always believed in the freedom of certain kinds of information. Official protestations of embarrassment do not sway me, and have never swayed my husband. Threats even less. The Goodman manuscript goes to Ms King. Perhaps you thought that your outpouring of bluster might distract me from noticing that you had failed to answer my question. I repeat: Do you know where Holmes is?
Mary Russell Holmes

M,
Treasury building
SW1

M – I have always believed in the freedom of certain kinds of information. Official protestations of embarrassment do not sway me, and have never swayed my husband. Threats even less. The Goodman manuscript goes to Ms King.

Perhaps you thought that your outpouring of bluster might distract me from noticing that you had failed to answer my question.

I repeat: Do you know where Holmes is?

Mary Russell Holmes

LADY BEEKEEPER - Searching for her partner? She might try the home of lost causes.

FROM *THE TIMES OF LONDON* ANNOUNCEMENTS COLUMN,
9TH MAY 1992:

> LADY BEEKEEPER searching
> for her partner? She might try the
> home of lost causes.

POST CARD

Billy—you saw Holmes' *Times* notice this am? Off to Oxford in haste tho' (thanks to the Americans) won't be at my own house. You could try St Hilda's—one of the young dons is Professor Ledger's great niece. Great-great? Or St Michael at the North Gate.

R.

Billy – you saw Holmes' <u>Times</u> notice this am? Off to Oxford in haste tho' (thanks to the Americans) won't be at my own house. You could try St Hilda's – one of the young dons is Professor Ledger's great niece. Great-great? Or St Michael at the North Gate.

R.

Round Pond, Kensington Gardens

Miss R–tried to reach you by phone but no answer at the flat and that ladies' hotel hadn't seen you. I've rung to the college, but in case you get one of these notes that I'm going to drop about the city, ring me immediately and I'll take you up to Oxford myself–I have a flash new motor that'll make you green with envy, we'll be there in no time. It may be a matter of grannies and eggs, but it didn't sound to me like you were taking into account that the _Times_ advert may be a ruse, and you could be in danger.

Wm

Miss R – tried to reach you by phone but no answer at the flat and that ladies' hotel hadn't seen you. I've rung to the college, but in case you get one of these notes that I'm going to drop about the city, ring me immediately and I'll take you up to Oxford myself – I have a flash new motor that'll make you green with envy, we'll be there in no time. It may be a matter of grannies and eggs, but it didn't sound to me like you were taking into account that the <u>Times</u> advert may be a ruse, and you could be in danger.

Wm

DOCUMENT SIXTEEN: TELEGRAM FROM
SHERLOCK HOLMES TO MARY RUSSELL

WESTERN
UNION

MARY RUSSELL

CARE OF ST HILDAS COLLEGE OXFORD

RUSSELL I AM AT THE OXFORD DIGS OF THE GREAT NEPHEW OF OUR MONACLED
FRIEND STOP SEEMS I HAVE HAD TO PULL OUT VARIOUS STOPS TO CONVINCE
HER MAJESTYS WATCHDOGS NOT TO PUT MY WIFE IN THE TOWER FOR CRIMES
AGAINST THE EMPIRE STOP YOU ARE EXPECTED FOR TEA STOP UNFORTUNATELY THE
SAME COOK REIGNS THUS BRING SCONES FROM COVERED MARKET OR RISK
ANOTHER

BROKEN TOOTH STOP HOLMES

MARY RUSSELL
CARE OF ST HILDA'S COLLEGE OXFORD

RUSSELL I AM AT THE OXFORD DIGS OF THE GREAT
NEPHEW OF OUR MONACLED FRIEND STOP SEEMS I
HAVE HAD TO PULL OUT VARIOUS STOPS TO CONVINCE
HER MAJESTYS WATCHDOGS NOT TO PUT MY WIFE IN
THE TOWER FOR CRIMES AGAINST THE EMPIRE STOP
YOU ARE EXPECTED FOR TEA STOP UNFORTUNATELY
THE SAME COOK REIGNS THUS BRING SCONES FROM
COVERED MARKET OR RISK ANOTHER BROKEN TOOTH
STOP HOLMES

DOCUMENT SEVENTEEN: POSTCARD FROM
MARY RUSSELL TO WILLIAM MUDD

OXFORD, UP THE CHERWELL

POST CARD

20th morning- The Sunday bells in Oxford, like no others!

Dear Billy, thank you for your concern but the advert was in fact from Holmes, whom I have (finally) retrieved from the household of a titled mutual friend (whose name I shall not commit to paper) who happened (coincidences do occur!) to be in Kew as Holmes passed across towards the taxi rank. They got into conversation, & Holmes asked him about the political repercussions of my memoirs. And as men do, they decided to pursue their conversation over various libations, in London, and then in Oxford. We are currently engaged in vigorous discussion concerning their proposed (slightly farcical and marginally offensive) solution to the situation, but I wanted you to rest easy and know that all is well, that the situation requires merely a trip to #10 to soothe ruffled feathers, and that we have seen no signs of the Americans.

Russell

10th morning – The Sunday bells in Oxford, like no others!

Dear Billy, thank you for your concern but the advert was, in fact, from Holmes, whom I have (finally!) retrieved from the household of a titled mutual friend (whose name I shall not commit to paper) who happened (coincidences do occur!) to be in Kew as Holmes passed across towards the taxi rank. They got into conversation & Holmes asked him about the political repercussions of my memoirs. And as men do, they decided to pursue their conversation over various libations, in London and then in Oxford. We are currently engaged in vigorous discussion concerning their proposed (slightly farcical and marginally offensive) solution to the situation, but I wanted you to rest easy and know that all is well, that the solution requires merely a trip to #10 to soothe ruffled feathers, and that we have seen no signs of the Americans.

Russell

WILLIAM MUDD INVESTIGATIONS

Dear Mrs Hudson,

Yes, I have heard from Mrs Holmes to say that they are in Oxford for a few days with a friend. I can't think why she didn't write to you, perhaps she did and the boy lost it again. But if I were you I wouldn't object to them not being in Sussex, since her reference to "vigorous discussion" between the two of them has overtones of rug-scorching, paint-blistering temper on both sides. You'd think that at their age, they'd have calmed down a bit.

If I hear further, I'll let you know.

Yrs, Wm Mudd

WILLIAM MUDD INVESTIGATIONS

Dear Mrs Hudson,

Yes, I have heard from Mrs Holmes to say that they are in Oxford for a few days with a friend. I can't think why she didn't write to you, perhaps she did and the boy lost it again. But if I were you I wouldn't object to them not being in Sussex, since her reference to 'vigorous discussion' between the two of them has overtones of rug-scorching, paint-blistering temper on both sides. You'd think that at their age, they'd have calmed down a bit.

If I hear further, I'll let you know.

Yrs, Wm Mudd

7 May 1992

PM Lifts Secrecy, Names Chief of MI6

Agency Comes in from the Cold

Breaking with longstanding government policy, Prime Minister John Major stood before the House of Commons today, the first of the new session of Parliament, and openly acknowledged the existence of Britain's Secret Intelligence Service, known as MI6. It is time, Mr Major said, to "sweep away some of the cobwebs of secrecy which needlessly veil too much of government business."

Earlier this year, the Home Office officially named Stella Rimington to be Director-General of MI5, the domestic security service. MI5 was similarly kept under official secrecy until the Security Service Act of 1989.

Mr Major took care to assert that operations under MI6 will remain secret. MI6 is responsible for intelligence gathering overseas, with officers based in British embassies around the world.

In his statement, Mr. Major named Sir Colin McColl as the country's chief spy. Sir Colin was appointed by former Prime Minister Margaret Thatcher in 1989, taking over from Sir Christopher Curwen, the agency's former "C", as the head is termed.

7th May 1992

PM LIFTS SECRECY, NAMES CHIEF OF MI6

Agency Comes in from the Cold

Breaking with longstanding government policy, Prime Minister John Major stood before the House of Commons today, the first of the new session of Parliament, and openly acknowledged the existence of Britain's Secret Intelligence Service, known as MI6. It is time, Mr Major said, to 'sweep away some of the cobwebs of secrecy which needlessly veil too much of government business'.

Earlier this year, the Home Office officially named Stella Rimington to be Director-General of MI5, the domestic security service. MI5 was similarly kept under official secrecy until the Security Service Act of 1989.

Mr Major took care to assert that operations under MI6 will remain secret. MI6 is responsible for intelligence gathering overseas, with officers based in British embassies around the world.

In his statement, Mr Major named Sir Colin McColl as the country's chief spy. Sir Colin was appointed by former Prime Minister Margaret Thatcher in 1989, taking over from Sir Christopher Curwen, the agency's former 'C', as the head is termed.

POSTCARD AND BANDSTAND, EASTBOURNE

POST CARD.

THIS SPACE MAY BE USED FOR PRINTED
OR WRITTEN MATTER

ONLY THE ADDRESS TO BE
WRITTEN HERE

19 May 1992

Dear Ms King,

I enclose the attached with the trunk of my memoirs, that you might understand something of its history. The Goodman case shook the intelligence community 68 years ago. As these varied correspondences show, its effects still reverberate through the corridors of power. Thus, I would strongly urge upon you the solution offered by the Oxford friend referred to in the communications: that this volume be published as fiction. Personally (although our current Prime Minister would disagree) I suspect any readers of my memoirs will be too intelligent to fall for the ruse. It rankles, to imagine my autobiography being published as mere entertainment, however I agree that in this one case, the world may not be ready for the truth about Mycroft's organisation. And if I may make a further suggestion? A whimsical title might be only appropriate. Something along the lines of, The Green Man, perhaps?

Yours, MRH

19th May 1992

Dear Ms King,

I enclose the attached with the trunk of my memoirs, that you might understand something of its history. The Goodman case shook the Intelligence community 68 years ago. As these varied correspondences show, its effects still reverberate through the corridors of power. Thus, I would strongly urge upon you the solution offered by the Oxford friend referred to in the communications: that this volume be published as fiction. Personally (although our current Prime Minister would disagree) I suspect any readers of my memoirs will be too intelligent to fall for the ruse.

It rankles, to imagine my autobiography being published as mere entertainment, however I agree that in this one case, the world may not be ready for the truth about Mycroft's organisation. And if I may make a further suggestion? A whimsical title might be only appropriate. Something along the lines of <u>The Green Man</u>, perhaps?

Yours,
MRH

STATELY HOLMES

A Christmas Conundrum

Unlike the other pieces in this collection, 'Stately Holmes' has never before appeared in any form. It owes its presence to the persistence of Barbara Peters, owner of Scottsdale's Poisoned Pen Bookstore, who just kept asking . . . Sherlock Holmes and Christmas may seem antithetical, but there is good precedence in Arthur Conan Doyle's 'The Mazarin Stone', a story in which the murder of a goose provides not only both mystery and solution, but a roundly satisfying meal as well. All it lacks is winsome young children and footprints in the snow.

To snicker at one's husband is never considerate, rarely wise, and went against all the precepts that governed this Dickensian season of hospitality and merriment. It was particularly misguided when the illustrious gentleman in question was Sherlock Holmes, but . . .

'Oh, Holmes, you look quite, er, stately.' I was trying to be reassuring, but I found it difficult to keep my face under control.

He looked like a man in a corset, although as yet it was only strapping bands.

'I am pleased my infirmity brings you amusement,' he growled.

'No, truly, I am sorry you've put your back out. I really think you should have stayed in London and submitted to a few days of pummellings and steamings at the Turkish baths. The climate here in Berkshire will do you no good at all. It is cold, bleak, biting weather; foggy withal . . .'

'What the deuces are you on about, Russell?'

'Nothing at all. Do you suppose we are slowing, or simply congealing?' It had clearly been some time since Holmes had refreshed his knowledge of *A Christmas Carol*, I thought, peering through the keyhole I'd kept chipped in the window's uncongenial frost. 'This may be us.'

The train was not exactly slowing, since we had yet to reach anything near full speed. However, our forward progress now felt even less assertive, suggesting either a huge drift across the tracks ahead or the leisurely approach of civilisation. It proved to be the latter – or at any rate, a rural facsimile thereof: Arley Holt.

I gathered our things. Holmes gathered himself, struggling to achieve an upright stance without my help. Stifling curses, he made it to his feet, then turned an accusing gaze at his hat, which remained on the seat, an impossible distance away. I handed it to him, transferred our smallest valise to his hand, so he might not feel completely useless, and helped the porter wrestle open the frozen door of our ill-heated first class compartment.

Even following the train's tepid interior, the late-afternoon air hit us like a fist. Ice daggers drooled off the eaves of the tiny station. The platform had been shovelled down to its frozen base; the porters resembled golems beneath their heavy garments. Similarly amorphous were the clots of snow clinging halfway up the lamp posts, which I thought might be holiday wreaths. The steamed-up windows of the station glowed with welcome while the blessed odour of woodsmoke tantalised with a promise of restored sensation to long-numb hands – but we turned our backs on the warmth to follow the laden porters down the platform to the car park, where a noble Silver Ghost limousine idled amidst clouds of steam.

The instant we came into view, the motor car exploded. The doors flew open, emitting a circus-act flood of heavily-bundled midgets and a chorus of shrieks and giggles. The children circled the massive fenders and skittered across the frozen slush towards us. I took Holmes's arm, so as to present a more unified target, and an instant later we were surrounded by a waist-high cricket team.

Well, perhaps one or two short of a full team.

I looked across the seething collection of knitted hats at the driver of the motor car, who had emerged with considerably less energy.

'Good afternoon, Mr Algernon,' I called.

'Oi!' he shouted. 'You little beasts want 'em to climb back on the train? Leave be, you lot. Back in the motor, now!'

The threat concerned them not at all, but they did draw back a bit. All but one.

Sherlock Holmes, that cold thinking machine, most solitary of men, stood gazing down at the child before him. Bright blue coat, porcelain skin, delicate features, black hair sticking out from under her woollen beret: the shape of the eyes came from her Chinese mother, their grey colour from her father's people.

'Hullo Estelle,' he said.

''Allo, Grandpapa. 'Appy Christmas.'

Somehow, the children were inserted back inside the motor car, most of them atop me in the back, while Mr Algernon provided Holmes a tactful arm to get him into the front, where – unusually enough for an estate car, which tended to assume a driver impervious to the elements – windows sealed the compartment all around. Estelle Adler was placed cautiously upon Holmes's lap, along with a heated brick, a fur-covered travelling rug, and a warning that Grandpapa's back was bothering him so she needed to sit very still.

I couldn't hear her words, buried as I was amongst a cacophony of village children, but as we slithered out onto the main road, I could see that they were talking. A pair of tiny gloved hands occasionally came into view, their gestures even more French than her accent had been. No doubt by the time we reached Justice Hall, this frighteningly intelligent child – daughter of an artist, stepdaughter of a doctor, granddaughter of the most formidable mind of his generation – would not only know all about his infirmity, but have a treatment plan in the works.

Two days earlier, a child-laden trip into the depths of Berkshire had been about the last thing on our minds. Certainly Holmes was no devotee of Christmas revels, and although I had fond memories of distant childhood (my mother, though Jewish, was deeply attached to family rituals), the holiday had faded considerably in importance. Holmes being of the *Bah, humbug* school meant that our long-time housekeeper, Mrs Hudson, tended to proceed blithely with her annual preparations, ignoring his grumbles. But Mrs Hudson was no longer in the house. Instead, our 1925 holiday itinerary had been built around a demanding and intricate experiment in the laboratory, with plans to ignore any tantalising aromas from the kitchen until our new (and decidedly temporary) housekeeper appeared to demand our presence at the table. We had drawn the line at a tree in the sitting room or Christmas music on the wireless. We ignored the whimsical cards on the mantelpiece and the sprigs of holly the young woman had stuck into any convenient nook. I did actually have two gifts prepared – a pretty scarf for her and a little book for Holmes, to be presented once he had grudgingly set aflame the inedible yet requisite Christmas pudding that had long been ageing on the pantry shelf.

On Boxing Day (our original itinerary continued) we would bow to the demands of the season and take the train from the South Downs up to London, to spend three days with Damian Adler and his family: Holmes's long-lost artist son, his half-Chinese daughter, and his copper-haired second wife, a Scots doctor Holmes had abducted from her coastal village to treat a bullet wound.[7] London offered both sufficient distraction for these visitors from Paris and sufficient distance between living quarters: relations between father and son were more formal than cosy.

Then Holmes wrenched his back moving a beehive, which promised to make bending over the laboratory table trying for both of us. And the next morning, a summons from Mycroft arrived, <u>blowing our plans</u> away like the wind over dry snow.

[7] The Adler family is introduced in *The Language of Bees* and *The God of the Hive*.

No doubt, in our absence, the housekeeper would enjoy filling the house with every seasonal fare the wireless had to offer.

'We had plans, Mycroft,' Holmes told his brother. He said it in the vestibule of Mycroft's London flat, unwrapping his scarf and dropping it atop his snow-flecked hat and fur-lined gloves, then turning his cold fingers to his buttons.

'No doubt,' Mycroft replied. 'Many happy returns of the season, Mary. Shall I take your things?'

I handed him my gloves, which he tossed onto the table, frowning as I turned to help Holmes out of his coat.

'What have you done to yourself, Sherlock?'

'Nothing. Just a minor – ow! A small misalignment of vertebrae. I've strapped it up. A night's sleep will put it right.'

'I have a brace if you'd like.'

'If it fits you, it would drop to the floor on me.'

'I am half the man I used to be, Sherlock. In any event, this is one of those with a lot of ties, infinitely adjustable. Shall—?'

'A shot of morphia would do,' Holmes suggested. 'Absent that, a stiff drink.'

His face was rigid as he eased onto the sofa, but, indeed, a generous dose of alcohol comforted his twisted muscles, if not his ravaged nerves: Sherlock Holmes was not one to admit readily to weakness.

Instead of brandy, I went into the kitchen to assemble a large pot of very hot tea, holding my fingers out over the stove as I waited for the kettle to boil. Fortunately, the fire in Mycroft's sitting room was well built up: I had no doubt I would need every scrap of comfort to withstand whatever demands my brother-in-law was about to make on us.

Back at the fire, I took a grateful swallow of searing liquid, stretching my numb toes towards the coals. The Holmes brothers were talking, not about Christmas plans, but about a shared investigation into a case of bribery in Turkey, currently stalled for lack of evidence. We all knew which government tobacco official had been taking money from the Régie Company, both before it was nationalised and – more disturbingly – since, but we had thus far failed to uncover any firm links.

With one cup of tea warming my internal person and a second pressed to my tingling hands, I interrupted the fruitless and oft-repeated discussion. 'Why did you summon us this time, Mycroft? An eggnog scandal in Belgravia? Attempted assassination by holly berries at Sandringham? Father Christmas found murdered on the Palace hearth-rug?'

No: the case in hand was far more diabolical than any government machinations. It seemed that coincidence and our far-flung responsibilities had joined forces against us, with Mycroft (naturally) leading the conspiracy.

'I, er, understand that Damian and his family have come over from Paris for the holidays,' he began.

'We told you of that some weeks ago,' Holmes pointed out.

'Yes. Well. I had a letter in October, from Gabriel Hughenfort's widow.'

'She wrote to *you*?'

I was surprised, too: did Helen even know Mycroft?

'Asking me to forward an enclosed letter.'

'Yet I do not remember you sending us a letter in October,' Holmes remarked.

'You were away. As usual.'

'Whereas you, Mycroft, are a famously permanent fixture in London.'

'And thus a logical intermediary for international communications, yes.'

'What did the letter say?' I interrupted.

My brother-in-law cleared his throat, frowning at the glass in his hands. 'It seems that the seventh Duke of Beauville expressed a desire to visit the family properties for the holidays.'

Holmes and I stared at him. The Duke was a seven-year-old child we had dug out from the wilds of the Canadian prairie, over the powerful objections of his mother, and nearly killed in the process. The repercussions of that episode, two years ago, were still being felt: we had recently learnt that Scotland Yard were seeking the boy's great-uncle (who was actually a grandfather, although very few people knew that) as a 'person of interest' in the death of another uncle. A death for which said grandfather was in fact responsible.

'I thought Helen planned on keeping the boy in Ontario until he came of age?' I said.

'The child seems to have developed a marked degree of single-mindedness.'

'He wore her down,' I translated.

Having known two of the child's blood relations quite well over the years – that murderous unacknowledged grandfather and his equally cut-throat second cousin, two English aristocrats whom I had met in the guise of Mahmoud and Ali Hazr, a pair of Bedouin Arabs – I could understand how even the most strong-willed of Canadians might have met her match.

'So Helen and young Gabe are here in London, too?' I asked. 'It will be nice to see them again.'

'Not precisely.' The fervour with which Mycroft was studying his glass warned me that life was about to get complicated.

Holmes caught on first. 'They want us in Berkshire.'

Mycroft's eyes came up at last. 'I happened to mention to Mrs Hughenfort that your son's family planned a visit, and she insisted that they come to Justice Hall.'

This was not at all what we had planned. However, it might take Holmes's mind off his inability to conduct any experiments. 'I'm sure Damian's family would enjoy a visit to Justice Hall, Holmes, if for nothing more than the art on the walls. Your back should be fine in a few days. We could go up together before New Year's.'

'In fact,' Mycroft said, 'I believe the Hughenforts are already in residence.'

Holmes and I directed a pair of identical scowls at his brother. 'Mycroft, what are you up to?'

'Not I. However, I am to understand that Justice Hall has a ghost.'

'Of Christmas past, or present?' I blurted out.

The two Holmes brothers stared at me blankly.

The letter Mycroft then handed us had been written the previous week by Justice Hall's butler, Ogilby. It was directed to Sherlock Holmes, an outside authority he knew from our time there two years before – but again, Mycroft had preferred to take command of it rather than send it on to Sussex. The letter read as follows:

Dear Mr Holmes,

I write concerning the long-anticipated return of the Duke of Beauville and his mother from their Canadian sojourn, on December 21st. Although we in the Hall are naturally overjoyed to have the Duke in residence once again, and the very last thing we desire would be to present any hindrance to his plans, I nonetheless require some advice.

It would appear that Justice Hall has [one could see the hesitation of his pen here] a ghost.

Beyond our usual spectral residents, that is. This one is rather more substantial than most of the spirits with which Justice Hall has been credited. We have never before had food disappear from the kitchen or clothing from the cupboards.

Naturally, this is a minor consideration that would best be dealt with by the Hall staff. Certainly, I have *no* wish to bring in the police. However, the disruption was first noticed ten days ago, and although I have had various of the footmen and maids, as the phrase goes, 'lay in wait' for the invader, we have seen no trace of him other than evidence of his presence.

I may be overly concerned. Still, I cannot keep from remembering the Duke's last visit here, and the dangers that ensued. On the one hand, I do not wish to say that His Grace and his mother should hesitate to return to their rightful home. On the other hand, I cannot put either of them at any further risk.

Thus I consult you, to ask if you might be able to assist me in discharging my duties to my young master and his honoured mother.

Respectfully yours,
Walter Ogilby,
butler and steward
Justice Hall, Berks.

I was not surprised to hear that Mycroft had promptly replied with a telegram to assure Ogilby that assistance would be to hand. And although I did not wish to spend a holiday with my brother-in-law, some freak whim of holiday spirit drove me to urge: 'Why don't you come with us, Mycroft? It's your family, too, after all.'

The big man merely raised an eyebrow at me.

'Old Marley was as dead as a doornail,' I muttered.

'I beg your pardon?'

'Oh, nothing,' I said. Neither Holmes brother, it appeared, was a fan of Dickens.

Mycroft took his disapproving gaze from me, and resumed his instructions. 'I should have liked you to be available before now, but this will have to do.'

Yes: the promised assistance was made up of Holmes and me. We were, it seemed, doomed to celebrate Christmas.

Thus it was that on 23rd December 1925, we sat in the crowded and noisy estate motor car, our tyres churning away the snowy miles to Justice Hall.

The passing countryside, which I remembered as being fields to the left and an endless high stone wall to the right, had been invisible from the moment the motor car doors closed back in Arley Holt. I could see the back of Holmes's head through the open window to the driver's compartment, but only Algernon's regular use of a chamois kept the windscreen from submitting to the fog of breaths, with a swipe at the side windows each time we approached an intersecting lane.

However, the moment the big motor slowed at the entrance gates, the energies within the motor car approached the boiling point. The lodge-keeper let us through with a tug at his hat, and the instant the gates fell behind us, a clamour arose, demanding that the windows be opened. Frigid air billowed in; the outside world came into view. It was indeed very pretty, the entrance drive of snow-scaped rhododendrons, but I could not see why small children should find it so thrilling – until I spotted a shape through a couple of excited heads.

The Justice Hall drive consisted of a straight run through formal landscaping followed by a gently curving track down the side of a perfect hill, designed to provide a long and leisurely view of the magnificent house. This initial straight section might be interesting when the huge old rhododendrons were in bloom, but that would not be for many months.

At present, the shrubs were small snow mountains – except that some of these shapes, I now saw, were not based on vegetation. They were figures. A long row of figures, perhaps twenty in all, shaped out of snow and given costume. The first snow blob was draped in red, defining it as Father Christmas; antlers thrust into a horizontal shape at its side made for a napping reindeer. The following mound was rendered human only by the bowler hat on its peak and a mock neck-tie below, but the next one . . .

By this time, the motor car was creeping at a slow walk, that we might admire the details: a heap of snow so tall and thin it must have been built over a series of sequential freezes, to overcome snow's tendency to collapse. It was swathed all the way to the ground in an ancient houndstooth-check cape, and something about the way the voluminous garment had been draped made for a remarkably . . . Holmesian stance (pre-back problems). On its 'head' rested a deerstalker, at an angle suggesting a disapproving tilt

I had seen a thousand times. Leaning against the houndstooth was a tennis racquet missing its strings: a Brobdingnagian magnifying glass.

Estelle squeaked and jumped up and down a bit, subsiding instantly at the involuntary noise Holmes gave out. 'Oh, Grandpapa, I am sorry – but do you see? *C'est vous!*'

'I see, *ma petite*. Did you make it?'

'*Papa* made it. I helped him. Do you like it?'

'It is very clever, Estelle.' And it was, thus proving that an artist's eye and hands could manipulate even the most unlikely medium.

I was somewhat relieved when the next figures did not include Mary Russell. Instead, there was a pair of sturdy figures decoratively wrapped in bright colours and snug Arab turbans. Again, the unlikely details were striking: pride in the set of the shoulders, a froth of dark coir for the beards, chips of charcoal eyes that even from a distance looked piercing. The taller of the two was draped in a dozen wide belts like bandoliers, and both wore the scabbards (empty, I hoped) of curved Bedouin swords.

Mahmoud Hazr and his 'brother' Ali: the two Bedouin Arabs from Palestine, also known as Lord Marsh, one-time heir and reluctant master of Justice Hall, and his cousin Alistair.

I laughed aloud.

The other figures were less specific, although the children in the car gabbled their identities: local notables; the King; Ogilby, the Justice Hall butler.

We came to the end of the flat and of the snow statues. Here the drive turned slightly left before it dropped, and there Algernon stopped the motor car – not, as the designers had intended, to admire the noble house, but so as not to mow down a collection of bundled figures standing on the road.

At this, all four doors of the motor car flew open and a tide of small figures began pouring out. Even Estelle abandoned us, although she moved with more caution than any of the four sets of shoes that left marks upon my flesh. At the top of the hill were arranged an assortment of sliding implements, from a gilded sledge as ornate as the Royal Carriage to dustbin lids with their handles bashed flat. The children flung themselves on the varied sliding apparatus, and with hoots of glee launched off down the perfect and unsullied hillside.

'I wonder if Capability Brown had sledding in mind when he laid out the landscape?' I mused.

'Certainly the angle encourages speed,' Holmes replied.

'And a nice touch of thrill,' I noted, seeing the sleds towards the left side of the run – the route chosen, I noticed, by the larger children – take to the air over a hillock, accompanied by shrieks and the ejection of at least one bundled figure into the pristine snow.

Algernon had been working his way around the motor, shutting up the windows and doors. He resumed his place behind the wheel and we continued our sweep down the drive to the elaborate (currently drained) fountain in front of the house itself.

The children had long since reached the bottom, and most of them were already trudging back up the hill with their sledges. But not all. By the time Algernon and I had extricated Holmes, Ogilby was to hand, with the house door standing open behind him. The small knot of figures there – women bent over small bundles – resolved into two women, two children, and a housemaid. The red-headed woman, Estelle's doctor mother, added a tiny bright blue coat to the load of garments in the maid's arms.

Ogilby was too professional to break his butlerian calm, but I did not think I imagined the trace of panic in his face, instantly stifled, as he realised that Sherlock Holmes, his promised rescuer, was less than fit. His features looked just a touch bleak as he watched Holmes climb the single step to the walk. I took pains to say in his ear as I went past: 'Don't worry, Mr Ogilby, things will be sorted.'

At the door, the transfer of diminutive clothing had been completed, leaving four figures to greet us.

Estelle Adler claimed her grandfather's left hand while her stepmother, Dr Aileen Henning-Adler, shook his right to make her greetings – and her apologies for a missing Damian, who'd been called to London to see about a commission. My own hand reached for that of the other woman, the Canadian ambulance driver who had mothered a Duke.

'Mrs Hughenfort,' I exclaimed. 'It's lovely to see you, I had no idea you were coming until Mycroft waylaid us yesterday.'

'Please, call me Helen. I only asked him to send the letter on to you, but I guess he thought he needed to be a bit more . . .'

'Manipulative,' I provided. 'And Your Grace, goodness you've grown since I saw you last.'

The lad blushed slightly, either at the title or at the cliché greeting of the adult world. He gave my hand a solemn shake, turned to Holmes with the same, and then stood back, a Duke welcoming his guests.

'Mama,' piped Estelle, *'Grandpère* has injured his vertebrae.'

The doctor's concern and Holmes's protests took us across the magnificent but icy entry hall with barely a pause to admire the broad stairway up which one could drive a coach-and-six, or the museum of furnishings against the walls, or the stunning painted dome high above our heads, or even the twenty feet of fragrant pine tree that loomed over a small mountain of crates, all of them bearing the label: XMAS DECORATIONS.

'It was good of you to invite us all,' I told Helen as we went.

'It's actually a relief, I was dreading these great echoing halls with no one but the servants. And I'm afraid I'm something of a disappointment to them – I draw lines through half of Mrs Butter's proposed menus, I've ignored Ogilby's pointed suggestions of a formal party, and we've more or less taken up residence in the library, even for meals.'

'Shocking,' I agreed. 'What about the others?'

'Oh, Phillida's taken her family off to the south of France, so we don't even have them to entertain us.'

I wouldn't have considered Mahmoud's sister, her dreary husband, and her intrusive children 'entertaining', but Helen was a better person than I.

'Oh, doesn't the south of France sound heavenly?' I asked.

'Oh, yes – I managed to forget how incredibly cold this place could be. But come, the library's not too bad.'

The so-called library (as opposed to the actual library, upstairs) had a considerably smaller tree, already anointed with its baubles, in one corner. More to the point, it had a fire like a blast furnace. We gratefully began to shed our many garments, Aileen peeling off Holmes's greatcoat with the efficiency of a ward sister before she tucked her hand under his elbow, easing his descent into an armchair. Helen set a well-filled glass on the table by his side. Estelle climbed onto the settee across from him to sit, heels dandling. Young Gabriel watched to make sure his guests were well cared for, then sat down beside Estelle, pulling a rolled-up penny-dreadful called *Chums* from his pocket and disappearing into its well-thumbed pages.

I waited until I could feel my toes again before I caught up a nice thick rug from the back of the settee and slipped into the frozen wastes of the great hall, in search of the apprehensive butler.

'Even Ogilby agrees that there isn't a whole lot to go on,' I told Holmes an hour later. We had retreated to the privacy of our rooms to dress for dinner, where I was acting the valet for my husband. 'You know, I really think you ought to try Mycroft's brace. Think of it as an exoskeleton.'

'I can't think why you brought the thing along, it will not fit me. Do you suppose the Hall has rats?'

'Very tidy rats, taking an entire loaf of bread from a cupboard and slices from a roast in the larder? It will fit you, we just need to adjust the laces. Try it. If it's not more comfortable, you can go back to your swaddling bands.'

He stared at the male corset with loathing, and gave a curt nod. Snugging up the laces made him wince, but once it was tied, he tested it by drawing breath, then rotating his shoulders. One eyebrow went up. 'Not bad,' he admitted. 'Although I resemble an automaton.'

'You merely look dignified, Holmes.'

Indeed, clothed in his dinner suit (informality at Justice Hall clearly had its limits), his posture was one of dignity and deliberation. As I'd said: stately. So long as he didn't drop anything.

And after dinner that night, he declared himself fit enough to wander the cooling halls with me, hunting ghosts. We did so until after four in the morning – the kitchen maids would come down by five, which would be sufficient guard.

'Not a creature was stirring, Holmes,' I yawned the next morning, following too little sleep. 'Not even—'

'If you say "a mouse",' he growled, 'I shall incinerate your copy of *The Pickwick Papers*.'

'—the cat. Maybe Justice Hall should get a dog.'

Breakfast was extraordinary, a vast spread of hot dishes that would have made Mrs Hudson envious. Or at least, the Mrs Hudson I had known. The two children were practically bouncing on their chairs, despite their innate dignity, and the instant Helen appeared, her son demanded to know if the pond was sufficiently frozen for skating.

She raised an eyebrow at the dark figure occupying the far end of the buffet. 'What do you think, Ogilby? Is the ice thick enough?'

'I sent the footman and two stable boys out on it this morning, my Lady, and it gave no indication of weakness.'

'Then finish your breakfast, Gabe, and you can take Estelle out for a time. I imagine the neighbour children will be waiting about for you,' she added, the second half of her statement accompanied by a furious rattle of spoons against porridge bowls.

Fond smiles all around, as the two children flew out of the door.

Morning was skating, and the two children were not the only ones to retreat for a nap before an only marginally less sumptuous luncheon. Then the family and the entire Justice Hall staff, indoor and out (this being Helen's radically egalitarian decree, ignoring

Ogilby's stony face), assembled in the great hall for the decoration of the tree.

Unfortunately, Damian was not back from London. A message had come on the telephone, to say he was on his way, but . . .

'Oh, let's go ahead without him,' Aileen declared. And with that, the XMAS boxes were flung open. Strings of modern electrical lights festooned the branches, followed by every shape of glass bulb one could imagine. In the end, a semicircle of participants, ranked from Gabriel and his mother at one end to the young son of the estate woodcutter at the other, stood back to sigh in admiration.

Even, secretly, Sherlock Holmes.

Then Gabe looked up at his mother. 'Could we go carolling?'

'Well, we can certainly sing some songs,' she replied.

'No, I mean real carolling. Door to door, like at home.'

'But, sweetheart, we don't have neighbours here, do we? It would be quite a trudge to the village.'

'There's a sleigh!'

Helen looked sideways at the servants' end of the gathering, evidently hoping for some degree of resignation on their faces, but there seemed to be only eagerness.

Still: 'It's a lot of work for Mr Ringle's men,' she began – Ringle was the estate manager – however, the two young men with the roughest boots were already shaking their heads.

'Mum, we've had it out and serviced, and the horses are shod, just in hopes . . . well, everything is ready, whenever you'd like.'

She blinked. Until that moment, I don't think Helen had the faintest idea how much the Justice Hall estate longed for their Duke, how violently they had thrown themselves into preparations the instant that news came of the Canadians' visit. Surely everything was always kept in such a polished state? After all, members of the family – Phillida and Sidney, Lenore and Walter – spent most of their time here.

Apparently not.

'I see,' she said. 'Well, if there's time before dark, that would be extraordinarily lovely. Shall we say, in an hour? Or would it take—?'

'Thirty minutes, tops, my Lady,' the youngest of the stable men blurted, and the two of them made a gesture at their forelocks and hurried out.

'Ma'am,' said Ringle, and followed.

Helen watched various maids and footmen scatter, bemused at the result of her mild decree. She was still looking bemused when she was settled into the high, and highly-polished, sleigh, handed a booklet of carols, and wrapped in a fur rug with a heated stone at her feet. The rest of us followed suit, and once we were swathed and warm, two of the Hall men clambered up in front (the footman, and a middle-aged stable boy proud of his baritone). Off we jingled into the snowy afternoon.

Two of our party stayed behind: Holmes because the jostling of the sleigh would undo all the good of Mycroft's corset, and Estelle because she preferred to remain with her grandpapa.

I managed to get one hand out of my swaddlings to wave a goodbye.

Holmes directed his grey eyes down at the small child. Her own grey eyes gazed back up at him, oddly appraising.

'You should have gone with them, child. I plan to sit and read.'

'That's all right. Ralph's voice hurts my ears.'

'Which one is Ralph?'

'The stable boy with the funny nose.'

The child was cursed with perfect pitch, he remembered. 'I'm no good at games,' he warned her.

'I am,' she replied. 'What do you do?'

'Do?'

'Papa paints, Mama makes people better. I go to school. What do you do?'

'I figure things out,' he said, and turned towards the warmth of the library. As he'd feared, she followed.

'What kinds of things?'

'If something important is stolen, I find who took it. Or someone is ki—is hurt, I find who did it. Who is selling things they shouldn't, telling secrets they weren't supposed to.'

'How do you figure those things out?'

'I watch, I listen, I think.' He hovered over the armchair, book in hand, wondering if there was someone on the staff better suited than he to entertain a five-year-old girl. 'Don't you have schoolwork?'

'No. I like to think, too,' she pronounced, plopping herself onto the hard settee and bouncing her heels. 'Like when someone stole Ines's puppy, and I figured out where it was.'

He sighed, and grimaced his way down to the chair. 'Who is Ines?'

'Ines Laurent. She lives next door, in Paris. Her uncle gave her a puppy for her birthday that was small and white and liked to lick everything, but it never stopped barking and then it went away, and Ines thought someone stole it. But I figured out where it went.'

'It got hit by a motor?'

'No. Her mama gave it to a friend. I could tell because

Madame Laurent was happy after the dog went. She pretended to be sad, but only when Ines was looking at her. And a few days later Madame Laurent's good friend came to visit and had some white dog hairs on her coat, but she hadn't had them before.'

Sherlock Holmes stared at the infant in the red dress with the bouncing patent leather slippers. He hadn't felt this astonished since the spring of 1915.

'Yes,' he said slowly. 'I can see you like to think. Do you also like to watch and listen?'

'Oh, yes,' she told him.

He laid aside his book. 'So tell me, Estelle: how many . . . ?' He paused. How high could a small child count? 'How many steps to the front door?'

'Three,' she said promptly, then amended it. 'Four, if you count the step at the end of the walk.'

The tired horses pulled up in front of the house that afternoon at dusk as our voices uplifted (we'd been well provided with lubrication along the way, even before we reached the Duke's Arms) in a final chorus.

God bless you, merry gentlemen.

May nothing you dismay!

I was surprised to see Holmes out on the snowy terrace with little Estelle. The two of them had been studying something on the ground – Holmes's rigid back angling off his hips, the child squatting on her heels – but when the sleigh came around the side of the house, Estelle leapt up and came skidding across the stones and down the steps, a grin on her gamine face. The half of her that was Chinese kept her face from going pink like those of most

English children, but today she'd been out long enough that her cheeks were bright with cold.

The moment young Gabriel had been lifted down from the conveyance, she seized his hand and demanded, 'Come and see the footprints.'

When the footman had unwrapped us from our many layers and handed us down as well, I walked up the steps to where the children were solemnly studying the terrace stones. 'Footprints?' I asked Holmes.

'The child has a remarkable eye for detail,' he said, and turned stiffly towards the French doors.

'Art in the blood,' I murmured, and followed, while Helen urged the two shivering children into the house, then upstairs to change their clothes. Holmes and I went up, too, and happened to come out again as the children were descending.

The electrical lights on the big tree had been turned on, throwing splashes of colour across the dim hall. In our absence, several large, colourful packages had appeared at the base of the tree. Estelle spotted them. 'Pwesents!' she squealed.

She darted forward to look – only to be halted by a voice from the door. 'No opening presents until the morning,' said a man in stern tones.

'Papa!' This squeal was even higher. Damian Adler, returned from London, caught his daughter mid leap and swung her in a circle.

'Look, Papa, the tree! See how its lights go! And, presents!'

'No opening until morning,' Damian warned again. 'If they get opened too early, Father Christmas might take them back during the night.'

This naturally led to a discussion on the nature of Father

Christmas, how he knew where they were (answer: Father C knows all) and how he came down chimneys if there was a fire (Justice Hall has far more chimneys than it does fires). The young Duke lingered at the edges of the discussion, clearly torn between sophisticated doubt and a yearning to believe, until his mother shooed us all into the warm library for drinks and an early supper for the children, and drinks before dinner for the adults.

Around 7 a.m., the other three took their young people up to an early bed. I would happily have taken to my own rest (most of the previous night having been spent hunting the Ghost of Christmas Pilfering) but I waited, and joined the others for an early dinner (a simple meal that I suspected had drawn Mrs Butter's scorn as a mere supper) before Holmes and I excused ourselves, retreating to our own beds for a couple of hours. We rose again at midnight. The house had gone quiet. I dressed in thick, dark clothing, helped Holmes put on his own soft-soled footwear, and we let ourselves into the still corridors.

A country house like Justice Hall generates its own electricity with a power plant, shut down at night because of the noise. The battery system, although no doubt generous, would not last the night if many lights were left burning, which meant that the halls held but the faintest and most distantly spaced of bulbs. And that was before we ventured into the hidden passages behind the walls that Ali Hazr – the cousin born Alistair Hughenfort – had shown us. Those passageways had a store of candles at their entrances, but Holmes and I carried torches as well, with a spare in our pockets.

We prowled the halls for hours, taking turns perched in a dark corner of the kitchens in hopes of catching the pantry's invader. Two o'clock came and went; three. The closest I came to a disturbance was when I paused outside of the nursery, hearing the whispers of conversation. I smiled, recalling the difficulties of sleeping through an endless Christmas night with my own brother, and went on.

Holmes and I met up on the great stairway, where the incongruous outdoors odour of pine lay heavy in the air. 'Holmes, if those two children are anything like Levi and me, they'll rouse the place at the crack of dawn. Surely we don't need to wait the whole night?'

'Give it another hour,' he replied.

'I must have coffee,' I said. 'And I saw some of Mrs Butter's rolls, leftover from dinner. Meet me in the kitchen in twenty minutes?'

It was a sign of his own need that he did not object.

Twenty-five minutes later, Holmes and I sat across from each other at the scrubbed deal table, between us a platter of well-buttered rolls. We had just buried our faces in the steam from our cups when a series of creaks broke the profound stillness – a sequence of noises we knew well from our trips up and down the servants' stairs.

Coffee sloshed out of both cups as they hit the table, and Holmes was not far behind me as I dashed out of the swinging door and up the narrow stairway. My feet automatically followed the path that would draw the least reaction from the old wood, but at the top, the probe of our torch beams gave no sign of intruder. We separated, Holmes into the servants' wing and me through the baize door to the family bedrooms: nothing moved.

We searched high and low, but found no indication of life. Even the nursery had fallen silent.

I was cold through and beyond exhaustion when Holmes and I found each other again, outside the butler's pantry. 'Nothing?' I asked. He shook his head. 'It must've just been the stairs settling in the cold. Old houses do creak. Can we get some sleep now?'

'We might as well.'

'I need something to eat first. I couldn't face that coffee, though. Tea?'

We had perhaps half an hour before the first yawning maids appeared to stir up the fires for this busy day. We went through the swinging door – and stopped dead.

The plate of buttered rolls held nothing but crumbs. Our two cups were now empty, but for a ring of brown at the bottom.

Shortly thereafter, the sound of girls' voices, thick with sleep, travelled down the stairs. We retreated to our rooms, and dropped hard into a too-brief sleep, awaking to the arrival of a depressingly festive tea tray. Heavy-eyed, we stumbled downstairs to the bustling (and warm) library, where we found two children ensconced in their new toys, and three adults in coffee and newspapers.

'A Merry Christmas,' I said.

A chorus of happy voices rose up, wishing us the same.

Estelle jumped up, wading through a lake of torn paper and ribbon to show us her prize. 'Look, Grandpapa – Father Christmas came! He bringed me a stefascope!'

'*Brought* me,' Damian corrected under his breath.

It was, as she said, a diminutive stethoscope. 'Most useful,' Holmes agreed, blinking in his attempt to focus on the object.

'He bringed – *brought* – you a present, too. It's in the tree.'

'Very good of him,' Holmes said, accepting a cup of coffee

from the too-cheerful maid, that he might warm his legs before the fire with it. I took one as well, discovering a drink so unexpectedly and blessedly strong it might have come from a Parisian brasserie. Damian's work, I thought.

'Do you want me to get it?' Estelle asked.

'Get . . . ? Ah, my present. Not just now, thank you.'

Young Gabe, kneeling on the floor in his pyjamas and dressing gown with a pair of child-sized field glasses around his neck and a cowboy hat on his head, was busy arranging a battalion, if not an entire brigade, of tin soldiers. They were currently taking up their positions along the corner of the room: artillery advancing upon the carpet, snipers occupying the high ground of the lower shelves. I took another swallow of coffee, then followed a thousand odours floating in the air to the next room, where I found an impromptu buffet set atop the billiards table – Helen's enforced informality must be giving Ogilby ulcers, I reflected. A fire almost as authoritative as the library's complemented the flames beneath a dozen or so silver chafing dishes. I worked my way down the offerings and settled with my laden plate before the hearth. Holmes came in and did the same, although his plate contained rather more pig products than mine.

After our second plates (and fourth cups of coffee), Estelle's head popped around the door from the library. 'Do you want it now, Grandpapa?'

Holmes's brain cells having been stimulated into something approaching their usual brisk pace, he did not reply, *Do I want what?* but merely hesitated a moment before noticing the white shape in his granddaughter's hand. He stretched out an arm, and she came skipping across the room to place it on his palm.

An envelope, the size and weight of a formal invitation, his name in block letters on the front: MR SHERLOCK HOLMES. She leant over his elbow as he examined it, and watched as he took out his penknife to run it through the flap.

Using the tips of his fingers, Holmes pulled out the contents: a photograph. Estelle picked up the envelope to see if there was something more interesting, then dropped it and went off to the more enticing entertainments of the library.

Not so Holmes.

'What is it?' I demanded.

He turned the photograph over, to check that there was no message on its back, then laid it on the damask before me.

It showed a crisp, clear image of a street-side cafe in what I recognised as Istanbul. Several of the tables were occupied, but to one side, separated from the main body of the cafe by two or three empty places, sat two men, bent together in urgent conversation. They had sat down with their backs to the cafe's wall, that they might keep watch on the street. Their faces were absolutely clear.

One was the man representing the newly monopolised Régie Company. The other was the governmental employee suspected of receiving his bribes.

'Where the hell did this come from?' I demanded. Holmes, breathing curses, fought his way up from the chair and set out across the room, with me on his heels.

'Child,' he demanded, 'where did you get that?'

His sharp voice caused the entire library to stop: children, tin soldiers, lifted cups, words on lips. Even the dancing flames seemed to freeze, just for an instant.

Estelle, wide-eyed, retreated towards her father's knees.

Damian's hand came to rest on her shoulder as he studied Holmes's face.

'Where did she get what?' Damian asked, his voice eerily like his father's.

'That envelope. Who gave it to you, child?'

'Nobody,' her little voice protested. 'It was in the tree. Where Father Christmas told me it was. He said to make sure you found it.'

Damian looked about two seconds from getting to his feet and thrusting a fist under Holmes's long nose. 'Holmes,' I murmured. 'It is a shame to quarrel on Christmas day. Gentle.'

After a moment, his shoulders went down, his voice relaxed. 'I simply need to know where the photograph came from, Estelle. It wasn't really Father Christmas that told you, was it?' he coaxed. Damian's bristling temper subsided a fraction at the change of tone.

'It was,' piped another voice. 'Really, it was.'

Little Gabriel was on his feet, as uncompromising as one of his tin soldiers. Chin up, black eyes flashing, the Duke of Beauville prepared to go to battle for his friend.

Holmes stared for a considerable time before abruptly realising that he was rather looming above the others. He cleared his throat, and moved with deliberation to the settee before the fire. The emotional charge in the room dropped considerably.

'When you have eliminated the impossible . . .' he reflected, *sotto voce*, then: 'Are you saying that you and Estelle had a conversation with a man who looked like Father Christmas?'

'He was Father Christmas.'

'When was this?'

'Last night.'

'Before you went up to bed?'

'No. We were asleep. I heard a noise, and he was there, so I woke up Estelle so she could see him, too.'

Damian and Helen looked at each other in alarm: a costumed stranger among the children was indeed worrying.

It was Aileen who asked the next question, her voice nearly as sharp as Holmes's had been. 'What did he do?'

'He talked. He sat down and talked. He made us stay in our beds because it was cold, but he said he wasn't cold, because of the fur in his suit.'

At the telling detail, the five of us stared, first at him, then at Estelle. She was nodding in agreement. Damian gathered his daughter up into his lap. Helen suggested that her son sit down and start at the beginning. 'Tell us what happened.'

What happened was: Father Christmas came, as the children had been assured he would. And clearly, he'd come down one of the cold chimneys as anticipated, since when he left, it was not past the low-burning coals in the nursery fireplace, but out of the door.

It took some time, and much circuitous explanation and backtracking, but in the end, we had a quite vivid image of this man in a fur-trimmed red suit, sitting on the nursery's low armchair with his legs stretched out before him, holding a comfortable and apparently quite lengthy conversation with the children. And not about their parents, but about their own lives: schooling, friends, and interests.

Primarily, it would appear, Gabriel's.

Estelle had dozed off after a while, leaving Gabe and the man to engage in solemn converse for what must have been an hour or more – the very conversation, I realised with sinking heart, that I'd overheard, and dismissed as sleepy mutterings.

At the end, he'd stood and said he had to leave.

'To go to the other children,' Estelle explained, as an aside.

He told them that he'd leave them each a present for the morning, then asked Estelle to make sure her grandfather found his envelope in the branches of the library tree. After shaking Gabriel's hand and giving Estelle a brief touch on the forehead with his gloved hand, he told them to go back to sleep, and let himself out.

'Which presents were from him?' Damian asked.

Estelle burrowed through the paper and came up with a slim, beautifully bound Moroccan-leather volume that she had politely set aside due to its lack of pictures. The title, picked out in gilt, caused every adult there to choke back an identical reaction of startled bemusement: 'A Scandal in Bohemia'. The story of how Damian's mother, Irene Adler, got the better of one Sherlock Holmes. We turned with some apprehension to see Gabe's revelation, but his was considerably less of a shock: Father Christmas had given him the field glasses. And even those, far from being a child's toy, were made by Zeiss, and very expensive.

The two children, seeing that we were finished with our demands, went back to their play. We listened to the crackle of the fire. After a while, Helen got up to ring the servants' bell. Ogilby drifted in the doorway, wishing us many happy returns of the day.

'Mr Ogilby, something . . . odd has happened,' she said.

'Madam?' he said guardedly.

'It would appear that the children had a visitation from St Nicholas during the night.'

'Madam?' This time his voice was startled – or as startled as a butler would get.

'Yes. Father Christmas. In the nursery. All in red.'

'The fur was white,' Estelle corrected, from where she lay on the hearth-rug, industriously applying artists' coloured pencils to a book of pictures.

'And his beard,' Gabriel added, back amongst his soldiers.

'You aren't aware of one of the servants being . . . behind this?'

'Madam, I am not. Is it perhaps possible . . . ?'

'I'd say there was a real man, wearing Father Christmas clothing, as they believe.'

Ogilby looked decidedly green at the thought of an invasion aimed at the most innocent members of the house. 'Madam, there is such a costume in the house. If you remember, I did offer to have one of the footmen dress in it for the evening festivities, however—'

'I turned you down,' Damian said.

'Where is the suit?' Holmes demanded.

'In the butler's pantry, sir. I saw it this morning. At any rate, the box is there.'

Holmes and I were delegated to accompany him, and the suit was there, in all its parts. The costume had been taken out and brushed the week before, and left hanging to dissipate the mothball smell. It had then been packed away again last night after Ogilby's offer of a Father Christmas was politely dismissed. There was no way to tell if it had been worn and returned to the box during the wee hours of Christmas morning.

The only thing Holmes discovered was one curly black hair in the backing fabric for the beard. He placed it in an envelope (he was never without the odd envelope) and we returned to the library. When we had delivered our report, the five of us studied the two children, blissful in their innocence.

'Gabriel,' Helen said. 'Honey. Tell me more about Father Christmas. What did he look like?'

He looked, it seemed, rather like Father Christmas.

'How big was he?'

Tall. Bigger around than either Damian or Holmes – although padding was, after all, a part of the costume. 'What about his accent?'

English, rather than Canadian. But beyond that, he sounded like anyone else here.

'What else did you notice about him? His hands, his shoes, his odour?'

He wore gloves; his boots were soft and unpolished; he smelt of mothballs.

'Father Christmas isn't rich,' Estelle noted from where she lay, stretched out on the hearth-rug.

'Sorry?' Holmes asked.

'He's not rich. He had a patch in his boots. Like Papa had, in the shoes that Mama gave to the man who begs on the corner, even though Papa said we weren't rich enough to give away perfectly good footwear. I s'pose Father Christmas needs all his money for the poor children's presents.'

At the revelation of his disappearing shoes, Damian shot his wife an accusing look; Aileen played with her ring; Helen stifled laughter; Holmes nodded.

'His eye colour?'

Dark. Black, Estelle specified, then added, 'His beard wasn't real.'

'Was so,' Gabe protested.

'It had stitches,' Estelle noted.

The Duke was troubled, but he did not argue – and I had to agree, Estelle Adler was as unassailably sure of herself as any Holmes I knew.

However: 'But he had a beard under the beard,' she continued.

'What do you—?'

'A beard *under*—' two voices began.

'How do you know that?' Holmes's question won out.

Estelle lifted her head, her grey eyes focusing on the details of memory – again, a thing I'd seen a thousand times. After a minute, she blinked and shifted around to look at him. 'It was too lumpy. And you could see under it, on his neck. There was dark hair, like Papa's.'

'It wasn't me,' Damian hastened to say.

Estelle burst into childish laughter. ''Course not, silly. It was Papa Noel hiding his real beard, 'cause in England they think his beard is white.'

The logic of children.

The two smaller members of our gathering readdressed themselves to their projects, leaving the adults to migrate out of hearing towards the windows. It had not snowed since yesterday, but there was still a pristine expanse of white between here and the frozen lake, broken only by the pockmarked trail of some passing deer.

Helen spoke first. 'I refuse to believe one of the staff could have done this without Ogilby's approval – or knowledge.'

Holmes, staring out at the snow, mused, 'Were it not for the dark eyes, I'd have begun to suspect an elaborate prank on the part of my brother.'

'The room was dark,' Helen pointed out. 'She could have been mistaken.'

'No,' Holmes said.

'Holmes, are you sure?' I asked.

'Unreservedly.'

All right, then. 'Well, I'm still finding it hard to believe that someone got past both Holmes and me. We were all over the house.'

'He must—' Holmes went still. He was staring out at the snow, his eyes doing precisely what Estelle's had done a few minutes before. And like hers, after a moment his gaze sharpened, and he turned to us – with, I was astonished to see, the kind of dancing amusement one only saw there when someone had got the better of him.

'What?' I demanded.

Instead of answering me, he crossed the room, saying, 'Estelle, get your coat, we're going outside.'

Obediently, the artist's daughter dropped her pencil and rose.

'Holmes,' I protested, 'do we really have to go outside just now?'

'Not at all. I merely require the assistance of Miss Adler in order to solve our case.'

Naturally, we all ended up donning our heavy outer wear and following him out of the front door.

Holmes and his grey-eyed granddaughter, hand in hand, turned to the right, with the rest of us trailing behind (along with two or three of the household staff, a number that increased as we went on). We followed Holmes's rigid back to the terrace steps, where he paused, two steps down, to speak to Estelle at the top. She listened to his quiet instructions, then nodded and walked slowly on, studying the ground as she had on our return from carolling. All along the terrace, then down again to ground level, crossing the well-trodden path that led to the kitchen, then over a second thoroughly churned-up section of snow near the stables.

And when that disturbance was past, it appeared: a solitary line of footprints in the snow, joining in from around the house.

Holmes idly studied the top of the hill where the drive vanished towards the main gates. Estelle, on the other hand, bent over until her nose nearly touched the snow, before straightening to say something to Holmes. He nodded, and the two of them continued along the line of boot marks towards its source.

The rest of us stopped to examine the snowy prints. They showed the passage of a pair of boots – not heavy or hob-nailed such as an estate worker would wear, but a man's nonetheless: longer and wider than my own, and pressed more deeply into the surface.

Even when I imitated the action of Miss Estelle Adler and laid the side of my face along the snow, I would not have sworn that the faint uneven portion in the centre of the right boot was a patch. Would Holmes's eyes have seen it, had he been able to get down and look? Probably. Possibly . . . I brushed off my knees and followed the two generations of grey-eyed detectives.

The man with the patched boots had come along the outside of the stables block. Before that, his path cut directly across fifty yards of perfect white snow to the walled-in kitchen garden, and from there to . . .

A patch of blank wall.

Except it wasn't, not quite. An ancient stone shed leant up against the outer wall of Justice Hall, a single row of footprints leading away from its ancient door. Either our Father Christmas had laboriously (and expertly) reversed his every step to hide his passage towards the house, or he had spent a very cold night in this frozen place. Or . . .

It took Holmes some time, but with the use of Damian's cigarette lighter, he traced a continuous crack through the crumbling grout. One of Helen's hairpins fit into an almost invisible hole; Damian's young shoulder shoved hard . . . and a section of stone wall gave way on massive, well-oiled hinges.

Damian squatted to peer inside the resulting black hole. Estelle looked worried as he ducked inside. Gabe would have followed but for Aileen's hand on his shoulder, while Helen, ever practical, said something about going for a torch. Holmes's words stopped her. 'There will be candles, just inside.'

And, of course, there were. As there had been in the hidden passages Ali had shown us.

The others followed Damian inside, and were soon swallowed up by the hidden passageway. Exclamations and reassurances echoed down the stones. The far end, I thought, would open up in the back of a cupboard, near the nursery.

'You go on, Russell,' Holmes said.

I shook my head. We turned and threaded through the press of astonished Justice Hall staff. When we were out of their hearing, I spoke. 'Father Christmas was Mahmoud.'

'He needed to give me that photograph, but when he got wind of his heir coming over from Canada, decided he might as well see something of the lad as well. Which he could not risk doing openly because of the recent Scotland Yard warrant.'

I considered this as we crossed the little walled garden towards the now-bustling kitchen. 'Holmes, I think you have it wrong.'

He stopped to fix me with a look. 'Really?'

'I suspect that for Mahmoud, any delivery of evidence came a distinct second to his wish to see the boy.'

After a moment, Holmes turned back to work the door's latch, and over his shoulder delivered one of the nicest Christmas presents I've ever been given. 'You're probably right, Russell. But then, you generally are.'

God bless us, every one.

ACKNOWLEDGEMENTS

EVEN MORE THAN A novel, a story collection like this depends on the voice of the community. My usual suspects – Alice, Merrily, Erin, John, and Vicki – keep an eye on aspects of Mary Russell's life that the author forgets. 'Mary Russell's War' and 'A Case in Correspondence' would have been impossible without the help of Bob Difley. 'Stately Holmes' owes its existence to Barbara Peters, who wouldn't take no for an answer. Zoe Elkaim sets me aright time and again. And thanks to the fabulous people at Random House, unparalleled at polishing the edges of rough fiction, especially Kate Miciak, Julia Maguire, Kelly Chian, Matt Schwartz, Carlos Beltran, Gina Wachtel, Erika Seyfried, and Ashleigh Heaton. Thanks also to Allison & Busby for bringing these books to UK readers.

Mary Russell loves you all.

Publication History

'Mary's Christmas': Originally self-published by the author in 2014.

'Mary Russell's War': Originally self-published by the author in 2015.

'Beekeeping for Beginners': Originally published by Bantam Books, an imprint of Random House, a division of Penguin Random House LLC, in 2011.

'The Marriage of Mary Russell': Originally published by Bantam Books, an imprint of Random House, a division of Penguin Random House LLC, in 2016.

'Mrs Hudson's Case': Originally published in *Crime Through Time*, edited by Miriam Grace Monfredo and Sharon Newman (New York: Berkley, 1997).

'A Venomous Death': Originally published in 2009.

'Birth of a Green Man': Originally self-published by the author in 2010.

'My Story': Originally self-published by the author in 2009.

'A Case in Correspondence': Originally self-published by the author in 2010.

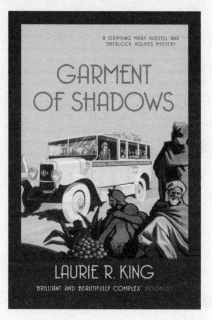
In a strange room in Morocco, Mary Russell is trying to solve a pressing mystery: Who am I? She has awakened with shadows in her mind, blood on her hands, and soldiers pounding at the door. She is clothed like a man, and armed only with her wits and a scrap of paper showing a mysterious symbol. Overhead, warplanes pass ominously north.

Meanwhile, her husband Sherlock Holmes is pulled into the growing war between France, Spain, and the Rif Revolt. He badly wants the wisdom and courage of his wife, whom he discovers, to his horror, has gone missing. As Holmes searches for her, and Russell searches for herself, each tries to crack deadly parallel puzzles before it's too late for them, for Africa, and for the peace of Europe.

Returning to their tranquil Sussex home, Mary Russell and Sherlock Holmes discover a beautiful rock mysteriously planted in the flower bed – a rock they last saw in the emperor's garden in Tokyo. Perhaps the dangerous investigation they carried out for him might not be as complete as they had thought?

One year earlier, Russell and Holmes board the Thomas Carlyle, bound for California with a visit to Japan on the way. A holiday, they think – but intrigue raises its head when a fellow passenger agrees to tutor the couple in her native language and customs. Young Miss Haruki Sato, they begin to suspect, is not who she claims to be. From the winding lanes of Oxford to the palaces of Japan, the ingenious duo embark on an utterly compelling adventure of politics and espionage.

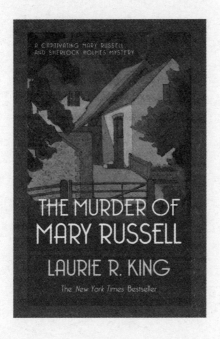

A CAPTIVATING MARY RUSSELL
AND SHERLOCK HOLMES MYSTERY

THE MURDER OF
MARY RUSSELL

LAURIE R. KING

The *New York Times* Bestseller

Mary Russell is used to dark secrets – her own, and those of her famous partner and husband, Sherlock Holmes. But what about the secrets of the third member of the Holmes household: Mrs Hudson? When a man arrives on the doorstep Russell cannot help but believe the revelations he has about their beloved housekeeper, just as she believes the threat of the gun in his hand.

When a frantic Sherlock Holmes discovers the scene left behind – a pool of blood on the floor, the smell of gunpowder in the air – the grim clues point directly to Clara Hudson. There is death here, and murder, and trust betrayed. And nothing will ever be the same.

To discover more great books and to
place an order visit our website at
allisonandbusby.com

Don't forget to sign up to our free newsletter at
allisonandbusby.com/newsletter
for latest releases, events and exclusive offers

Allison & Busby Books
@AllisonandBusby

You can also call us on
020 7580 1080
for orders, queries
and reading recommendations